The UNDECIDED

ROBIN DONARUMA

Mechanicsburg, Pennsylvania USA

Published by Sunbury Press, Inc.
50 West Main Street, Suite A
Mechanicsburg, Pennsylvania 17055

www.sunburypress.com

NOTE: This is a work of fiction. Names, characters, places and incidents are the product of the author's imagination or are used fictitiously, and any resemblance to actual persons, living or dead, business establishments, events or locales is entirely coincidental.

Copyright © 2014 by Robin Donaruma.
Cover copyright © 2014 by Sunbury Press.

Sunbury Press supports copyright. Copyright fuels creativity, encourages diverse voices, promotes free speech, and creates a vibrant culture. Thank you for buying an authorized edition of this book and for complying with copyright laws by not reproducing, scanning, or distributing any part of it in any form without permission. You are supporting writers and allowing Sunbury Press to continue to publish books for every reader. For information contact Sunbury Press, Inc., Subsidiary Rights Dept., 50-A W. Main St., Mechanicsburg, PA 17011 USA or legal@sunburypress.com.

For information about special discounts for bulk purchases, please contact Sunbury Press Orders Dept. at (855) 338-8359 or orders@sunburypress.com.

To request one of our authors for speaking engagements or book signings, please contact Sunbury Press Publicity Dept. at publicity@sunburypress.com.

ISBN: 978-1-62006-396-5 (Trade Paperback)
ISBN: 978-1-62006-397-2 (Mobipocket)
ISBN: 978-1-62006-398-9 (ePub)

FIRST SUNBURY PRESS EDITION: April 2014

Product of the United States of America
0 1 1 2 3 5 8 13 21 34 55

Set in Bookman Old Style
Designed by Lawrence Knorr
Cover by Lawrence Knorr
Edited by Janice Rhayem

Continue the Enlightenment!

Also by Robin Donaruma:

Sweetest Confection

Death surrounded me. Cold fingers scratched along my back causing my breath to chaotically spew from my lips. My spirit recoiled as I pressed into a tree offering me shelter from my pursuer. The bark dug into my skin, and I welcomed the pain.

They were coming. I could feel them. The darkness, so sultry in its dance to destroy, sailed silently through the night in search of its prey, in search of me. Sweat coursed down my back, casually introducing itself to the bark that was fast becoming one with my flesh. My mind raced as quickly as my eyes, which darted around the dense forest searching for an escape. If I stayed where I was, they would find me.

Hysterics threatened as fear subsided and panic took its place. A menacing growl dripped from the pine needles above my head. I shook off the icy film that paralyzed me where I stood and slapped both hands on the tree trunk in an attempt to push away from it. Pain exploded through my hands. I bit my lip, swallowing my scream. The tree's trunk was wrapped with thorn wielding vines. I scraped the thorns from my skin watching my blood as it seeped from my flesh adding a new color, emotion, and scent into the thickened air. As I pulled myself away from the tree, I knew that my back wasn't much better, but I took comfort in the pain; it meant that I was still alive.

I looked back at the tree and its massive vines that strangled the bark appearing as if it were being held prisoner. I pitied it. Fisting my injured hands, I turned from the tree that was once my savior and ran.

I could feel death as it approached. The scent of my blood betrayed me. My throat closed and my vision faltered. My legs became numb. I felt as though a heavy cloak was thrown upon my shoulders slowing me from my fast-paced gait to a shuffled walk. I stumbled to the ground as something cold grabbed my ankle.

"No!" I screamed attempting to crawl away. "No!"

ROBIN DONARUMA

The grip tightened as a black oily mass moved over my body hovering just above me. Frigid, dank air assailed my nostrils and I gagged into the mossy soil. Deep laughter void of frivolity echoed around me.

"Wake up, Lucas. The game has only just begun."

CHAPTER ONE

    My head whipped up from the mossy ground into something hard, my bed. My sheet was wrapped around my legs making it impossible to stand up, so I opted to stay there and take inventory of my surroundings to make sure that I was really awake. Luckily, the only faces lurking in the dark were the familiar ones from my Foo Fighters poster. My heartbeat finally began to slow as I realized that the smell of earthy soil was really just a dirty sock that my face was so fortunate to have landed upon. Confident that I was back in reality, I slowly untangled myself from the sheet and stumbled over to the window. I swallowed a shallow slice of nerves as I reached for a handful of my slightly faded navy curtains and in one quick jerk-like motion, ripped them away from the glass.
    Warm, golden light showered over me as I rested my forehead against the window waiting for the chill that still lingered to subside. Begrudgingly, I pulled away from the morning and turned towards the bed. I ran my hands through my russet hair hoping to find some sort of rewind button so I could start this morning over. No luck with that, so I picked up some faded Levis and a white tee shirt off the floor and threw them on. I headed for the door but hesitated before opening it, not really sure that I was up to facing my parents just yet. The dream was back. After more than a year, it was back. But this time it was different. It was stronger, darker and a lot more real. A shiver trickled down my spine as I remembered the touch of the cold *thing* that grabbed my leg. I walked to my bed and picked up my old, beat up acoustic guitar that I lovingly named Layla.
    "Good morning, beautiful." I sat on the bed and began mindlessly strumming chords.
    Why did the dream come back? Why now when I was just on the verge of feeling like I actually fit in somewhere?

But this one was different. It felt too real. And this time, they called me by my name.

A cold breeze shot across my bed causing the hair on my skin to stand on end. I jumped up and decided that it was time to eat. Propping Layla against my dresser I put on three black bracelets, one for every school I've been to in the past three years. I'm not sure why I started wearing them; maybe they're some sort of subconscious tally of the nightmares that always seem to come back just before my parents shuffle us off to some other town, but they do make a pretty cool contrast sitting against my birthmark—a thin white line encircling my left wrist.

As I turned the knob of my door handle, the reality of my dream hit me between the eyes. My gut hit my feet and I knew, without a doubt, what I would find when I went downstairs, because it's happened three times before. I looked down at the black bracelets. It can't be a coincidence that every time I have one of these bad dreams my parents come up with some reason to move out of town. It's not as if I tell them every time I have a nightmare, but they always seem to know.

"Well, time to put my theory to the test." I took a deep breath, opened my bedroom door and walked into the living room. I stopped dead in my tracks and stared at my dad, who was attempting to tape up one very large and very brown moving box.

"I can't believe it," I mumbled, looking at the box. "I can't freaking believe this." I didn't know whether I wanted to laugh or to scream. I glared back and forth between my father's guilt ridden expression and the moving box and slowly backed into the kitchen hoping to make a quick escape through the back door. No such luck. Blocking my getaway was Mom as she carefully wrapped our cheap drinking glasses with newspaper. I blew out one of the safer curse words causing her head to snap up.

"Lucas! Good morning. I didn't know you were awake yet." She approached me, speaking slowly in soft tones as if I were a dog that might attack at any moment. The humor in the situation disappeared and was replaced by the weighted reality of the situation, but the last thing I wanted now, the last thing I wanted to deal with, was a pep talk from mommy. I needed to get out of here. I made a line for the door but a small, five-foot, 100 pound wall jumped in front of me. I slowly raised my eyes to my mother's and found them a cool mixture of concern and fear, and it was enough to delay my escape plan. I backed up and crossed my arms attempting to appear casual and only slightly furious.

"So. Where to this time?" I uttered between clenched teeth.

"Lucas, please understand. Joey!" she yelled for my father. Great. There is no way this can be a good sign. I could hear my dad. No, I could *feel* my dad standing behind me waiting for the secret signal to enter.

I guess my mom's expression was the entry ticket. Dad slowly walked into the kitchen and slapped his hand onto my shoulder in a reassuring, don't worry son and oh, don't freak out either kind of way.

"Luke, I'm sorry. We planned on talking with you before we got this far, but circumstances have been changing. Circumstances *have* changed," my dad stuttered as if he didn't know what to say, or was afraid to say it. His eyes darted between the floor and my mom, and I was seriously starting to get a little creeped out.

"What your father means, Lucas, is that we knew this was a possibility but didn't realize that it would happen quite this fast."

"What circumstances have changed? What circumstances?" I shot out.

Mom looked at Dad questioningly as her hands tried to rip themselves from her arms. Dad must have gained some courage over the past forty-five seconds, because he finally looked me in the eye. What I wasn't prepared for was how deadly serious his demeanor had just turned. I backed up until I hit the table and grabbed the edge for support.

"What's going on? Dad? Mom?"

"Tell me something Lucas, and whatever you do, do not lie to me, do you understand?" My dad moved closer to me, and I gripped the table harder.

"Of course, Dad." I looked between the two of them as I wondered what had happened to my tough guy attitude when I walked into the kitchen a few minutes earlier.

Suddenly, I felt as if I was eight years old and they were about to tell me my hamster Moe died. It was that same look, sadness with a trace of fear over my reaction.

"Have you been having the dream again?" my dad asked me.

My head started to hurt, and my stomach felt like it just dropped into my socks. I froze. All I had to say was yes, but for the life of me, I couldn't figure out how. Did he just ask me about the dream? I nodded once and watched the color of my dad's face change from a light pink to gray. He looked at my mother then back to me.

"Last night?"

I nodded again and struggled to remember how to form words. I didn't know what any of this meant, but I knew that it meant something. I also knew that somehow I was involved and I was not liking it, not one bit.

"It was the first. Last night. The first time in a long time, since we moved here actually." I looked to my mother for encouragement for finally remembering how to speak, but she was staring at my dad with a stunned and pretty freaked out face. Some color had returned to my dad's face, which is a good thing I guess, until he looked at me with his blue eyes that seemed to bore into my skull.

"Impossible," he growled.

"Um. No?" I whispered. "Last night was the first."

"Lucas, there is no way that you have only had that dream once!" my father took a step closer to me.

"Okay, look, you guys are really freaking me out." I stepped back.

"Joey, maybe he doesn't remember the other dreams," my mother offered my dad, trying to calm him down. Unfortunately, I took this time in the conversation to finally find my voice.

"No, this is the only one, believe me, there is no way I could have forgotten if there were other dreams like the one last night." My parents whipped their heads towards me.

"What do you mean? It was different? Different from the others?" my dad asked, moving in closer with eyes that I swear were now glowing.

"No, it's the same, just more real is all. Look, someone tell me what's going on here. Why is everybody freaking out and looking at me like a science project gone wrong? And what do my dreams have to do with anything, especially with us having to move again?" My parents looked at each other with glazed expressions.

"Someone tell me what's going on!" I pushed away from the table and confronted my dad. "Tell me."

My dad wearily rubbed his hands over his face and grabbed one of my hands and one of my mother's. My mother, with tears in her eyes, grabbed my other hand and took a deep, heavy breath.

"Lucas, you're turning eighteen this month. Each year you grow stronger in ways that you aren't fully aware of."

"Mom, please tell me that this isn't turning into one of *those* talks." I'm thinking that if there is anyway this is going to turn into a puberty talk I'm forgetting the door and going for the window.

My mother caressed the birthmark around my wrist.

"Our family. We aren't exactly like other families."

"Mom..."

"We're special, Lucas. We're part of the chosen ones."

I looked at my dad to see if he was buying this, but he was staring at my wrist.

"Chosen by who? What are you talking about?"

"By whom," my mother corrected me then cleared her throat. "Chosen by the White Army."

I ripped my hands from theirs and backed up a few feet. The air was definitely thinning out right alongside their sanity. Time to bolt. I eyed up the door, thinking it a quicker and cleaner exit, but my dad was one step ahead of me.

"You're not safe here anymore, Lucas." Glancing at the door and then back at me. "Forget it."

"Okay fine. I'm not safe anymore. *What does that even mean*? Not safe from what? Is this some government thing?" I looked to my mother who was looking at the clock. "What is Dad—a spy or something?"

"This has nothing to do with the government Luke. It's much bigger than that. Bigger than you can imagine, right now," my dad said as he skillfully placed himself between the door and me.

"What? Big like the oh-so famous White Army? Come on Dad, give me a break here. You know, I'm actually a pretty smart kid. I get good grades, pay attention in school, I watch the news, and I'm telling you I've never heard of any *White Army*. And I've never heard you talk about it before. So why is it so important now?" I stood there admiring my little speech not realizing that no one was answering me. They were just staring at me waiting for me to finish my little tirade.

"There's a war going on Lucas," my dad finally spoke.

"Well, that's not exactly news Dad and, I'd call it more of a sandy ecru kind of skirmish than white."

My dad slammed his forearm against the wall.

"The time for joking is over Lucas. We've tried to protect you for as long as we could, but it's out of our hands now. It's up to you. That's why you're being called."

"I'm being what?"

"They know that you're almost of age, and they are after you. They will stop at *nothing* to make sure you fail," my mother so lovingly added.

"Who? Fail how? Fail at what?" I was beginning to wonder if maybe this was a dream too.

"The Dark Army," my father injected.

"The Dark Army, of course, I should have seen that one coming," I mumbled sarcastically.

The next thing I knew my dad was on top of me holding my wrist in front of my face. I didn't even see him move.

"This is no joke, Lucas. Do you know what this is? Do you have any idea what this means?"

"Joe, please," my mom said, trying to calm down my dad. "We don't have as long here as we thought."

He released my hand and looked at my mother.

"I'm sorry, Lucas," my father said sincerely. "Your dreams, we've never talked about them before, but it's important now that you tell us about them. What exactly do you see?"

"I, um, I don't know really. You know how dreams can be. Sometimes it's not what I see so much as what I feel, but it's pretty much always the same. I'm being chased."

"Chased, by whom? Can you see them?" my mother asked me.

THE UNDECIDED

"I don't know who it is. I've never seen them. It's always too dark. I just sort of feel them." I didn't like the understanding that was washing over my dad's face. Especially since I still had no idea what was happening.

"You had said that this last dream was different from the others. How so?" my mother gently nudged.

A shudder traveled down my spine, and I could feel all of my hair follicles standing to attention.

"Well, because this time they actually caught me." My mother gasped out loud, and my father took a step back.

"What?" I nervously laughed. "It's just a dream! I'm right here, see?"

My father looked at my wrist again and then back to my face.

"It's much more than just a dream, son. It's like a game of Chess, only you didn't know you've been playing. But you're on the board now and, it sounds like they've just made their first move."

"What, the Dark Army?" I shook my head not believing what I was hearing. "Okay, but why me? What's the big deal with me?" I was really getting over this conversation.

"Because, Lucas, you are the leader of the White Army. Our only salvation."

CHAPTER TWO

Time had stopped. My parents were still talking, but I couldn't for the life of me understand anything they were saying. They sounded like the teacher in a Charlie Brown cartoon. A line of sweat was threatening to break free from my hairline. The kitchen lights began moving in circles, and I decided it might be fun to join them. I began to sway and hoped that if I were going to pass out, it would happen soon before my stomach took over. Darkness edged its way in with a cool sparkly star like effect. I was enjoying the light show and even welcomed the opportunity to check out for a while until I got slapped from behind by something cold and wet.

"Lucas! Can you hear me? Joe, do something!" Panic laced my mother's words.

"He's fine, Mary, stop hovering. Lucas, son, can you hear me?"

The cold wetness left my back and slapped me in the face shooting me back into reality. I tried to talk through the wet cotton.

"Mom. Do you mind?"

It dropped immediately only to be replaced with two sets of very concerned eyes. Good grief.

"I'm fine. I'm fine." They looked at me as if I were about to explode into thousands of tiny pieces at any minute. "I swear. Could you back off, please?" Reluctantly they both stepped back. Mom's concern still lingered, but I could tell that Dad was switching gears.

"He's fine Mary. We've got to get moving." Then he looked at me. "I know you have a lot of questions, Luke. Some of them I have answers to, some of them I don't. Everything will be answered in time. You've just been given more information in five minutes than most people digest in their lifetime, but for right now, today, we need to get going."

THE UNDECIDED

I looked at him like he just grew another head. I couldn't believe what he was telling me.

"Let me get this straight. You're telling me I'm in the middle of some big bad battle, oh and I happen to be your only hope of winning. People are trying to kill me, I think there was an almost happy birthday thrown in there from mom, thank you very much, let's see, oh yes, and I'm also the fearless leader of the White Army, now go pack some boxes?"

Without skipping a beat, Dad looked at me, said "Yeah, that's right," and threw a roll of tape at me. From the other room I heard him yell, "You may be our only hope, but you're also still my son. Start with your room."

I looked at my mother who was back to packing the cheap glasses.

"Don't worry, Lucas, I promise we'll explain as much as we can soon, but we really do need to hurry."

I didn't really have anything to say. And though I had questions that spiraled me back down that black hole I just crawled out of, I knew I wasn't ready for any answers. I still wasn't sure that I even believed any of this. But there was one question I did want an answer to.

"So can you at least tell me where we're going?"

"Of course. Branford, Connecticut," my mother happily supplied.

"Connecticut? Why there?" I've never been or really even thought about Connecticut before; all I knew was that it sounded cold. Much colder than Florida, that's for sure.

"Aren't people supposed to like move *from* Connecticut to Florida, not the other way around?" I asked my mother with only a tinge of sarcasm.

"Lucas," she responded with a slight hint of warning. "You'll love it, I promise. It's beautiful up there. Branford is right on the Long Island Sound, water as far as the eye can see."

"As opposed to Florida?" I rolled my eyes, and my mother gave me that warning look that let me know I was treading on thin ice. "Okay, fine, there's water, what I meant was why there? Why Branford?"

"Your father and I knew that our time here was up, so to speak, we just didn't realize until this morning how little time we really had left." She continued to pack glasses, and I sat there hoping that she wouldn't realize that I hadn't begun to help yet.

"A friend of your father's called last week asking for his help in investigating the sudden dying off of wetlands in Branford. Apparently, it's become a full-blown phenomenon and no one can pinpoint the reasons behind it. So they called the best Benthic Ecologist around and offered him the job." She paused and gave me one of those aren't you so proud of him smiles. "There also happens to be an opening for a counselor at the high school." My mother looked at me sheepishly and I saw the pieces of the puzzle starting to fit together.

"What you don't understand yet Lucas is that our lives are being led by something much bigger and more important than you could ever begin to imagine. Once you know the truth, you'll realize that the decision to do what we *need* to do rather than what we may *want* to do is absolutely vital. Don't you see? First your father's job offer, then the counselor's position."

"Wait. Just because there's a couple of job openings, doesn't mean we have to move. That's not a sign from God or anything, that's just luck."

"It's more than that Lucas." She nervously looked to the living room, and I leaned forward knowing that she was about to divulge something she probably didn't want to.

"Like what? Don't tell me taxes are better 'cause Florida doesn't have any."

"Oh Lucas, honestly." She paused and took a deep breath. "I have dreams too."

Now we're getting somewhere. "You do?"

"Yes, but they're not like yours. They're more like instructions."

"Instructions from who?" I asked, completely riveted.

"From *whom*, dear," she corrected. "From the Council."

"The Council?"

"The Council is a group of elders, very, very wise souls that direct the battle for the White Army. They've been protecting you through us."

"So this *Council* who is protecting *me* is telling you that we have to move to *Branford, Connecticut?* Okay. Does this

Council tell you why Branford or does it just say jump and you jump?"

"I have no reason to question what they show me. We still have free will, Lucas, nothing makes me do the things we do except for our desire to keep you safe," she answered quietly with deep emotion.

"What did you see?"

"It's not always what I see as much as what I don't see."

"I don't follow."

"Lucas, this really isn't the time for this." She turned back to begin packing. A feeling of desperation rang through me, and I gently grabbed her arm turning her back toward me.

"Please," I managed to whisper. My mother's eyes reflected my desperation, and she clutched my hand that was keeping her from packing. Her eyes darted to the living room where my father was faithfully packing our lives away. I knew this wouldn't be the long explanation, and I was fine with that. "Please Mom, I need something to help me make sense of all this. Anything."

She introduced her explanation with a deep, weary sigh. "All right, but then promise me you'll start packing."

"Fine, yeah sure." I let go of her arm and picked up the roll of tape that Dad threw at me earlier as a testament of good faith.

"My dreams are more like visions than actual dreams. Usually, I am shown an image, similar to a map, you know, like the kind your teacher pulls down from the blackboard?" She looked to me for acknowledgment, and I eagerly nodded my head encouraging her to continue. "Sometimes it's a map of North America, or sometimes a specific state or group of states. After the map is shown to me, waves of dark and light masses begin to float on top of it, swirling around like a giant hurricane until they eventually still and settle onto the map."

"Let me guess, The White and Dark Armies?" I asked tongue in cheek. But apparently the joke was on me.

"Precisely. It shows me where we stand in the battle and where the dark ones grow the largest."

"So what exactly are we supposed to do with this information? Move from state to state to avoid all those big dark voodoo daddies?"

"We used to, yes. But now it seems there is another plan for us. One that does not include avoiding the darkness."

"But I thought you were supposed to be saving me from them, now it sounds like you're serving me up for dinner," I replied shakily.

"Lucas, I know this is all new to you, but you must trust in the Council to show us the right path."

"And that path is in Branford, Connecticut with a huge army of bad-asses?"

"Watch your language. I told you before Lucas, I don't question the Council. But I will say that there was something very different about this vision."

"Like what?" I asked cautiously.

"Well, this time instead of the map being defined by dark and white, there was an unusually large infusion of gray."

"Gray?"

"Gray patches. I've seen spots here and there before but never such a large amount," she said wide-eyed.

"And that means what exactly?"

"The grays represent the undecided. Those who have yet to choose their side, be it on a conscious or subconscious level."

"So what, that's a good thing, right? At least they're not working for Darth Vadar, right?" I tossed the tape up in the air and gave her a little smirk. This conversation was so surreal that I began doubting that it was actually happening, at least until my mother eyed me with another one of her freaky stares.

"Lucas, you must never underestimate the grays. The grays are even more dangerous than the dark." I looked at her questioningly and she continued. "At least with dark entities you know where they stand. The grays are hard to track, even the Council never gets a fully accurate account of their numbers. They're like ticking time bombs that can go off at any minute, to either side. Anything could set them off in one direction or another."

"So where exactly do I fall into all of this?"

"I don't know, at least not exactly. In the past, we've always run away from the darkness to keep you safe. This is the first time we're being sent toward the darkness, the same year that you are coming of age." My mother picked up my hand and rubbed my birthmark. "Surely that can't be a coincidence," she mumbled to herself. "This is all much bigger than either of us imagined."

I rubbed my free hand through my hair. "This is definitely not the way I imagined today would start off."

"It will all make more sense to you soon, I promise, but for now..."

"Yeah, I know." I tossed the tape up into the air. "Time to rock-n-roll."

CHAPTER THREE

Branford met me much like every other town I've ever rushed into, filled with the same types of people and the same types of buildings.

Unlike Florida, Branford seemed pretty tame. There was definitely a vibration strumming through the area, but a very subdued one. Everyone was properly dressed, properly mannered, and properly reserved. Walking through town made me feel as if I stepped into the opening scene of Disney's *Lady and the Tramp*, with perfectly manicured lawns, lampposts that were always turned on, and a golden retriever lounging on every front porch. It's great, don't get me wrong, just different, very different.

My favorite part of Branford is an area down by the water called Stony Creek, a little seaside village reminiscent of a scene right out of *The Perfect Storm*. I spent a lot of time walking around, watching people, and searching for clues, any clue as to what the heck my mother is talking about, but so far no luck. All I see is Americana at its finest, no dark shadows lurking behind buildings or under cars. It has become a struggle to keep my anger in check over the move to Branford. Yes, it's beautiful, our house is cool, and I love the whole water thing, but my friends and my life were left down south and for what?

I'm still having the dark dreams, but they've been much fainter since moving. They're nowhere close to what they were before we moved, but they're still there nonetheless. My solution is to not sleep. I don't require that much sleep anyway, and spending more time awake gives me more time to play my guitar.

Looking around Stony Creek, I'm just not feeling anything, definitely not feeling any evil army sneaking up behind me.

THE UNDECIDED

    My days had become routine. Sleep very little, get up very early, and try to tap into the vibe of the town. So far, all signs pointed to my mother's need for psychiatric care, 'cause I wasn't feeling anything close to negative in Branford. And that started to make me feel down right pissed off.
    I stopped walking and leaned against an old lamppost adjacent to the docks and watched as two older men loaded their skiff with fishing supplies. They maneuvered the boat and all the stuff they piled in it as if they have been doing it all their lives, and I guess they probably have. One man paused to look up at me and gave me a curt nod. The other man looked up, then quickly looked away without any sign of acknowledgment. For a split second it seemed that the unsmiling man wasn't happy to see me standing there. But that didn't make sense. I shook my head feeling like a fool and perhaps a bit like my mother and crossed the street to the Stony Creek Market.
    Stony Creek Market, a local favorite around Branford, is usually so crowded that I'm never able to approach it. But it was early enough this morning and I was hungry enough that I thought it was worth a shot to see what all the hype was about. The outside patio had several tables with big red umbrellas, most of them still closed. There were bicycles parked alongside the railing (a popular form of transportation around these parts since parking can be hard to come by) and planters full of vibrant red flowers that beautifully offset the brown and weathered shaker shingle construction. It was, as my mother termed, quaint. Every step offered a groan or creak from the wooden deck as I walked onto the patio. I thought about how in a town where very little is kept secret, my coming up to the front door of this market would later become fodder for the three witnesses sitting on the patio slowly sipping their coffees. I looked up apologetically to the one couple for my disturbing entrance into their once tranquil morning, but they hardly took notice, or at least they were polite enough to pretend not to notice me. I addressed the other patron with my rueful stare and found myself immediately engaged in a staring match.

ROBIN DONARUMA

All I could think of was The Gorton's Fisherman. This guy looked like he had been driven hard and put away wet after a few years of battling it out with Moby Dick. His hair was two shades lighter than his beard and held together by an old weathered cap. He wore a thick cable knit sweater that covered his entire upper torso, except for his dark, thickly veined hands. In one hand he held a navy mug where steam danced out of the top melding into his beard. In his other hand, he gingerly tapped an old pipe on the table in a slow, steady cadence.

Our eyes were locked and I became transfixed by the monotonous tapping and the smooth, silky lines of the steam. A small gust of cool wind ran across the patio ruffling his paper and blowing his beard in an intimate manner. He used his pipe to still his paper as I attempted to get closer to the door. He was still watching me so I offered him a small nod of my head then looked away. I made it to the door and the tapping stopped. I turned back around and he was reading his paper and drinking his coffee just like everyone else.

A jingle from a bell on top of the door rang as I entered the market, and my nostrils were assailed with the most wonderful aroma that I had smelled in what seemed like forever. My stomach finally caught up to me and made an audible "hello." Luckily, there were only a few patrons this early, and they were all sitting down and concentrating on their food. The market wasn't big, just a few tables and chairs for those who dare not brave the elements outside. The counter was stacked with old newspapers, salt and pepper shakers, bottles of ground cinnamon, and a pile of napkins. It was a very homey help yourself type of place. The air was filled with the vintage tunes of Pink Martini, a cool band out of Oregon that my friend, Billy, turned me on to last year. They're not exactly something I would listen to all the time, but they've definitely got a unique sound. Billy described their music as something you can listen to whether you're sad or happy, cleaning your room or seducing your friend's grandmother. I didn't get into the last part with him too much, but it did get me to listen to them and like I said, pretty cool.

THE UNDECIDED

Billy is still in Florida along with the rest of my life. Kind of strange that the first music I hear playing would be an obscure group that reminds me of where I wasn't. Maybe this is some sort of sign. A sign of what, I have no idea but something to definitely think about later. Right now, the only sign I was interested in was the one with the menu listed on it hanging above the front counter. It was an old chalkboard that listed like twenty different kinds of sandwiches. I grabbed a bottle of Nantucket Nectar apple juice out of the cooler beside me and looked around for someone to take my order.

"Funny, you've got a lot of sandwiches here," I mumbled under my breath in my best John Cleese imitation. I set down my juice to walk around the counter and find someone when an apron flew across the market hitting me in the face.

"Oh jeeze! I'm sorry," came a voice from beyond the white veil. I was about to remove the cinnamon scented garment when it was ripped from my head as abruptly as it landed there. Though the event lasted only a few seconds at most, my mind was already racing with clever quips and complaints. I was ready for the attack with hopes of maybe getting a free sandwich out this.

Hopes of a free sandwich and a clever comment were gone in a blink of an eye. Literally. Because after the apron was (none too gently, by the way) taken back by its owner, I was left staring into a pair of the most beautiful green eyes I had ever seen.

"I'm really sorry," she said through her laughter. "I didn't realize anyone was out here."

I mentally shook myself and tried to pull away from her eyes, but that only left me staring at her hair, which was the most beautiful, long, wavy, deep red hair that I had ever witnessed. She was quite possibly the most beautiful girl I had ever seen, and I knew without a doubt that in this one moment my life would never be the same.

"You're new around here, aren't you?"

Focus Lucas, focus. She's talking to you. "Um, oh yeah, moved here about a week ago."

"Cool. So where from? New York?" she asked me, tapping her pencil against her left cheek complete with dimple. Good Lord, what's happening to me?

"Nah, actually Florida." I tried to appear cool by sticking my hands in my pockets as if I hadn't a care in the world.

"Florida? What are you crazy? You're supposed to move *to* Florida not away from it!"

"Believe me, this wasn't my idea."

Understanding and a little touch of sympathy washed over her face, her flawless face. "Ah. Parents?"

Parents and then some you could say. But all I did was nod my head. "Yup, something like that."

"My name's Marianne, but everyone calls me Mare."

"Lucas. Lucas Aarons," I said, reaching across the counter to shake her hand.

"Well, very nice to meet you Lucas Aarons. And welcome to Stony Creek."

We held hands for one second longer than necessary, and suddenly, I didn't care if my mother was certifiably crazy, and I didn't care about the reasons we moved. I was just happy that we did.

"I'm sorry. I guess you didn't come in here to meet the local town folk, you probably want to eat something, huh?"

"Yeah, actually. So what do you recommend?"

"Well, we make a mean breakfast sandwich."

"Breakfast sandwich it is then. With bacon."

"Ah, a man after my own heart. What kind of roll? Never mind, you need a bialy."

"A what?"

"A bialy roll. Trust me."

She swiftly collected my money and then set out to make my breakfast sandwich on a bialy roll, whatever that was. I walked to the window and looked out into the sound. Things were picking up. There was more activity on the water and in the street. The couple that was sitting on the patio earlier had left, but the old man was still there. As if he could hear my thoughts, he slowly turned his head towards the window where I was standing and pinned me down with his stare again. I helplessly stared back. He began tapping his pipe, but this time the only sound I

THE UNDECIDED

heard was the faint tunes of Pink Martini floating around the market. This guy was really starting to freak me out. I watched him watching me and decided that this wasn't just my imagination. The little hairs on my neck stood straight up. First the guy in the boat, and now this guy, and maybe the boat guy was a coincidence, but this definitely was not. There was only one thing for me to do. Confront him. I swallowed the big lump in my throat and went for the door at the same time Mare approached me with my sandwich, which I proceeded to knock out of her hand.

"Whoa. Sorry." I bent down to pick up the bag.

"No, I'm sorry. I didn't mean to sneak up on you," she said, bending down to help. "I called your name, but you seemed pretty entranced by something out there." She looked at me questioningly.

"Oh what? No. I mean, yeah, I was looking out the window, but just kind of zoning out I guess. Sorry."

"You know, we've spent a good portion of our conversation saying sorry to each other."

"Yeah, I guess we have." I paused and then looked directly at her and together we both said "Sorry."

I took the bag and my Nantucket Nectar and held them up.

"Thanks for the sandwich. I guess I'll see you around?"

"Goodbye Lucas Aarons," she said smiling as she walked back to the counter.

I went for the door, psyching myself up for a confrontation with the old man, but when I opened it, he was gone. Just like that.

I looked around, but he was nowhere to be seen. I let out my pent up breath and with a careless shrug of my shoulders continued down the street towards my new digs. I thought about the old man for a while but not nearly as much as the red headed girl from Stony Creek Market with the stunning green eyes. Marianne.

CHAPTER FOUR

"Anyone home?" I yelled, walking into a room full of familiar things in an unfamiliar place. I found my mom sitting at the kitchen table with a cup of Joe and a crossword puzzle.

"If I was a robber he'd have cleaned us out by now," I stated, startling my mother who jumped and spilled some of her coffee.

"Lucas! What have I told you about sneaking up on me!"

"If you call sneaking up on you walking through the front door yelling, then you got me. Won't happen again." I kissed her on her forehead and sat down slinging my sack onto the table.

"Sorry. I guess I'm just in my own little world this morning." She eyed up my sack. "You're certainly up early. What do you have in there?"

"A breakfast sandwich." I was trying to think of the name of the bread that Marianne, or Mare made it on, but all I could remember were two amazing green eyes that seemed to look right through me.

"From Stony Market?" my mother asked, shaking me out of my reverie.

"Yeah, I was walking down by the harbor and thought I'd try it out."

"A couple of girls over at the school were talking about their pizza. I didn't know they were open for breakfast too," she said, looking back to her puzzle. "We'll have to try it out sometime."

I opened the bag and pulled out a sandwich wrapped in white paper. I slowly opened the package being careful to not pull off all of the cheese that annoyingly stuck to the sides. The roll looked similar to a bagel minus the hole, only it wasn't as heavy. I took a bite and had to admit that Mare had done me right. Maybe I was exceptionally

THE UNDECIDED

hungry, or maybe I was associating it with the stunning chef that created this meal, but this was one of the best breakfast sandwiches that I had ever had.

"So what had you up so early today? You only have a couple more days of sleeping in before school starts."

"Yeah, I know. I just wanted to take a look around the town, and I was having trouble sleeping, so I put the two together and ended up with an awesome sandwich."

My mother put the crossword down and drilled her eyes into me. She better not be after my sandwich.

"Is it the dreams, Luke?"

I shoved the last of my breakfast into my mouth and crumpled up the bag. I leaned back in my chair and threw a three pointer into the trashcan.

"He shoots, he scores," I mumbled through a sticky bread and cheese mixture.

"Lucas?"

"No, Mom, it's not the dreams. Not really, anyway. I haven't had a real dream since we got here. But there is a sort of uneasiness that kind of creeps in, and that's what wakes me up. It's hard to explain." My mother raised her eyebrows and tilted her head silently demanding that I continue. "Okay. It's like you're sitting in the dark, alone, and all of a sudden you think that you hear something, or someone, only you know that no one else is in the room. You can't help but get a little freaked out and want to reach for a light, right?" She nodded her head in understanding. "Well, that's how I feel sometimes, and though it's really nothing, there is this tiny nagging feeling that it very easily could turn into something. So, I find it much better to walk around town and eat a sandwich." I stood up and went to the sink to wash the grease from my hands.

"Well, I'm glad that the dreams aren't back, it's much too soon for that." My mother stood up and refilled her coffee cup adding half and half and raw sugar that she insists tastes different than regular sugar. "So what do you think about Stony Creek? It's nice, isn't it? I know your father loves it, he's in seventh heaven working in those marshes, God love him."

"Well, that is his job, so I guess it's cool that he likes it." My mother rolled her eyes and shrugged her shoulders. She would rather have him home with her all day. And actually, my dad would rather be home with her too. If there is one truth in this world that I am sure of, it's how much my parents love each other. Most of my friends' parents are always doing things separately, or one is working all day or all night and then they just come home to watch TV. My parents have been married for eighteen years and act like it's only been eighteen months. You can't meet them and not feel their tremendous love for each other. It's definitely off the hook."

"I guess the town is kind of growing on me," I answered.

"Well it's certainly beautiful, you have to admit that. A little different from what you're used to in Florida I suppose, but once you're back in school I'm sure you will feel as if you've always been here."

"Yeah, nothing like starting a new school in your senior year. That should be fun."

"Lucas, you know we had no choice."

"Yeah, yeah, I know. Forget about it. I'm just giving you a hard time."

"You should be nicer to your mother," she said with a wink and then went back to the table. I debated whether to tell her about how the fisherman on the dock and the old man were staring at me. But I still wasn't a hundred percent sure that it wasn't all just my imagination. Now that I was home and my hunger satisfied, it all seemed kind of silly that two men would care what I was doing, or who I was. Nah, info to just stick in my back pocket and see if anything else comes to life.

"Oh, come now Mother. You know you are the best mother a boy could ever ask for. And I thank God for you every day of my life," I said, holding one hand over my heart.

"All right, all right, enough. Go on. What are you going to do with your day?" she asked with rosy cheeks and a heartfelt smile. Works every time.

"After I write an ode to you, I believe I shall spend some time with Layla. It's been far too long."

THE UNDECIDED

"Since last night you mean? You had better hope that you never get a girlfriend or she's going to be mighty jealous of a piece of wood that's held together by a few strings."

"Mother, she is much more than mere wood and strings. She is my life, my link to the other side, my salvation, my best friend, my..."

"Guitar. Yes, I get it. Don't turn your music up too loud with those little things you stick in your ears, you could really damage your hearing."

"What?"

"Ha ha!" My mother rumpled up a piece of newspaper and hurled it at me across the kitchen.

"Love you, Mom!" I yelled as I escaped to my bedroom in search of my best friend, a piece of wood held together by a few strings. Layla, my escape route from reality.

CHAPTER FIVE

I closed my bedroom door and moved around the few stray boxes that I had yet to unpack. After cranking open my window, I looked out into the backyard. The day was warming up, but the trees kept my room from heating up. Living in a two-story house was pretty cool. My room was upstairs at the end of the hall, a fairly decent amount of distance from my doting parents. I had two windows, one overlooking the backyard and one above the driveway. I couldn't see the front yard, but I could just make out the mailbox by the main road. I felt totally secluded and safe up here, almost untouchable. The only bummer was the view of the house next door, which was way too close for my liking. My bedroom window offered a clear view into their kitchen and a room upstairs. Lucky for me, no one lived there. According to my mom, the house has been on the market for about a year. My dad checked out both houses before settling on this one. He said that it all came down to low-lying land or something like that.

Grabbing my iPod and guitar, I fell onto my bed, and turned on some Stevie Ray Vaughn. Stevie soulfully sang about the water rising in Texas, and I gave my dad props for keeping us off of low-lying land. Listening intently, I was transported into the lone star state's torrential downpour. The guitar solo creating an eddy that kept me entranced in his flooded world. This music was more than just licks recorded in a generic studio. This was nothing short of a man's soul reaching out and testifying.

The music became one with the landscape, and I become one with it. I felt invincible, strong, a part of the infinite. With each tone a new array of colors opened up, each note holding a key that unlocked spaces yet discovered. Here, there was no fear, no pain, only light. Everything was brighter and stronger, and it fed me. The

THE UNDECIDED

light moved into and through me, and I became awash with a sense of peace.

The song ended, and I came crashing back to reality. I pulled out my headphones, pausing my iPod. My pulse was racing, and I was slightly breathless. Slowly, I sat up and looked around my room in wonder.

"That was different," I mumbled to myself, smiling.

I felt as if I could run a marathon and had just downed an entire case of Monster energy drink. My wrist began tingling, and when I looked down, I found my white birthmark *glowing*. I held my arm out in front of me and turned it from side to side, studying it from every possible angle. With my other hand, I rubbed my eyes and shook my head in an attempt to clear my vision. Music has always been an experience for me, but this was pretty extreme. I scrolled down my song list ready to try out another song. I propped myself up against my headboard, selected The Foo Fighters' "The Pretender," leaned back, and hit play.

The licks came up smooth and familiar, and I played along with Layla, feeling my way into the song. When the lyrics began I felt myself sinking into the song just like I did with Stevie's, but this time I was waiting for it. I was transported into the song. Darkness rushed around me, but not in a threatening sort of way. I welcomed it and looked for what was held within it. With the song's acceleration I walked into the swirling dark bands of emotion. They turned into a murky shade of gray and were encompassed by shadowy figures shuffling aimlessly. I played along with Dave Grohl and attacked the darkness with each strum of my guitar and each note of the song. I felt a rush of power and a wave of concern for the faceless people held within the gray. Holding out my left hand towards them my birthmark began to glow. The shade of gray lightened to a dingy white. They slowed their shuffling and turned towards me. As the music reached its end, a bolt of light shot out of me and into the gray, forming a bond between us.

I didn't want the song to end, but it did. I ripped off my ear buds feeling powerful and alive. I felt as if I was going to burst into a million pieces.

ROBIN DONARUMA

    My wrist was glowing again, and everything in my room seemed a little bit brighter. I rubbed my eyes and shook my head in an attempt to clear my thoughts. I wasn't sure what any of this meant, but it definitely was not a figment of my imagination.
    During the song, the darkness turned from gray to white. Eerily close to my parents' explanation for the war of light and dark. As much as I hated to admit it, I knew that this couldn't be a coincidence. A tingling sensation ran from my wrist to my neck. My wrist was still faintly glowing, but when I stopped playing the guitar, it faded back to normal. I started playing again and watched it become more prominent. It didn't take a genius to figure out that the music was creating some sort of change in me. But what that meant, I had no earthly idea.
    I set Layla on my bed and opened my bedroom door. I guess the only thing to do is to talk to my mom about this new development.
    She was in the kitchen. I hesitated in the doorway wondering what exactly I was going to say. It's hard to explain something that you didn't even understand yourself. What if it just ended up freaking her out even more? I looked down to my iPod that I still had clutched in my hand then walked back to my bedroom. I grabbed my headphones, hit shuffle and lay back down on my bed. Mom could wait.

THE UNDECIDED

CHAPTER SIX

About five hours later I walked out of my room ready to eat whatever got in my way. I was starving, and very pumped since I had just spent the last five hours in the heads of some of the most amazing musicians that have walked the planet. I didn't know their thoughts, but I could sense their emotions. I could feel all of the love and hatred and fear and passion that they used to create their music. I became a part of it, and it became a part of me. I felt energized. I felt like I could conquer the world. But first, I needed to scarf down a couple of sandwiches and a bag of chips.

My dad was talking with Mom in the kitchen as I rounded the corner.

"Hey Pops," I said, bee-lining my way to the fridge.

"Hey yourself Lucas. Mom says you've been getting around town huh?"

"Yeah, it's pretty cool," I said as I stuck my head inside.

"I think we're all going to really like it here," my dad said, hugging my mother and kissing her on her forehead.

The cupboard was bare. All I found was some left over pasta, so I shut the door.

"Do we have anything to eat around here?" I asked, turning towards my parents who were staring at me as if I had just spoken Vulcan.

"Lucas?" my mother asked tentatively. "What's happened to you?"

My dad stepped closer. My mother was staring at my wrist. I looked down and saw that it was still faintly glowing. At least now I knew it wasn't all in my head.

"What have you been doing?" she asked again as my father gently grabbed my wrist studying it from all sides.

"Nothing really, just listening to music in my room." Which was the truth.

"Lucas, you look like you've been, I don't know, plugged in!" my dad said.

"You're glowing Lucas! You're eyes, your wrist, you!" My mother grabbed my other arm. "It's coming from the inside, I can feel it, it's coming from within you."

"What kind of music were you listening to?" Dad asked with wonder and a hint of humor.

I pulled my arms out of their grasps and walked to the living room to find a mirror. Considering my parents' history of over reacting, I wasn't really concerned, but I did notice my wrist glowing earlier, so who's to say I didn't glow anywhere else? I approached the mirror and with one quick upwards jerk of my head, looked at my reflection. It wasn't like I was actually glowing, at least not like a nuclear reactor or anything. It was more like light was seeping out of me. My eyes looked electrified and ready for anything. I was looking on the outside exactly like how I was feeling on the inside.

"Pretty cool," I mumbled to myself. Behind me my parents were staring at me as if I was about to explode.

"Well, here's something you don't see every day," I offered.

"Do you feel okay?" Mom asked timidly.

"I feel amazing. I feel like I could run a marathon while doing calculus. I have never been better. I swear."

"You mean to tell me that all you have been doing is listening to music in your room?" Dad asked.

"Yeah." I couldn't keep from looking at myself in the mirror. It was a scene out of the movie *X-Men*, and I was one of the mutant kids coming of age. Cool.

"When you were walking around town this morning, did you go anywhere unusual? Did you go near any power lines, or..."

"Dad, I swear. I walked around Stony Creek and the docks for a while, but other than that, I've been in my room, listening to music. Ask Mom."

My mother shook her head confirming my story.

"I will admit though, as weird as this sounds, listening to music is a whole new experience."

"What do you mean a whole new experience?" Dad asked me, moving closer.

THE UNDECIDED

"Well, when I listen to the music, it's more than hearing just notes or lyrics. I actually don't really know how to put this. I sort of become one with the music."

I looked to my parents expecting them to be as jazzed as I was but instead saw two sets of blank eyes staring back at me. I was waiting for tumbleweeds to come blowing across the floor.

"I'm not following," Dad slowly said as he took my arm and led me into the living room motioning for us all to sit down.

"Okay, like earlier I was listening to Marley's "Redemption Song." My dad was following, but I'd already lost my mother.

"Bob Marley Mom, come on, keep up."

"Lucas," my mother scolded.

"So I'm listening to the lyrics and before I realize it I'm there. In the song. In the moment. I saw it. I saw men being dragged onto ships. I felt the fear, the shame and the anger, anger like I have never experienced in my life as these souls were taken and put on these filthy ships."

I sang some of the lyrics for my mom, who was still staring at me with a blank expression.

"Then I actually see a movement of light and dark. I feel a surge of spirit that they're using to bring up their people and fight back. It's like the entire nation was singing, and I was there to witness. And it becomes a part of me, or maybe I become a part of it, I don't know." I sang more of the song.

"You see? It's a plea for help from humankind to stop the killing and enslavement and to help lift up and elevate, and I was there! I was there in Bob Marley's head, spirit, mind, whatever you want to call it, and I felt where he was coming from, and felt his pain and his joy, which are kind of all meshed together. Does any of this make sense?" Tears were streaming down my face, and I carelessly wiped them away.

"I don't know what is happening here Luke," my dad slowly started, "but I think it's safe to say that it has begun. This is nothing less than a miracle. I still have no idea what it is, but..."

"But it's something wonderful," my mother interrupted with tears in her eyes. "Lucas when you sang, you were, it was, I don't know, it was you and then something more. It was like I could feel you when you sang, your words triggered something inside of me."

"Look at your wrist," my dad noted. It was definitely glowing more brightly. "We may not understand what's happening just yet, but I think it's safe to say something is definitely happening. And you're sure you feel good about this?"

"I've never felt better in my life. Well, I'm starving, but other than that, I feel amazing."

"Okay, well we knew we would see signs sooner or later, and I guess that time has come. Let's just take it slow and think this through. Lucas, I don't recommend listening to too much music before school on Monday."

"School. Right. Totally forgot about that small detail."

"But Lucas is right about one thing, it's time to eat, and we don't have anything in the house. How about pizza?"

"Awesome," I said as I felt my stomach start to cave inward.

"I heard that the Stony Creek Market has good pizza, should I order from there?"

My stomach forgotten, I jumped up.

"I'll go get it!" I went for the door, glowing wrist forgotten. All I could think about now was the possibility of catching a glimpse of a pair of haunting green eyes.

CHAPTER SEVEN

The market was livelier than it had been earlier this morning. There were three people behind the counter, an older guy making pizzas and two identical female twins who were taking the orders, moving and laughing in unison. They were dressed alike and had straight, blonde hair. As far as I could tell, there wasn't a single identifying mark that separated them, and I've got to admit that as pretty as they both were, it was a little creepy.

I looked around hoping to catch a glimpse of the redheaded Mare, but no such luck. My excitement bubble deflated, but all was not lost, since I was still going to walk out with a pizza. As I stepped up to the counter the twins both looked at me, cocked their heads to the left and said "Hi." Again, creepy.

"Um, hi. I'm here to pick up a pizza, the name's…"

"Lucas Aarons!" they both announced together with perfect smiles.

"Yeah, that's right," I answered, slightly embarrassed by their zealous greeting.

"Trudy, he's the new boy Mare was telling us about," one twin said to the other.

"Like duh, Judy," she replied and then followed with a not so private whisper. "He's super cute."

"Totally."

"So is Mare working tonight?" I dared to interrupt. They both looked at me as if they had forgotten I was still standing there.

"No," they answered in unison. "She got off about fifteen minutes ago," Trudy answered.

"Yeah, fifteen minutes ago. She might still be out back," Judy added.

"She likes to feed the stray cats," Trudy finished with a disgusted wrinkle of her nose.

"Cool. Um, so is the pizza ready?"

ROBIN DONARUMA

"Oh! I'm sorry, it's right here, half cheese, half sausage and onion right?" Judy asked as she slid a big white box in front of me.

"That sounds right."

"That's twenty-two even," Trudy said.

I handed them twenty-five. "Keep the change."

"Awesome!" they exclaimed at the same time.

"Thanks Luke!" Trudy said.

"Hey, see you at school on Monday!" Judy added.

"What's up with calling him Luke as if you're his best friend or something?" Judy squabbled with Trudy as I headed for the door.

"Why can't I call him Luke? And maybe we will be like best friends one day. He's really cute isn't he?" Trudy replied.

"Totally," Judy said, her voice drowned out by the tinkling of the door chime as it closed. I opened the box and took out a small slice of cheese as Judy and Trudy frantically waved to me through the window. I motioned back before stepping off the patio and decided to take a detour around the rear of the building, just in case they knew what they were talking about and Mare was still hanging around.

I rounded an overgrown bush and saw someone bent over and petting a cat. Bingo, and kudos to the Bobbsey Twins. I shuffled my feet in the crushed gravel as I walked towards her so that I wouldn't startle her. No luck. She jumped up whirling around defensively. I held up my free hand that wasn't holding the pizza box.

"Whoa. I didn't mean to scare you. Mare right?" I offered. She walked closer squinting up at me. I realized that I was standing in front of a large floodlight that darkened my features beyond recognition, so I slowly moved to my right and into the light. Her body softened, and she drew in a deep, shaky breath.

"Lucas Aarons," she stated.

"I'm sorry if I scared you. I was just picking up a pizza and then saw someone back here." I lifted my pizza box in my defense. "Thought I'd come check it out, make sure everything's okay."

THE UNDECIDED

She looked back at the three stray cats that were busy eating food off of the ground.

"So is this how you spend your evenings? Walking around town, eating pizza and looking for people to save?" she suggested with a small smile.

"Well, it's not always pizza. Sometimes I like a cheeseburger. Less cumbersome, you see."

"Yes, I can see how a cheeseburger would be much more convenient. But, alas, as you can see, I'm in no danger. Your powers are useless here."

"Well, at least we have pizza!"

Rolling her eyes "Ugh, no thanks. I've been cooking and smelling that pizza for four years and haven't been able to eat any of it in three. It's all yours," she said, picking up her bag from the ground and walking towards the street.

"So where are you headed?" I asked, catching up to her.

"Home."

"Mind if I walk with you?"

"This isn't Miami you know, Branford is about as safe as it gets."

"Fort Myers," I corrected. She stopped and looked at me, so I stopped too.

"What?"

"Fort Myers. That's where I'm from, not Miami." She shook her head dismissing the fact as lame.

"Whatever."

"Well, Miami is the east coast and Fort Myers is on the west coast of Florida. Very different. Different sand, different surf, different fish, the color of the water is different..."

"Okay, I get it." She held up her hand. "You can walk with me if you want, you never know there might be a piece of glass on the sidewalk that will require removal."

"Excellent."

We walked in silence, but it wasn't awkward the way silence can sometimes be. I shifted the pizza box to my other hand remembering that I was supposed to be delivering this to my parents, in the opposite direction. Oops.

"So I take it you met Judy and Trudy tonight?" She looked at me with a knowing smile.

35

"All at once. Are they always so, um, excited?" She laughed, and I was entranced.

"Excited is a good word for them. Their dad owns the market."

"They knew who I was as soon as I walked in the door."

"No doubt. Not a thing goes by in this town without them knowing about it first."

"Really? Well they said they heard about me through you." I looked at her expectantly.

"Did they now? I told them you had come in this morning, but they knew that you had moved into the Taylor's place." She looked at me slyly.

She took a right and pointed to a small white Cape Cod style home across the street.

"Well, that's me."

"The one with all of the bushes?"

"That's right," she said, trying to contain her laughter. "The one with all of the *award winning hydrangea* bushes."

"Ah. I take it that's a big deal?"

"It is to my mother anyway. Apparently we have really acidic soil that creates this rare red color. Most of the hydrangeas you see around here are either blue, white, or pink."

"So you have some magical dirt that grows red flowers? Interesting," I chided. She lightly slapped my arm, and I had to clutch the pizza box to keep it from falling.

"Your pizza is going to be cold by the time you make it back to your house."

"No, it's not that far from here, really. Just up the road a bit."

"Lucas. Judy and Trudy, remember?"

"Right, nothing is sacred, is it?"

"Well, not your address anyway." she turned before she reached the front door "See you on Monday!"

"Monday?"

"School. See you at school?"

"School, right. See you at school."

I started my twenty-minute hike home wondering if I should just stop and order another pizza. I thought about Judy and Trudy and bagged the idea. So it's a little cold, that's what microwaves are for, right?

THE UNDECIDED

I imagined my father pacing alongside the living room window while my mom conjures up every sort of horrible scenario that she can think of. I began to walk a little faster than usual. Maybe a little run would do me some good.

CHAPTER EIGHT

I was already awake when Mom came bursting into my room with a flaming donut.

"Up and at 'em birthday boy! It's a big day! Joey!" she yelled into the hallway.

"Thanks Mom, but don't you think this could have waited until I got dressed?"

"Of course not. I have always been the first one to wish you a happy birthday, and I always will."

My dad popped his head into the room still using his electric razor.

"Happy Birthday kiddo. Don't be late for school."

"Thanks Dad. I won't be late unless Mom decides to burn the house down with that donut." The donut was practically engulfed in flames.

"Oh!" She tried to blow out the flame. "You finish getting dressed Luke, there's more where this came from."

"Right, Mom," I said laughing. I got up to find a shirt as she popped her head back in the door.

"Happy birthday, Lucas," she said with a wink.

"Thanks, Mom."

I could hear her in the kitchen frantically extinguishing the now *refried* dough. I must say that if there is one thing this family isn't, it's dull. I finished getting dressed and mentally prepared myself for the first day of my senior year. I wouldn't say I was nervous, but I wasn't exactly looking forward to walking into a school full of strangers either. As a birthday bonus, Dad was letting me use the old Saab, which was very cool. No bus for Lucas. I lovingly gave Layla a final pat farewell and headed to the kitchen, my last stop before Branford High.

School came across like most other schools I've been in. Same smells (desk cleaner mixed with cafeteria French fries), same water fountains, same cinderblock walls, same

THE UNDECIDED

skylights over the library, same people. Yeah, they're all different from my friends down south, but they all faintly resemble each other in an eerie, clone-like way, especially the girls. One year every single girl had curly hair, wore way too much makeup and wore ridiculously tight clothes (not that I minded that part too much). This year it seems everyone is into flat hair, light makeup, and flip-flops. Maybe it's a territorial thing, who knows? I definitely liked this look much better though.

The halls echoed with conversations, which came out sounding like one universal chant. There was a monotone thread to the conversations that only occasionally expelled bursts of alternative sound like a squeal of laughter or a jocular taunt.

As I walked down the hall, the fluorescent lights cast weird shadows along the lockers as well as everyone around them. It reminded me of Peter Pan's shadow that followed him around moving a second later than he did. I stopped in the middle of the hall and rubbed my eyes trying to will away the headache that was threatening to break through. This morning definitely came too early. Before I could open them, a hand grabbed my left shoulder.

"You okay there? A bit lost perhaps?" said a tall British man who looked just like William Shakespeare.

"Yeah, no, I'm just looking for room 216," I answered.

"Well, by Jove, I think you've found it! Come in, come in!" He stepped aside and with one arm ushered me in as if he had been waiting for me all morning.

"Thanks."

"Pick a seat anywhere, it doesn't matter where you sit, be assured, I shall find you." He winked, pointed to the desks, and then went back into the hall in search of other lost souls.

There were fluorescent lights in the classroom too and not only were the shadows still hanging around, now they were pulsating like our old TV did right before the tube blew out. Maybe a seat close to the window would be a good idea. As I turned towards the windows I saw a familiar head of red hair. She bent down to pick up a piece of paper off the floor, but I beat her to it.

"Lucas! I thought I'd see you today, just not first thing today," she said with the most perfect smile God ever created.

"Lucky me, I guess," I said. She laughed and pointed to a desk beside her.

"Sit down," she said as she gestured to a petite blonde sitting in front of her. "Becca, this is Lucas Aarons, he just moved here from Florida."

"What are you crazy? Ugh. I would give anything to live in Florida."

I reluctantly turned my attention to Becca. She was real pretty in a very earthy way. Straight blonde hair and blue eyes, great skin and an even better smile. But there was something else, too. There was a haze around her, a bright haze. I looked back and forth between Becca and Mare who were now talking about the pros and cons of living in Florida. Maybe it was the reflection from the sun coming through the window, but Mare didn't seem to have it. I looked up at the lights again and got poked by a pencil.

"Ow!" I looked at the guilty party who motioned with her head to Becca. Apparently, I slipped into my own world and was completely ignoring Becca, the bright blonde (as I was calling her). "I'm sorry, I'm just zoning out. Becca, right?"

"Yeah. So why'd you move from Florida?"

"My dad's job."

"Bummer. What part of Florida?"

"Fort Myers."

"Hey, my grandpa lives in Naples, that's near there, right?"

"Yeah, just south by about twenty minutes."

"Cool." She smiled a perfect smile, and I was mesmerized by the bright glow around her.

"Attention! Attention!" said the man from the hall as he walked into the room.

"Is it just me, or does this guy look just like Shakespeare?" I whispered to Mare who giggled under her breath.

"Mr. Holland is the best. Just wait," she said out of the side of her mouth while Mr. Holland ceremoniously pushed a cart of books over to the opened doorway.

THE UNDECIDED

"Before we proceed any further, hear me speak." He opened his arms to his sides then quickly dropped them. He furtively whispered to the class "Shakespeare, *Coriolanus*, opening line, write that down. "Open your ears! *Henry IV, Part II*, so that you may immerse yourself into the wonderful world of written word. Words that so tiny on the tongue or miniscule on paper, when formed together become more lethal than the sharpest blade, mightier than any man made weapon of destruction. More beautiful than any God created visage and more inspiring than the creation of life itself. Welcome, my dear friends, to Branford High School's British Literature course for honors. You may now take out your book, which you each will find safely nestled under your seats."

I shot a look at Mare and Becca. They seemed to be equally as enthralled with Mr. Holland as I was. If nothing else, this class promised to be anything but boring. I grabbed the big book entitled *Shakespeare's Works* and slapped it on top of my desk along with the rest of the class.

"Turn to page eighty-four where we shall have the privilege to begin our journey together with the world's most famous couple, *Romeo and Juliet!*"

I found the page almost immediately. Whoever used this book before me left their mark via highlighters and ripped pages. I opened my notebook just as Mr. Holland approached my desk.

"Good show, Lucas, you found it. That indeed is the first step in reading the classics, finding the correct page."

I looked up at him in acknowledgment and noticed the same white haze hovering around his head, just like Becca. He was practically sitting on top of my desk when he flipped the pages in my book trying to find a particular passage. When he did, he pointed it out, looked directly at me and read it aloud.

"Wisely and slow. They stumble that run fast."

Mr. Holland then straightened, walked away and began addressing the class. I looked around. No one else seemed to have noticed our special moment that I was thinking was pretty strange. Maybe that's just what he does.

"I know most of you have already read about our star crossed lovers; however, it never hurts to remind ourselves from whence we came."

We spent the next forty-five minutes with the Capulets and Montagues until the bell rang for the next round of classes. I put the book back under the seat, as instructed by the highly entertaining Mr. Holland, and gathered the rest of my gear.

"So what do you have next?" Mare asked as she and Becca got up to leave.

"Uh, looks like Music Theory," I answered, reading my schedule.

"I have Calc," said Becca.

"I wish I had Calc I have P.E. Can you believe it? P.E. for second period?"

"That totally sucks," said Becca. Mare looked at me, which I guess meant that I was supposed to add my own opinion.

"Yeah, bummer," I flatly stated. Personally, I had no idea why P.E. would be a bad thing for second period, but Becca and Mare certainly did.

Mr. Holland was at the door ushering out the old class and welcoming in the new one. Mare and Becca went out before me, and just as I was about to leave, Mr. Holland grabbed my arm.

"Welcome to Branford, Lucas."

"Thanks Mr. Holland."

"I know you'll get along just fine here. It's a pleasure to have you in my class." He looked directly into my eyes a little too intensely for this early in the morning.

"Thanks again. See you tomorrow," I said, trying to leave for my next class. By this time Mare and Becca were long gone.

"And Lucas? Happy Birthday," he said with a wink. Before I could respond, he engaged another student.

I started thinking it kind of strange that he wished me a happy birthday. Or was it? Teachers have access to all sorts of personal info like that on students. I need to make sure not to read into every strange nuance that comes my way. At the rate things are going today, I won't even make

THE UNDECIDED

it to lunch. Time to move on to music theory, one of the few classes that I am actually looking forward to.

I got to the room just as the bell rang. Everyone was still shuffling around trying to find a seat, and I took a minute to scope out where I would plant myself. There weren't any windows in this room, and the walls were baffled. There were a couple of cellos and trombone cases sitting up against the wall and a Branford High Band State Champs 2009 banner hanging on the back wall.

I thought that maybe the lack of windows might help with my vision ailment this morning, but no such luck. The fuzziness, for lack of a better description, was even worse in here. Not only was I seeing bright areas, but there were dark areas too. Two girls in the front were both enveloped in a bright haze while one boy in the back was sitting in darkness. A couple people didn't have anything around them at all. Ugh. This was going to be a long day. I headed towards an empty seat in the back next to a kid sporting a Meat Loaf tee shirt.

"Nice shirt," I said, sitting down beside him. He plucked out his earphones that were hidden behind a huge head of wavy brown hair. He looked like he just stepped out of a '76 Frampton concert.

"You dig the Loaf, man?" he asked, perking up.

"Yeah, Meat Loaf's cool," I agreed, instantly liking this guy.

"Excellent! You wouldn't believe how many people haven't even heard of them before. It makes a boy want to cry. For them, not for me."

"Of course. What else do you listen to?"

"The Who, Yes, Rush. Gotta love Rush, man. Am I right?"

"Absolutely."

He sat up straight and put out his fist for me to knock knuckles with.

"The name's John. Not Johnny, not Jonathan, just John like my dear mama named me." I met his fist with a small tap and a flare of whitish light surged then floated around his body.

"Lucas. Lucas Aarons," I said, staring at the brightness surrounding him. I looked around the class noticing shadows ebbing and flowing around everyone else. I was beginning to think that this wasn't just a side effect from fluorescent lighting anymore. There was something much heavier happening here. Of course it could be my eyesight, but it *felt* like it was more than that.

The teacher came bursting into the classroom startling everyone into silence. Even if he had come in quietly, this guy would be hard to miss. He had to be over six feet tall with a full head of white hair. He had a guitar strapped to his back and a stack of papers tucked under one arm. He threw the papers on the desk, swung the guitar around, leaned against the front of the desk, and started playing. Everyone was staring at him, not sure how to react. I thought it was awesome, as did my new friend John who looked at me with his thumbs up. I tuned in to the chords trying to remember the name of the song as the teacher began singing.

Bob Dylan, excellent. Some girls in the front were whispering to each other, but most of the class sat entranced. He finished the song, and we all clapped.

"Whoever can tell me who I was just playing gets their first A." The class was abuzz talking with each other, trying to figure it out. I looked to John, thinking he would have this one, but he looked at me in frustration.

"Ah man, I know this. I know this one. My mom used to play it like all the time. Ugh this is killing me." He was lightly knocking his fist on his desk trying to conjure the answer that sat so close to the forefront of his memory.

"Dylan. 'Shooting Star,'" I whispered to him.

"Yes!" he yelled and raised his hand. The teacher propped his guitar against the blackboard and looked at John.

"Meat Loaf in the back," he said, neatening the papers on his desk.

"Bob Dylan, Shooting Star," John proudly answered. The teacher stopped shuffling his papers and walked to the front of the desk, staring at John. He looked at me, then back to John.

"Nice job, you have a good ear. Unfortunately, you used it to listen to your friend there give you the answer. Kudos to the both of you, A's to neither of you." He then

THE UNDECIDED

addressed the rest of the class. "Welcome to Music Theory, I'm Mr. Kenzie." He handed the pile of papers to a girl in the front row instructing her to pass them out.

Class went by pretty fast, and before I knew it, I was back in the hall making my way towards my next class. John gave me a peace sign as he left in the opposite direction, and I was once again left to my own navigating skills.

The next two classes breezed by since all we did was go over the syllabus, and before I knew it, I was headed towards the cafeteria for lunch. Walking into the overly loud lunchroom, I was assaulted with the aroma of food. My stomach growled in response, and I eagerly headed over to the lunch line, picked up a tray, and started piling on the food.

"Whoa, eat much?" said a voice behind me, a beautiful, melodious voice that I would know anywhere.

"Hey! I'm starving," I said with a big smile, handing her a tray.

"So I see! You're not even gonna have time to eat all of that," she chided.

"Oh, never doubt me, Mare. I will do this lunch tray proud." She shook her head as she put a small green salad on her tray.

"So how's it going? Get lost yet?" she asked, grabbing a carton of chocolate milk.

"Nope. But the day is not over yet." I knocked on the wooden table that I was sliding my tray on. "I see you survived P.E."

"Ugh. Barely. We start swimming next week, can you believe it?" she said with a disgusted roll of her eyes.

"Swimming? That really bites! Is there anyone you can talk to about this? I'm sure they're breaking some sort of law." She lightly punched me on the shoulder then pointed behind me.

"You're next smartie," she said with a little push. I turned towards the attendant, who was staring at me with wide eyes.

"Hello," I said for lack of anything else to say. Maybe people don't eat this much around here.

"Hi," she said, clearing her throat. She looked around for a pen and started adding up my meal on a small piece of paper. She appeared a little flustered, and I looked at Mare who was noticing the same thing. We both shrugged our shoulders.

"That'll be $3.75, Lucas," the attendant said, ringing the price into the register.

"Sure thing." I handed her four dollars.

"Twenty-five cents change," she said. As she dropped the quarter into my hand, she discreetly brushed the outside of my hand. I looked up and noticed a rush of bright light surrounding her. She smiled.

"Welcome to Branford, Lucas. Enjoy your lunch." I nodded and grabbed my tray, allowing Mare to pay for hers.

"Looks like someone has the hots for you," Mare teased as she led me to a long table by the window. Becca from British Lit., along with two of the biggest kids I had ever seen, were already sitting at the table.

We put our trays down and Becca offered me a huge smile, her whitish haze dancing around her.

"Who has the hots for who?" Becca asked.

"The cashier has the hots for Lucas," Mare answered, giggling.

"Ooh! This is quite a first day for you, huh?" Becca laughingly asked.

"You don't know the half of it," I mumbled as I started to throw down a handful of fries.

"Hey, you know what was really weird?" Mare asked.

"What?" I asked.

"She called you by your name," she stated as she inspected my shirt.

"What?" I asked with a mouthful of food. "What are you looking for?" I looked down at my shirt hoping I hadn't dripped ketchup on it.

"Have you ever met her before?" Looking at my blank stare, she continued. "The cashier. Do you know her or something?"

"I've never seen her before in my life," I said, gulping down my milk. For some reason, I didn't like where this conversation was going.

"Because she knew your name. She called you Lucas." Becca and Mare were both staring at me now.

"She probably heard you say my name in line," I quickly said. Becca silently nodded her head in agreement. Thank you Becca.

"No," Mare cut in. "I didn't say your name in line."

"You probably just forgot," Becca said.

"I didn't forget. I know I didn't say your name."

"Okay, Mare. You're salad's gonna get cold if you don't eat it."

"It's just strange, that's all," she said, stabbing a tomato wedge with her plastic spork.

"Look," I said, holding up a folder with my name written on it. "She probably just read it from this." I was silently congratulating myself on my quick thinking. I knew that my folder was tucked under my tray, but a white lie was worth this conversation coming to an end.

"Yeah, she probably just read his name on his folder, Mare," Becca added as she dunked one of her fries into ketchup.

"Whatever," she said, stirring her salad. "Even though I don't remember you carrying a folder, and I think it's weird how gaga she was acting around you. But whatever."

"No need to be jealous, Mare. You know I've only got eyes for you," I teased, holding a hand over my heart.

"Awe. How sweet," Becca said.

"Oh stop. Fine, forget I ever mentioned it!" She looked at me out of the corner of her eye turning a charming shade of pink.

"Hey Jeff, Scott, this is Lucas. He's just moved to Branford from Florida," Becca said to the two hulking teenagers to her right. They had already demolished their lunches and were into a deep conversation about a Patriots football game. Like some other people I saw today, these two guys didn't have any haze around them, light or dark. I looked at Mare and confirmed that she still didn't have any either.

"Luke, what's up man?" Jeff, slightly taller and bigger than Scott stood up and offered me his fist to knock knuckles with.

"What's up?" I replied. Scott leaned over and offered his big beefy fist to me.

"You're a long way from Florida, bro."

"Tell me about it," I half mumbled to myself. Scott and Jeff both stood up with their trays and announced that they were "outta there." I looked at Becca who was sweetly telling them that she'd see them later. Becca looked at me and laughed.

"They're really sweet guys," she said to me.

"Oh, I'm sure they are. They're just really big guys."

"The pride of the Branford Hornets!" she happily exclaimed.

"They're on the football team, in case you didn't guess," Mare added.

"I would be concerned if they weren't," I added as I stood up to throw away my trash. "Well, two hours to go." Becca and Mare followed me to the trashcan.

"Good. I'm so tired," Mare said.

We dumped our trays and set them on top of the trashcan. Mare and Becca led the way out as another wave of eager eaters were coming in. Just before walking out the door, I looked back and found the cashier watching me with a serene smile pasted on her face.

This was definitely one wacked out first day.

CHAPTER NINE

    I sat at the dinner table eating my traditional birthday dinner of loaded nachos as my parents drilled me with every question imaginable about my first day of school. I don't know what exactly they think takes place during the first day of school that is so different from every other day of my life. If anything, there is less possibility of anything interesting happening. The questions died down, and I could tell they were disappointed by my lack of interesting responses. I debated whether to tell my parents about the light fluctuations that I experienced at school. They grew stronger and more prominent as the day went on, and by seventh period, I knew that it wasn't a problem with the lights or my eyesight.
    There was a brightness around my parents, not hazy like some of the kids today, but a solid aura of white surrounding them. Feeling the need to escape to think this through, I stood up. So did my parents.
    "Whoa. Not so fast, Luke!" Dad said.
    "We haven't had cake, and you still have presents to open!" my mother said, hustling off to the kitchen.
    "Oh right. What's a birthday without cake, right?" I asked my dad, who was piling the dishes on top of each other.
    "You okay, son?" he asked, his voice echoing concern.
    "I'm fine, just tired," I answered honestly.
    Mom entered the room, and I flashed back to this morning. Hopefully this celebration would end better for the cake than it did the donut. They both sang "Happy Birthday," I blew out the candles, and my mom cut me a huge slice of chocolate cake.
    "Okay, present time!" my mother exclaimed, pulling out two small packages from the chair beside her, handing me the smaller one.

ROBIN DONARUMA

"Nothing too big, just something to open," she explained.

"Mom, I don't expect anything, really," I answered.

"Good, you shouldn't since you've commandeered the Saab," my dad chimed in.

"The Saab is awesome and I love it. Thank you." I opened the first box. Three iTunes gift cards. "Excellent! These will come in handy in about five minutes."

"Just be careful you don't use them all up then go to school," my dad said. I think he was trying to make a joke about my "glowing" incident. Dad was never much of a comedian, but I always appreciate the attempt and happily offer up my conciliatory chuckle.

"Absolutely. Thanks, Dad. Thanks, Mom. These are awesome," I said. My mom handed me the other package.

"This one, Lucas, is yours by birthright." I smiled at my mom, who, along with my dad, were looking at me very seriously. She continued, "It has been handed down for several generations to the eldest son on their eighteenth birthday." My mother placed the small package in my hand and gave my fingers a subtle squeeze. I looked at both of my parents curiously. This was the first I had ever heard of this family tradition. I opened the package.

It was a small wooden box that looked as if it had been hand carved. It also looked really old. I gingerly pulled off the top. Inside laid a strange looking necklace on a piece of purple silk. The chain wasn't really a chain at all, but a piece of darkened leather that looked like it had been around a while. There wasn't a clasp, just a knot and a loop on either end. The pendant was a round, silver medal embossed with intricate carvings. It had two sides to it, each with different markings and was hollow in the middle so you could see right through the design. I held it up to the light. The leather cord laced through my fingers, and I felt as if I had just found something that had been lost to me. Tears pricked my eyes as I wrapped my hand around the pendant. Breathing deeply, a beautiful silence washed through me, and I was filled with serenity. I turned it over, looking at both sides. I still couldn't make out what the design was, and I know that I had never seen it before, but I also knew, without a shadow of a doubt, that it was *mine*.

THE UNDECIDED

My parents were sitting very still, observing my reaction. My mother had tears in her eyes and one hand over her mouth. My dad was going back and forth between my mother and me.

"Lucas?" my mother asked. "Do you know what this is?"

"It's mine," I simply stated.

"Yes, it's yours. Have you seen it before? You seem as if you know it, as if you've seen it before."

"I don't know," I said, staring at it. "I don't think I've ever seen it before today, but I know that it's mine. I feel it."

"Do you know what it says?" my dad asked.

"It says something? No. I just thought it was a design."

"It's Hebrew. It says, *I Am Who I Am. I Am has sent me to you*. The other side is a silhouette of a tree."

"Where did this come from?" I asked my dad.

"It was given to us at your birth, Lucas," my mother added.

"From who?"

"It was at the hospital," my mother said meekly, "after you were born. They had taken you away to get you cleaned up. Your father went with you. He never left your side," she said through the fog of a fond memory. "I was resting in my bed when a beautiful, tall orderly came in. He was the most beautiful person I had ever seen. He smiled at me, and I was completely entranced," she said, looking off into the distance.

"He asked how I was feeling, and asked about you, then said that he had something that belonged to you. I remember I was confused thinking that you were just born, so how could he have anything that was yours? But then he took my hand and placed that box into it." She pointed to the box and then looked at the necklace. "He said that I was to give it to you on your eighteenth birthday, not a day before, not a day after. He said that it will mark the path that you will one day lead. And then he was gone. Just like that. One minute I looked down at the box, the next minute he was gone. It was as if he vanished into thin air. I asked the nurses if they knew of anyone by his description,

ROBIN DONARUMA

I asked the doctor, your father searched the entire hospital, but no one had either seen or heard of him."

"Who do you think it was?" I asked, staring at the necklace.

"He was a messenger sent by the Council," my mother answered. "Of course, I didn't find that out until much later when I began having my visions on your first birthday."

I looked at my parents, then back to the necklace. It was warm in my hand. I fastened it around my neck. It fit perfectly. I set the pendant on my skin and heat flowed through me. My eyes closed, a soft smile curled around my lips and the most beautiful music I had ever heard filled my head. I felt as if I had been reunited with a long lost love. I was completely and utterly content. Slowly, I opened my eyes and placed both hands on the table in front of me. My birthmark was glowing, and I lifted it for my parents to see.

"I think it has begun," I said with a huge smile.

THE UNDECIDED

CHAPTER TEN

They were getting closer. I could feel them. Like a silent wave in the middle of the ocean, the darkness rolled towards me, relentless in its pursuit. My legs were beginning to tire and the moist, thick earth slowed me down. The wind shifted making the reeds dance in a peculiar fashion appearing alive. I stopped and looked around, wondering which way would offer safety. The reeds, as if in answer, shifted creating an opening. I ran aimlessly, not knowing where I would end up. The water was deeper in the grasses and the coolness seeped into my shoes. I stopped to gauge my surroundings and listened for my pursuers. It was eerily silent. They were near.
    I crouched down to feel how close they were. The darkness surrounded me in an arc; they were trying to flush me out. I closed my fist around the silver pendant tied around my neck. A rush of power moved through me. Light filled me and surrounded the cold, muddied hole where I crouched like a wayward animal. I slowly stood as light poured from me onto the surrounding area. The darkness ebbed, and I felt its anger. I had control and was pushing the darkness away. I became giddy with the power and let go of my necklace. The light returned to me and I knew I no longer had to run. I was safe. I walked back through the reeds to the main path, not caring as they tore at my flesh. I stepped onto dry soil energized by my newfound power. I was in control and no longer afraid. I kicked a rock into the grass and stopped. My smugness faded. It was too quiet. Something wasn't right. I slowly turned and a massive black form came moving towards me at lightening speed. I stared helplessly at its approach and held my hands up to shield myself. It stopped. My hands emitted a soft glow that encompassed me like a bubble. The darkness stopped just before the threshold of my light. I walked forward, the darkness shrunk. I backed up, the darkness pursued. It

ROBIN DONARUMA

was a stalemate. I stared into the faceless void that wanted to destroy me. I felt its hatred, and I knew that it wasn't going to stop until it destroyed me. The battle lines had been drawn.

CHAPTER ELEVEN

I woke from the dream knowing that my life would never be the same. And I was okay with that.

Before heading to the kitchen I glanced in the mirror to look at my new necklace fastened securely around my neck. I grasped the talisman and was overcome with a sense of calmness. It was the most perfect emotion I had ever felt.

Mom was in her usual spot with a cup of coffee and a crossword puzzle. A shimmery white glow danced around her.

"Lucas! Good morning and happy day after your birthday!" she said, taking a sip of coffee.

"Thanks, Mom." I walked to the pantry.

"So, do you feel any different now that you're eighteen?" she joked.

"Uh, actually, yeah," I answered honestly."Well you look great!" She forgot her crossword, walked over to me and hugged my back.

"Thanks, Mom."

"No, I mean it. There's something about you. You look, I don't know, relaxed or well rested. You've been sleeping well I take it? No dreams?"

This was definitely not the time to get into my REM facts, so I opted with the fabricated truth.

"We all dream, Mom."

"Oh Lucas, you know what I mean," she chided.

"I know what you mean. And you will be happy to know that I have been sleeping fully every night."

"That's great, Luke." A look of relief washed across her face as she filled up her mug.

"So how's the life of Branford's newest high school counselor?" I asked.

"Oh, same as most other places, I imagine. Everyone's nice enough and so far, well behaved enough," she answered with a smile.

"Glad to hear it. Well, I better run." I put my bowl in the sink.

"You really eat too fast, Lucas. You don't give your body enough time to digest anything."

"Love you Mom." I picked up my backpack and kissed her goodbye on her cheek. "See you later." I was anxious to get to school. I had a theory that my necklace made the light flares stronger and was ready to check it out first hand.

The buses had already dropped off their loads of under eager kids and were headed out of the school. I picked up my pace and headed through the front of the school and onto British Lit. not needing the assistance of a map or friendly custodian. I glanced around at the few faces that had yet to find their way to their first period and definitely noticed a pronounced glow around them, well *some* of them. Just before I reached my class, a gawky kid was frantically racing from locker to locker looking pretty lost. White light bubbled up from his core showering over him. It enveloped his entire body and moved with him as he moved. Drawn to his light, I walked towards him just as his folder dropped causing papers to explode all over the hall.

"Hi. The name's Lucas," I said, helping him pick up the papers.

"I'm not available for tutoring until next week," he said without looking up. I touched his shoulder and felt his fear. Fear of disappointing his parents, fear of being late for class, and fear of everyone laughing at him. I gripped his shoulder with more force than I probably should have.

"I don't want you to tutor me," I said as gently as I was able to after swallowing his innermost thoughts. He looked up.

"Then what do you want?" he meekly asked. I handed him the rest of his papers as we both stood up.

"Not a thing." His name was written on his folder. "Peter. You just looked like you could use a little help."

THE UNDECIDED

"Thanks. I'm sorry, I'm just not used to people being nice to me without wanting something." He looked at the lockers, then back to me. "Thanks."

"Lucas," I said. "The name's Lucas. And you're trying to open the wrong locker." I pointed to number 432 written on his folder and then to the locker 423 that he was trying to open. Peter dropped his hand with an exasperated sigh.

"Your locker is over there." I pointed further down the hall.

"Thanks, Lucas." He shook his head in disgust. "Really, thanks for helping me."

"Anytime, Peter." The bell rang and he forgot about his locker and ran down the hall. *"Chill Peter, you'll be fine,"* I whispered. Peter slowed to a walk then went to his locker and calmly opened it and pulled out a book. Forgetting about my own tardiness, I turned towards my classroom to find Mr. Holland watching me from the doorway. A sparkling bright glow floated around him, brighter and broader than any I had seen before.

"Sorry, Mr. Holland. My friend, Peter, needed a little assistance," I offered, trying to float past him and through the door. No luck. He gently tugged my arm just as I was about to cross the threshold.

"A friend is one that knows you as you are, understands where you have been, accepts what you have become, and still, allows you to grow. Perhaps the greatest treasure given to man, that of a true friend. Excused this time Mr. Aarons, next time one may not be as lucky," he said with a wink. Still holding onto my arm, I felt love pouring out of him and into me. It was the touch, first Peter now Mr. Holland. As I was contemplating my new discovery, Mr. Holland's light grew brighter. He had stopped talking and was staring at me.

"Um, sorry. It won't happen again," I said, hoping that was a good enough response. He let go of my arm and ushered me through the door.

"Very good! Carry on then, and as you do, we shall all get out that very prized possession lying most snuggly under your arses," he announced to the class. I sat down, and Mare threw questions at me with her eyes. I shrugged my shoulders in a nonchalant manner and got out my book.

It was much more prominent today. Light and dark orbs pulsated around everyone. Mostly everyone anyway. Towards the front of the room there was a real pretty girl who looked perfect on the outside but was teeming with darkness. I must have been staring a little too intently, because she turned and caught me, her cloud darkening even more. She offered me a smile, which made my hair stand on end. I smiled back trying unsuccessfully to appear as if I was watching Mr. Holland who happened to be standing in front of her. The class spent the next forty minutes going over iambic pentameter while I spent it watching people. To my left was an overweight girl who was obsessively biting her fingernails. When she dared to make eye contact with anyone, she did so out of thick dark rimmed glasses. Her dark hair fell dully down her back and failed to detract from her clothes, which were too small and way out of date. She was the kind of girl, much like Peter I suppose, that people probably didn't talk to unless they needed something. I stretched back and leaned over her desk trying to read her name. Ruth. Ruth had light around her, but unlike Becca's vibrant hue, hers was feint. I experimented by trying to connect with her without using any physical touch. In my mind I repeated over and over, *"Ruth, stop biting your nails. Relax. Relax, Ruth. You're happy with who you are."* I envisioned her light brightening, and within a few minutes from the corner of my eye I watched Ruth gently drop her hand from her mouth and place it in her lap. She sat up a little straighter and her light visibly brightened. Everyone slammed their text books closed, snapping me out of my little world.

"Lucas did you pay attention to anything today?" Mare amusedly asked as she shoved her folder into her backpack.

"What? Of course I did, what do you mean?" I asked, looking around for my pencil that had disappeared from my desk.

"Oh nothing," she said with a smile. "It just seems like you spent the whole class daydreaming about something,

THE UNDECIDED

or *someone*." She motioned to the girl with the dark aura sitting in the front of the class. I shivered involuntarily.

"Don't worry, Mare. You know I've only got eyes for you," I said with a wink. She rolled her eyes and walked to the door with Becca. I picked up my backpack and called off the search for my pencil.

"Is this yours?" Ruth was holding my pencil.

"Yes, cool. Thanks." I took it from her hand.

"No problem," She shyly smiled and turned three shades of pink.

"I'm Lucas," I offered.

"Yeah, I know," she eked out as she started for the door. I followed her. "I'm Ruth," she offered when she realized that I was still beside her.

"Well, very nice to meet you Ruth. Thanks for rescuing my pencil." I headed towards my next class, but not before glancing back to see Ruth's light now beaming.

I got to class the same time as John, who was sporting a Pink Freud tee shirt. The front of the shirt had a big pink head of psychologist Sigmund Freud while the back read "From the dark side of the moon to the shrinks couch, Pink Freud lives." Awesome.

"Lucas, my man, what's up?" John greeted me with a laid back smile and his hand raised just enough for a high five contact without having to exert too much effort.

"Just ready to rock out day two, man," I answered, making contact with his hand. As soon as my hand struck his, I felt John's energy course through my own, and I was struck with an overwhelming sense of happiness. John was a pure, a very pure, all around, good guy. Excellent. We walked into class at the same time and headed to our desks. As soon as the bell rang, which was about thirty seconds after we found our seats, Mr. Kenzie closed the door and walked to the front of his desk.

"Okay. I assume that you're all here because you like music, yes?" Some of us nodded our heads, which didn't prove a sufficient enough answer for him. "Yes?" He asked again. "Yes," we all answered in unison. "Good, because between you and me, theory is boring. I know your mommies and piano teachers will be hunting me down come dinner for saying that, but it's true. And if I stand up here, day after day, talking about how many beats you can fit in a measure, half of you would fall asleep and the other half would want to date me. So this is the plan. We're going to talk, breathe, write, listen, and perform music instead of you just listening to me talk about it. How many of you play an instrument, I don't care what it is?" About more than half of the class raised their hands. "Okay, good. Now how many of you listen to music?" The entire class raised their hands. "Exactly. Is learning to read music important? Absolutely, unless you don't play an instrument. Hell, lots of famous musicians can't read a lick of music. To name a few, Tom Petty, Lindsey Buckingham, Paul McCartney, Stevie Ray Vaughn, B.B. King, Jimmy Page, and none of them could read music, and they seemed to do okay. And I'm pretty damned sure Ray Charles didn't read music either, by the by. But my point is that you don't have to *play* music to have a passion for it. You listen to it, sing it, dance to it, *talk about it*, do things I probably don't want to know to it, and *that's* what I want to tap into. Well, all but the last part that I don't want to know about."

Everyone was sitting up a little taller in their seats and excitedly whispering with each other while Mr. Kenzie walked to the blackboard and started writing on it.

"Music has been referred to as the heart of our soul. Plato once said that 'music and rhythm find their way into the secret places of the soul.' Victor Hugo is known to have said that 'music expresses that which cannot be put into words and cannot remain silent.' Music is the bridge that links us together as human beings, as spiritual beings. It doesn't matter what language you speak, or what color your skin is. You can love music whether you're Donald Trump or some aboriginal kid in the Outback. Music ties us all together, and understanding that is laying down an amazing foundation for your future in this world. It will change how you interact with people, the decisions you make, and quite frankly, it will make you a more interesting person." He wrote Van Morrison on the board. "I hate to even ask this, for fear of the answer, but who here has heard of Van Morrison?" Four people raised their hands, John and I included. "Oy Vey. That's what I was afraid of, and precisely why you need to be in this class.

THE UNDECIDED

    Van Morrison, Van the Man, is one of the greatest, transcendental, and inspired musicians to have ever graced this planet. Now, I could stand up here and tell you how he's won six Grammy Awards and has been inducted into the Rock and Roll Hall of Fame and the Songwriters Hall of Fame, but who cares? That means nothing if you don't know who the hell I'm talking about. So time to listen up kids. You're about to hear one of the greatest songs of all time. Van Morrison's "Into the Mystic," originally entitled "Into the Misty," but that's another story. The album was *Moondance*, the year was 1970. In 2004 *Rolling Stone Magazine* quoted this song as being number 480 on their list of the 500 greatest songs of all time." Mr. Kenzie grabbed the remote control for the stereo and walked to the back of the class. "As a matter of fact, according to a BBC survey, this song is one of the most popular songs for surgeons to listen to while performing operations because of its cool, soothing vibe." He stopped in front of me. "This song is about a spiritual quest." He walked behind us and leaned against the wall. "But enough of my voice, time to hear some magic, kids. Turn off your brains and just— simply listen." The soft strumming of a guitar filled the room. I relaxed listening to the familiar dulcet tones that I knew were about to build into an ethereal love story.
    I let go and listened with more than just my ears. The rush of the ocean echoed around me as a distant foghorn yelled to the sailors in warning. The rush of the salted air assaulted my lungs, but it didn't matter to me, because I knew my true love waited for me on the other side of the dense fog and rough surf. I rode the wave of emotion that Morrison created. I kept myself aware of the fact that I was sitting in class and not in my bedroom, making sure that I didn't fall too deeply into the song. It slowly faded away, much like a wave on the shore, and I crept out of my reverie. Mr. Kenzie, still behind me, put his hand on my shoulder as he passed by.
    "Pretty awesome, huh?" he asked. Emotion coursed from him into me. Much like Mr. Holland, overwhelming feelings of love poured out of him, but unlike Mr. Holland, it was laced with a thread of anger. I glanced at the white, very bright, air swirling around him.

ROBIN DONARUMA

    "Definitely," I said. He squeezed my shoulder in a fatherly way and the tinge of anger was replaced by music. He winked then headed back to the front of the class.
    "Into the Mystic," he said to the class. "A song can mean a lot of different things to a lot of different people. Is one right or better than the other? Of course not. On December 22, 1971 I was hanging out at Frist with my roommate pretending to study something or other, I don't remember." He stopped his stream of thought to clarify. "Frist is in Princeton. A campus community, if you will, a place to hang out, listen to music, watch theater, meet with groups, or whatever. I was there. And I remember this song coming on and thinking this was a really cool song. I had heard it before, of course, but it was getting a lot of play and becoming really popular around this time. So, in the back of my mind, I'm hearing this song and watching my friend pointing to his biology or something book. And I remember feeling so pissed off that he wasn't getting it. I thought, how can this music be on and you're just not hearing it? It infuriated me so much that I just had to get up and walk away. And it was at that moment that I ran into, quite literally, ran into the most beautiful brunette God had ever created. I lost my soul and my heart to this woman in that one moment that some would call a careless footstep. And this song, because of that moment, will always be more to me than just some notes on a page or some iTunes download. Music is personal, but it's meant to be shared. Which brings me to your first official assignment. I want you to bring in a song that has shaped your life in one way or another. Be it good, bad, sad, happy, I don't care. But I do want you to take your time and actually think about it. I'll even give you till next Monday. I want to know what *rocks your gypsy souls*." A girl in the front row raised her hand.
    "Mr. Kenzie?"
    "Yes?"
    "We were wondering." She looked to the girl next to her. "Whatever happened to the girl you bumped into?"
    "Ah. Well, Mrs. Kenzie is doing just fine and looking just as beautiful as the first day I saw her." The bell rang and a mixture of *awes* and *sweets* ricocheted around the

THE UNDECIDED

room as everyone stood up and started the slow shuffle to the door.

"This has got to be one of the coolest classes I've ever had," John commented.

"Definitely," I agreed.

"So, what's your song? What rocks your gypsy soul?" John asked with humor.

"No offense, but it's not Meatloaf."

"None taken, my friend." We got to the door and went our separate ways. "See you, *mañana*," he yelled, raising his fingers in a peace sign.

I spotted Mare as she entered the lunch line. I grabbed an empty and slightly dirty tray off of the nearest table, shook off the crumbs and slid in behind them.

"Ladies," I said with a flourish and half bow.

"Hi Lucas!" Becca smiled.

"Sir," Mare answered with a bow, showcasing her perfect smile and perfect teeth.

"Aren't you in Mr. Kenzie's, music class?" Becca asked me, reaching for a chocolate milk.

"Music Theory, actually. It's a pretty cool class, so far anyway. Definitely one of my favorites," I answered taking a bite of my pizza.

"I've heard that's an awesome class if you like music. If you don't, you're lucky to get a C," Mare added.

"Who doesn't like music?" I asked, the mere thought of someone not liking music turned my stomach. I prayed that Mare wasn't one of those people.

"Oh not me, I like music, I'm just saying that I heard Mr. Kenzie is kind of like a music maniac. If you love it, he loves you. If you don't, well, I guess you'd be better off taking P.E. second period."

"You're still griping about that?" Becca asked, laughing, as she paid for her food.

"Easy for you to say Becca, you don't even have P.E." Mare moved up in line and handed her money to the lunch attendant who was looking over Mare's head at me. She handed Mare her change without ever having made eye contact. I looked over my shoulder to see if maybe her attention was directed behind me instead of towards me, but there was no one there. I was hoping Mare wasn't noticing this, but of course, she was. I took another bite of pizza and got out my money.

"Good afternoon, Miss Muriel," I said, reading her nametag.

"Good afternoon, Lucas. Glad to see you back with your hearty appetite!" she responded giddily.

I handed her my money and she gave me change without even looking at the change drawer. She was watching me intently, but not like the way I wished Mare would look at me. More like the way my mom looks at me. Kind of strange, but it came across as very comforting and made me feel at ease.

"Thank you, Miss Muriel," I said, pocketing my change.

"Call me Muriel, Lucas. I'm much too old to be referred to as a miss," she said with a warm, glowing smile.

"Muriel it is, then. Be well, Muriel." I said.

"We will be now, Lucas," she said with a wink. Signs of change seemed to be greeting me at every turn, surfacing like tiny bubbles in my Coke. Obviously the game is in play, and I'm not the only one on the board. Who we're actually playing against is the question now, that and what exactly I'm supposed to do as the leader.

I walked over to Mare and Becca who were gathering an arsenal of napkins and salt packets. As we continued to our usual table by the window I noticed Ruth from British Lit. sitting by herself.

"I'll be right there," I said. Becca continued without a hitch, but Mare stared at me with question as I approached Ruth's table.

"Ruth, right?" I asked, setting down my tray. I guess I caught her by surprise, because she choked on a sip of milk. Luckily, Mare put half of her pile of napkins on my tray. I handed one to Ruth.

"You okay?" I asked, trying not to laugh. I patted her between the shoulder blades and her light flared brighter. I took my hand away and sat down. Her face, though red from coughing, radiated happiness.

"I'm fine. You just startled me, that's all." She blew her nose with the napkin I gave her.

"Sorry 'bout that. I just wanted to say hi, that's all," I said as I stood up.

"Hi," she answered shyly but through a huge, bright smile. "Thanks," she demurely added.

"Are you sitting by yourself?" I asked looking around. "You can come sit with us, over there." Ruth looked over at our table with trepidation.

"Oh, that's okay. Thanks though. I'm almost done, and I really need to study. I have a pop quiz in Economics next period."

I put my hand on her shoulder. She was afraid they wouldn't know who she was. And yes, she did have a quiz that she was nervous about. I decided to let it rest.

"Okay, well, maybe next time?" I squeezed her shoulder affectionately then picked up my tray.

"Maybe next time," she echoed as a blush ran across her cheeks.

"Good luck on your quiz, Ruth," I said, walking to my table, ready to devour my lunch.

"Thanks, Lucas," she faintly replied.

I reached the table and was met with two pairs of female eyes boring into me.

"What was that all about?" Mare asked.

"Isn't she in our British Lit. class?" Becca asked.

"Yes, she is, and her name is Ruth," I answered, folding my slice of pizza in half.

"And?" Mare baited.

"And what?" I downed the pizza with a small carton of milk. "I saw her sitting by herself, and wanted to see if she'd like to sit over here, with us."

"Aww, that's sweet, Lucas," Becca honestly reacted as she picked the onions out of her spaghetti.

Mare looked at Ruth who now had her nose in an Economics book.

"And what did she say? Why didn't she follow you?" she asked, truly curious.

"Well, what she said was that she had a test to study for. What she meant was that she was terrified of being rejected by you guys." I took a bite of chocolate cake.

"She said that?" Mare asked.

"No." I washed down the cake and wiped the crumbs from my face. "She felt that."

"How do you know what she feels if she didn't say anything?" Becca asked.

"Because I can read people. She looked over here, saw Jeff and Scott and then you two, whom I assume have never spoken a word to her in your lives, and turned a charming shade of pink. She then had a hard time making eye contact with me and started shredding her napkin." I took another bite of cake. "This cake is really amazing. You have to try this next time."

"Lucas, I have never known anyone to eat as much as you do and stay so thin. It's so unfair," Mare said.

"Totally," Becca chimed in.

Mare looked back to Ruth who had packed up her books and was emptying her tray.

"I'm not scary, am I? Why would she be afraid of Becca and me? Jeff and Scott I understand since they're like the biggest kids in the entire school."

"Maybe it's not the things you do but the things that you don't do. Ruth is a good person with a good heart, it's just that no one has taken the time to notice." I finished the last of my lunch feeling quite sated and satisfied. "I really love lunch." Becca laughed, and Mare rolled her eyes.

"Yo, Bec, you're Branning it this weekend, right?" Jeff asked Becca.

"Absolutely! Are you guys?"

"You know it." Jeff and Scott knocked knuckles. "What about you guys?" Jeff asked Mare and me. I looked at Mare, totally confused as to what the question was. Mare explained that *Branning* was a term they used when locals hung out.

"This weekend is the annual Branford Festival. It's so awesome. Everyone will be there," Becca added and looked at Mare. "Right Mare?"

"Just about. It's kind of a big deal around here. You would love it, it's a total food fest," she said collecting her stuff.

"Are you going to be there?" I asked Mare directly.

"Oh, I'll be there. I have to work in the morning. The market has a booth selling pizza by the slice. I have to work that for a couple of hours with Trudy and Judy."

"But after that?" I asked as we all stood up.

"After that, she's totally free!" Becca added then walked away to throw out her tray, smiling.

I looked at Mare who was looking rather flustered.

"Well, then, I'll definitely be there."

CHAPTER TWELVE

It was barely eight o'clock in the morning, and my parents were dressed and ready to head out the door, pretty unusual for a weekend morning.

"Where are you two off to this morning?" I sleepily asked.

"Good morning, Lucas," my mother sang, blowing me a kiss from across the kitchen.

"You look tired, son," my dad said through a sip of coffee.

"Yes, you're up early for the weekend." Sobering immediately, my mother approached me. "Are you sleeping okay?" I knew what the underlying question was. I thought it best not to worry them with the ones I have had, especially since they now seemed to have super sped up to being interactive. But the fact of the matter was that the best way to avoid any of those dreams, dark, interactive, or a little of both, was to not sleep a whole lot. I guess it was starting to show.

"I'm sleeping fine, I just heard you guys in here and thought I'd see what was going on." I pulled out a box of Reeses Puffs cereal. "Excellent," I commented to myself.

"Lucas, you know there is absolutely no nutrition in that whatsoever. Let me make you an egg or something."

"Mary, we don't have time for that. If he wants an egg, he is fully capable of making an egg," my dad interjected.

"It's made with whole grain and essential fiber, it says so right here." I pointed to the box. My mother rolled her eyes. "So where are you off to?"

"The Branford Festival," my father answered.

"Doesn't that start later and go all weekend? It's eight in the morning," I asked, pouring milk into my bowl.

"Yes, well, your father took it upon himself to sign us up at the pancake tent. So we're off to flip jacks."

"I think you mean flip cakes, dear," my father teased.

THE UNDECIDED

"I don't know, Dad. I was thinking she meant flap jacks." My mother looked back and forth between the two of us.

"Be nice, you know I've only had one cup of coffee. I don't care what you call them. Or what I called them. Let's go before I change my mind. You're coming down to the green, right Lucas?"

"Definitely," I said with my mouth full.

"Make sure you're there in time for the parade. There's an amazing lineup of classic cars," my dad added. He was a big car fanatic, though you wouldn't know it from the cars that were in our driveway. My mother kissed me on the forehead.

"And don't forget to make yourself an egg."

"Sure Mom. I'll see you guys there a little later." They said their final goodbyes, and I went to the refrigerator and pulled out the eggs.

***

The festival was going strong by the time I arrived, just before noon. Kids were running with American flags held high while mothers pushed their strollers along the green. Older festival goers seemed satisfied rocking in chairs, wistfully watching the youth. It was Americana at its finest. Red shiny tractors, circa 1940, drove kids around the square while they threw candy to those lucky enough to look up.

The vibe around town was good. The majority of people at the festival were enveloped by glittering, white light. A few dark energies were peppered amongst them, but nothing too alarming. What surprised me most was the large amount of people milling about who had nothing around them at all.

They were the grays, the in-betweens, ones who have yet to decide which side they were on. Mom said that the grays were the most dangerous, but I just couldn't wrap my head around that. There was no way that Mare could ever be considered dangerous, not to me. My necklace warmed, and I clutched it in my left hand. A vibration tickled my fingers and a beautiful, low tone, like the purr of a really good engine, filled my head.

ROBIN DONARUMA

I saw the pancake tent first and thought I'd check in with Mom and Dad. Standing behind a huge griddle the size of our kitchen table, Dad squeezed out batter while Mom flipped the cakes, talking the whole time. I don't even think she was talking with anyone in particular.

"Mr. and Mrs. Buttersworth, I thought I'd find you here," I said, walking up with an empty paper plate.

"Hey! There he is!" my dad happily exclaimed.

"Lucas! Not bad, huh?" my mother said, motioning to her flipping technique.

"Not bad at all, Mom. You do me proud."

"Just don't ask her how high she can flip them." Dad rolled his eyes and gestured to a trashcan behind them that had a pretty decent amount of battered (no pun intended) cakes decorated with blades of grass and dirt.

"No problem. I'll have two," I said, putting my plate in front of my mother.

"Just two? Are you feeling okay?" my mother joked.

"Perfect. I'm just pacing myself," I said, motioning to the rest of the tents. I took out two dollars to pay for the hotcakes.

"Oh put that away Lucas. Your father will pay for them," said Mom.

"Hey, wait a minute!" my dad exclaimed as I put my two dollars back into my pocket.

"Thanks, Dad! See you later, gotta keep moving." I rolled up my pancakes and dipped them into a small plastic cup filled with syrup. I looked back just as Dad patted my mom on her behind and kissed her cheek. That wouldn't have been a big deal, but that caused my mother to drop another pancake onto the ground. I watched as she tossed another dead soldier into the trash bin and thought how cool it was that after all their years of being married they could still make each other laugh.

I threw my empty plate into the nearest trash bin and leisurely strolled around the green. The sun was warm and soothing and the breeze was consistent and light. I listened to the music that was intertwined with children's laughter and absorbed the happiness that came with those sounds. This was a good place. There was a beautifully blinding light that surrounded the mass of people. There were a few

THE UNDECIDED

dark spots, kind of like sunspots, but the majority was light, and it felt right. With a lighter step, I walked the row of tents in search of the Stony Creek Market pizza tent. I recognized her auburn ponytail immediately.

Trudy and Judy were there, one standing on each side of Mare, talking at her like a pair of stereo speakers. As I approached, the conversation became quite animated.

"So, have you kissed him?" Judy asked Mare.

"I bet he's a good kisser," Trudy chimed in.

"Totally," Judy said to her sister.

"Guys, please," Mare pleaded. The twins looked at each other and rolled their eyes.

"Look Mare, we think you're being pretty selfish."

"Yeah, selfish."

"Selfish, about what?" Mare asked. "You guys are supposed to be helping me, not harassing me."

"Oh, chill out Mare. Geeze," Judy said, grabbing a paper plate.

"Yeah, geeze," Trudy echoed placing a slice of pizza on the plate. Mare took the plate and turned to the next customer in line, which happened to be me.

"You read my mind!" I exclaimed, taking the pizza. All three girls stared at me as if they had just conjured me out of thin air.

"Lucas!" Trudy and Judy said in unison.

"Ladies," I answered, and they giggled. "Mare."

"Lucas. You must have just gotten here, because the tents haven't run out of food yet," she teased.

"Ah, how right you are, dear Mare. The day is still young and my appetite quite hearty. How long do you have to work here?" I folded the pizza in half and took a bite.

"Actually, I'm done in about fifteen minutes."

"Excellent!" I said with a full mouth and upraised eyebrows.

"A bunch of us are going to meet down at the old Puppet House," Mare suggested as she continued to hand out pizza. Judy and Trudy were now attempting to help, but keeping a very close eye, or eyes, on us.

"Puppet House? That sounds kind of creepy."

ROBIN DONARUMA

"Only at night," she teased. "Actually, we hang out in a courtyard right beside the Puppet House, not actually in it."

"That's a relief. I kind of have a thing about clowns," I said with a shiver.

"Don't worry, I'll protect you," she said laughing.

"Ah, well then, in that case, I'm in," I said with a wink. "I'm going to check out the gelato tent next door, meet you there?"

"Sure."

"Excellent. See you in a few." I walked towards the aforementioned tent thinking what a great town this was turning out to be and then ran into a bag of popcorn. There was a guy walking with his little boy attached to that popcorn, and before I knew what had happened, there was popcorn everywhere.

"Whoa!" the man said as we careened into each other. The little boy, maybe five years old, laughed and began eating popcorn off of the grass. I started to apologize but was hit with such a sickening wave of dread that it rendered me speechless. The man was enveloped with darkness. I took three shallow breaths forcing words into my mouth.

"Um, sorry. I'm sorry sir. Really sorry." I looked at the boy and was relieved to see him surrounded in white light, happily eating the popcorn. I glanced around the green to see if anyone else was watching. I felt trapped. There were no other dark ones near, just the man in front of me. With much effort, I looked into his eyes, which appeared friendly, but the darkness oozing around him told me differently.

"Oh, not a problem, I should have watched where I was going," he kindly offered. "Besides, Adam there doesn't seem to mind, do you son?"

"Popcorn!" the boy excitedly exclaimed. The man laughed at his son.

"See there? No problem at all."

"Well, at least let me buy you a new bag, for Adam." I got out two dollars and offered them to him.

"No, don't be ridiculous. These things happen, put your money away and save it for that cute red head I saw you talking to." He winked at me and moved a little closer. "Hey, believe it or not, I was a young man once too." He grabbed me on the shoulder in a friendly manner, but it felt like cold talons piercing into my flesh. I looked at my feet willing myself to not fall into a full-fledged panic. Unable to stop myself, I connected with his energy. A wave of nausea hit me as I saw a vision of him walking into Adam's bedroom. He closed the door and unbuttoned his shirt raising one finger to his lips motioning for Adam to be quiet. He sat down on the bed then turned off the bedside lamp.

I was going to throw up. I whipped up my head and backed out of his grip. I tried not to look at Adam as he sat innocently eating the soiled popcorn.

"Okay, if you're sure. I better get going, I'm meeting some friends." I backed away slowly. He laughed and waved to me as if I were a long lost relative.

"You go on. Don't let us keep you. Come on Adam, Daddy will get you some more popcorn, or how about some ice cream? You want some ice cream?" Adam popped up and ran towards his dad's extended hand stopping to look at me before grabbing it. I gave him what I hoped was an encouraging smile, but the closer he got to his father's hand, the more faint his light became.

"How 'bout some ice cream, huh Adam? You want Daddy to get Adam some ice cream?" The man gave me one final nod and turned towards the ice cream tent as the small boy put his hand into his father's. His white light was extinguished. Adam watched me until he was swallowed up by the shadow of the ice cream tent. I stood motionless, not sure what to do or think. My appetite was gone, and I was debating whether I should just head for home.

"There you are. I thought you were getting gelato," Mare said bouncing around me, taking out her ponytail.

"I changed my mind," I said, trying to put on a brave smile.

"What's wrong? Did something happen?" she asked, immediately concerned.

"No, nothing happened. Well, I knocked a huge bag of popcorn out of some guy's hands." I pointed to the popcorn

ROBIN DONARUMA

all over the grass. "I just thought I had better pace myself. I'd hate to burn out early." The look on her face clearly stated that she wasn't buying my story.

"All right. As long as you're sure you're okay."

"Hey, you should see the other guy, it wasn't pretty, believe me. Butter, popcorn, as far as the eye could see." She looked back at the spilled popcorn, then back to me. Finally giving up, she smiled and grabbed my elbow.

"Let's go.

CHAPTER THIRTEEN

"That's it?" I incredulously asked as we approached a small wooden house that looked like it had been around for a few centuries.

"That's it. What? Are you scared? Because we can turn around..."

"You're a cute girl Mare. And funny. Anyone ever tell you that?"

"Hey Mare! Lucas!" Becca yelled from a small courtyard that attached the Puppet House with a small art gallery. "I didn't think you guys were coming!" She wove her way through about ten other kids and met us at a white picket fence surrounding the buildings.

"Becca's dad owns the art gallery so he lets us hang out here whenever we want."

"Very cool," I said, walking through the small gate. I recognized most of the kids from school, and was relieved to see that there weren't any dark energies among them.

"Lucas!" John from Music Theory shouted. He was sporting an old Rolling Stones tee shirt and had an acoustic guitar strapped around his shoulder. Excellent.

"John. What's up?" I said meeting his hand in a low five. "Nice G man. You play?"

"A little. Nothing to get the folks too excited about, but enough to keep the ladies interested." Mare walked up beside me.

"Hey John. Lucas, come here, I want to show you something." She took my hand and led me to the side of the Puppet House.

"I wanna hear you play, man," I yelled to John.

"I'll be here," he said as he strummed a chord.

"Here, jump up on that crate," she said, pointing to an old crate sitting on top of two pallets stacked against the puppet house.

"Are you sure?" I kicked the crate to make sure it was sturdy.

"Oh good grief, Lucas. Here, follow me." She stepped on one of the pallets, crawled on top of the crate and jumped up and down. "See? It's totally safe. Come on." I bypassed the pallet and jumped onto the crate beside her. She used her sleeve to wipe dirt off of the small window in front of us.

"Look in there," she said with a huge grin.

"Whoa," I said while peering through the glass. "Are those the puppets? They're huge!"

"Yeah, aren't they cool? Most of them are around five feet tall. My parents used to take me here every Sunday afternoon when I was a little girl. I used to be convinced that they were real, no matter how much my parents tried to talk me out of it. I had the biggest crush on that knight, right over there." She pointed to a medieval knight in full battle armor.

"I can see that. He's a good-looking guy. Aside from the twenty strings and metal rod coming out of his back." Mare lightly chucked me on the arm.

"Hey, I was like five, give me a break! They were brought here from Italy. Sicily, I think, and are supposedly some of the last of their kind."

"They don't make them like that anymore, I suppose."

"Nope." We both removed our noses from the window. Mare had a smudge of dirt on her nose, and I wiped it off.

"Hey, Mare, Jeff and Scott are here!" Becca yelled.

"Great!" she yelled to Becca. "Well, I guess we had better get down before this old box collapses underneath us."

"I thought you said it was safe," I said, jumping down.

"The last time I climbed up here was two years ago," she said, hopping off of the pallet smiling. "Come on, Becca's dad usually sets us up with a limitless supply of chips and soda."

"Now you're talking. Lead the way," I said with a gallant bow.

"Mare!" Jeff, or Scott, I still can't get their names straight, yelled picking her up and swinging her around.

"Ahh! Hi, Jeff. Okay, you can put me down now."

THE UNDECIDED

"Lucas!" Jeff bellowed towards me. I prayed he wouldn't pick me up, thank goodness he offered a high five instead.

"W'sup Jeff. Scott."

"Aw, you know, just Branning it old school," Jeff responded as he howled another greeting to someone across the yard. Mare looked at me stifling a laugh.

"We all used to meet down at the fair, but after we outgrew the face painting and balloon animals, Becca's dad was cool enough to let us hang out here instead. It's sort of become a tradition."

"And when did this tradition start?" I asked, looking around.

"Fifth grade. Thus, the old school comment." Mare started talking to a friend, and I took a moment to look around and take in the vibe. Becca was sitting in a chair in the shape of a large hand and talking to someone leaning against an oversized, concrete toadstool. Pieces from her dad's gallery, I assumed. John started tuning his guitar, so I walked over, anxious to hear him play something. He was sitting in an old yellow metal chair that looked like something you would find on your grandmother's front porch. Other kids sat on the ground or leaned against the wall, eating out of huge Dorito and Sun Chip bags and gulping down Mt. Dews and Diet Cokes. I walked over to a cooler, grabbed a bottle of water and leaned against the wall to John's left listening to him strum some chords.

"Come on John, play something," a cute dark haired girl sitting by his feet said, grabbing his leg and shaking it.

"Free Bird!" Jeff yelled from across the yard. Everyone laughed and John began playing the opening.

"Only if I can play the whole thing!" John yelled back. I walked in front of John, really enjoying the day, the music, and the positive energy surrounding me. I sat on the grass in front of him holding my bottle of water up as a salute as John melded his "Free Bird" chord into a blues riff from Eric Clapton's *Crossroads*. I closed my eyes and became absorbed. He sang some of the lyrics, but mostly worked his strings. As it turns out, John was a pretty decent guitar player. When I opened my eyes Mare and Becca were sitting beside me.

"He's really great, isn't he?" Mare asked me.

"Definitely," I answered with a huge smile.

"I remember when we were like in second grade and he would bring this big box wound up with all these rubber bands and constantly play it. It was so annoying," Becca said laughing.

"Wow, I totally forgot about that. Didn't he used to go around calling himself Eddie Van Halen?" Mare asked Becca.

"Yes, he did!" They both fell back laughing, and I continued to watch John as he approached his big finish. He stood up and pounded out the last few chords leaving everyone whistling and clapping for him as if he were a big rock star. This was turning out to be exactly what I needed. I approached John and shook his free hand, since his other one was still holding his guitar.

"Excellent job, man. Really, that sounded really great," I said.

"Thanks man. You and I are probably the only two here that could recognize the song, but they all seemed to dig it," John said as the cute dark haired girl brought him a Pepsi.

"Definitely" I said, raising my eyebrows and gesturing to the girl.

"That's Maggie. She's cool," John said as he gulped down his drink.

"She seems to think you're pretty cool too." John shrugged his shoulders.

"What can I say? Chicks dig me," he said seriously, then looked at me and cracked up. "I'm just kidding man. Hey, you wanna go?" he said offering me his guitar. "You play, don't you?"

"Yeah, I play," I said taking his guitar. "But usually at home, in my bedroom." Mare walked up beside me.

"Come on Lucas, play something."

It's not that I was nervous to play in front of people, but I was a little concerned with how I might come across. The last time I sang in front of my parents, I turned on like a light bulb. But right now, holding John's guitar and being surrounded by everyone created a heavy feeling inside me. I *needed* to play.

THE UNDECIDED

"All right. I guess I can come up with something." I sat in the yellow chair that John had played from and strummed a few chords appreciating that it was perfectly tuned. "Nice, man," I said to John. I didn't think about what to play, instead I just let my fingers walk along the strings and my mind go. I started thinking of the little boy from the fair. Anger welled up within me and inside I cried for the boy and without conscious thought, I began singing.

Queensryche's "Silent Lucidity" flowed from me as smoothly as a psalm from a pastor's mouth. I stood up looking out to the faces of my new friends and watched the light surrounding them expanded and meld with each other. The grays, there were three in the crowd including Mare, had developed white sparks that danced around them.

I finished the song feeling energized and refreshed. Light joyously eddied around making our crowd appear as if we were one entity.

Hands clapped me on the back. John made his way to me first by pushing that cute dark haired girl out of the way. He stared at me wide-eyed as if he'd never seen me before struggling to find his voice.

"Dude. That was freaking amazing!"

"Thanks, man. I think it was the guitar." I handed it back to him and he moved his eyes from me to the guitar staring at it as if it were made of gold.

"No, I'm totally serious. That was..."

"Awesome!" Becca butted in, giving me a huge hug. "I'm so glad you moved here, Lucas! You're so great!" She hugged me again.

"Thanks, Becca." I looked over the heads of everyone to find Mare staring at me with tears streaming down her face. I made my way over to her.

"What's wrong? Are you okay?" I grabbed her hand. She wiped a tear away with her free hand and stared into my eyes.

"Who are you?" My heart fell into my stomach.

"Come on, you know who I am. Are you feeling okay? Do you want me to take you home?"

ROBIN DONARUMA

"You're like no one I've ever known before. You're different." She looked down at my hand holding hers. She noticed my birthmark and inhaled sharply. I shrugged my shoulders trying to pretend that it wasn't slightly glowing.

"It's a birthmark. Kind of weird huh?"

"It looks like it's glowing," she said rubbing her thumb over it.

"Glowing? Are you sure you're okay?"

"I've never heard anyone sing like that before," she said, looking up at me.

"That bad?" Luckily, she took the bait and laughed, which lightened the atmosphere tremendously.

"Stop, you know it wasn't bad. Not even close. There is something about you that draws people in. Something..." She looked back down at my birthmark. "Different. I sound crazy, I know, but look at the way everyone reacted to you. The way everyone always reacts to you."

"Okay, I think I know what the problem is." I dropped her hand and put my arm around her shoulders. "I think you need some cotton candy stat."

"What?" she asked laughing.

"I think that it's time to tackle the rest of those tents, I'm beginning to feel faint." I put my hand dramatically against my forehead.

"All right, I need to meet my parents soon anyway."

"At the green?"

"Yeah, they're working the Italian tent, and I need to watch my sister."

"Ooh, an Italian tent?" I said excitedly. Italian food was one of my favorites.

"The best. But let me warn you now, if you even so much as mention The Olive Garden, you'll be wearing the food, not eating it."

"Whoa. Hard core."

"You have no idea. We Italians take our food very seriously, it's our passion." We waved goodbye to everyone as we left through the small gate.

"Your passion huh?"

"Like it or not. My grandmother used to do most of the cooking. She came here from Salerno."

"Cool."

THE UNDECIDED

"Yeah, her name is in the books on Ellis Island. She was the typical matriarch. She would cook for days without ever sitting down once, I swear. We would all cram into her small house, and I'm talking cousins, aunts, uncles, like twenty of us, and just eat and laugh and listen to stories about each other, one crazier than the other. My grandmother would always sort of be standing off to the side ready to refill a plate or take an empty one away, at least when she wasn't in the kitchen cooking." She smiled as she sifted through her memories. "I remember one morning we got there really early, my parents had just taken us out of bed and put us in the car, so when we got there, I really had to use the bathroom. So I ran upstairs having gotten there just in the nick of time, if you know what I mean." She gave me a sly wink out of the corner of her eye. "And as I was washing my hands, I saw something dark moving in the bathtub. I thought maybe it was her cat, Sniffles, so I walked over to get him out, but it wasn't Sniffles. They were eels. Live eels swimming all over the bathtub. I screamed bloody murder, and my dad comes crashing through the door with my mother right behind him, and while they're trying to calm me down, my grandmother, all ninety-eight pounds of her, walks in, reaches into the tub, grabs an eel in each hand, looks at me, and says 'dinner,' then walks out. After like half an hour, I finally calmed down enough to go back downstairs. So I went to the kitchen, and just as I walked in my grandmother pounded a huge nail through one of the eel's heads. I passed out."

"So much for passion," I said laughing.

"It was disgusting. To this day I can't stand eels or snakes, or anything that slithers," she said with a shiver. "Grammy died three years ago, and since then, everyone has sort of gone their own ways, with their own families. It's kind of sad, but I guess a natural progression of things, huh?" She looked at me, and I shrugged my shoulders, not coming from a large family. "But Grammy's recipes have been passed down and whenever we cook, it's more than just making food, it's like we're visiting with someone we love."

ROBIN DONARUMA

We reached the green, and I was again thinking what a really great place this was turning out to be and not just because of the red-haired Italian by my side. I was searching for the Italian tent when I spied the old man with the pipe from the Stony Creek Market as he was staring right at me. Again. I slowed down hoping to avoid getting closer to him.

"Hey, do you know that guy over there?" I asked. "He's smoking a pipe."

Mare looked around the green. When she found him, a huge grin lit up her face.

"What? The guy that looks like the Gorton's fisherman?"

"Yes!" I answered.

"Of course. Everyone around here knows him. That's Captain Bob. At least, that's what we all call him. His real name is Robert Sariel. He's been here like forever and knows everything about this town that you could ever want to know. I swear he's looked the same ever since I can remember. When we were little we used to think that he was a real pirate. He used to run this sightseeing tour around the Thimble Islands, thus Captain Bob."

"Tell me something," I asked Mare with my back to the Gorton's Fish—Captain Bob. "Is he looking at me?"

"Looking at you? Right now?"

"Yes, right now. I know this sounds crazy, but when I saw him at Stony Creek sitting outside on the deck, he stared at me, point blank."

"Yeah, he's a regular fixture most mornings."

"And just now, I caught him staring at me again."

"Did you ever think maybe it's because you're the new guy in town?"

I shrugged, starting to feel a little foolish.

"Maybe you're right. I don't know. But it's not just that he was looking at me, it was the *way* he was looking at me. It was pretty intense." She looked at Captain Bob then back to me.

"Well, he doesn't seem to care too much now. Come on." She took my hand.

"Wait. Where are we going?"

THE UNDECIDED

"There's only one way to figure this out. I'm going to introduce you to him."

I tried to come up with a reason not to go, but realized that this was actually the best solution to find out if this guy had it out for me, or if I was really starting to lose it. He was watching us approach, and I tried to shake off the unease that was creeping in.

"Hi Captain Bob!" Mare said perkily. He took his pipe from his mouth and smiled an unsettlingly beautiful smile full of straight white teeth.

"Good day to you Marianne." He held out his hand, took hers and gave it a familiar squeeze. "I see you brought a friend for me to meet?" He put his pipe back in his mouth and folded his arms in front of him.

"Captain Bob, this is Lucas. Lucas Aarons. He just moved here from Florida."

"Nice to meet you, sir." I presented my hand and he stood straighter, offering me his large, weathered hand in return. His grip was firm, yet gentle.

"Lucas Aarons." He removed the pipe from his mouth with his free hand and stared into my eyes. I tried to tap into his energy but couldn't feel anything. He chuckled as he dropped my hand and moved closer to me. "You're not quite there yet, son. Give it time," he whispered. He put his pipe back in his mouth and addressed Mare who was looking at something across the green.

"Looks like your parents are looking for you, Marianne." He gestured with his pipe to a tree just beyond where we stood. "You better get on. You're needed." Then he looked at me. "I will see you again, Lucas. Soon. You walk Marianne over to her folks. They're good people."

"Yes, sir," I responded lamely.

"See? He's sweet" she whispered.

"Yeah, I guess he's not a stalker after all." She laughed walking towards her family. Why couldn't I *hear* him? A light glow wafted around him, not brilliantly bright, but more like a thick fog different than any I had seen before.

"Lucas? You coming?"

I caught up with Mare just as she met up with her parents. I was about to introduce myself but was paralyzed

ROBIN DONARUMA

by the most beautiful, brightest light that I had yet to encounter.

CHAPTER FOURTEEN

The resemblance between Mare and her mother was unmistakable. The only difference being that her mom was surrounded by white light. Her dad, also standing amid a swirling mass of white light, was a good-looking guy with dark black hair and a natural smile. I liked them immediately. But it was the small girl standing between them that captured my attention. She couldn't have been much older than six or seven, but the large Boston Red Sox baseball cap and big denim jacket that were two sizes too big for her made her appear even younger. But it wasn't her clothes that held my attention, it was the light surrounding her. It came from deep inside and beautifully erupted around her leaving her swimming in light. She appeared angelic, and I was mesmerized until a quick jab to the ribs refocused my attention.
"Lucas. This is my family. That's Mom and Dad." I shook both of their hands and mumbled a greeting. "And this is my bratty little sister, Grace," she said smiling.
"Ha ha, Mare. Very funny." Grace stepped towards me. She looked at my wrist and grabbed my hand, peering at my birthmark by turning my wrist one way, then the other. Everyone was watching with interest, as was I.
"Who are you?" she asked with a raspy voice, craning her neck to look up at me.
"I'm Lucas," I answered, knowing that that was not the answer she was looking for. She giggled.
"I know that, I've heard Mare talk about you. You're from Florida."
"Yes, I am. So your sister was talking about me, huh?" I looked at Mare who was beet red.
"You're beautiful," she whispered.
"Thank you, Grace. You're not too bad yourself." She laughed looking back at her mother with a huge smile. She stepped closer making a gesture for me to bend down.

"I don't have any hair," she whispered into my ear. I pulled back to look at her wondering if she was pulling my leg, but then she placed her small hand on my shoulder and whispered again. "It fell out." Her energy shot through me like a lightning bolt. Her love came first, beautiful and pure without an ounce of malice. Then I felt her fear and sadness. Not for herself, for her family. Grace was a very sick little girl. Images of doctors, nurses, and medications, went flying through my head as well as visions of her parents crying uncontrollably. Grace was worried about how her family will be once she is gone. That thought caught me off guard, and I fell back onto the grass, tears stinging my eyes. She watched me knowingly, and held out her hand.

"It's okay," she said. "Truly." I nodded, not knowing what else to do. "Maybe you can come visit some time?" She looked to her parents who were watching us with interest. Her mother slowly stepped forward.

"That's a wonderful idea, Grace. Maybe you and your parents would like to come over for dinner this Sunday?" she asked me.

"Best Italian food you've ever had," Mare added, lightening the strange encounter.

"Well, how can I turn that down? I'm sure my parents would love it, thank you Mrs. Rossi, Mr. Rossi."

"Great! Maybe around seven?"

"Seven sounds great."

"Okay. Mare?"

"Yeah, I'll be right there, Mom."

"Okay honey. Bye Lucas, it was very nice to meet you." She took Grace's hand.

"Same here, Lucas," her dad said, shaking my hand.

"Nice to meet you too, sir," I said as Grace shook off her mother's hand wrapping both of her arms around the lower half of my legs.

"See you tomorrow, Lucas," she said, looking at my wrist as her mom pried her away from me.

"Bye Grace," I uttered, watching her float across the green with her parents.

"Okay," Mare started. "Now don't tell me I just imagined that!"

THE UNDECIDED

"What, that your sister has a crush on me? How can she resist?" I teased.

"You know what I mean. Look, I don't have time to get into it now. I have to take Gracie home."

"How sick is she?" I whispered. Mare sighed and all of the light flares that were around her disappeared.

"Very." We stood in silence for a moment, neither of us really knowing what to say. "So, give me a call and let me know if your parents want to come over tomorrow?"

"Definitely." I smiled.

"See you Lucas. I'm glad you came today." She kissed me on the cheek and walked away.

This had turned out to be one heck of a day, for a host of reasons. I was thinking that it was definitely time for a parental powwow, because something is definitely going on in the serene scenery of Branford.

I went in search of my parents and spied my mom walking out of The Beanery, a local coffee shop across the green, toting a large paper cup of coffee. She took a sip then quickly pulled back from the heat.

"Careful, it's hot," I said, kissing her on the cheek.

"You would think after thirty years of drinking coffee, I would know to wait until it cooled down. Where's Mare? That's her name, right?"

"Yeah, Marianne Rossi to be exact. She had to watch her little sister while her parents worked their tent. They were really cool, though. They invited us over for dinner this Sunday night." My mother stopped and looked at me.

"They did? Well wasn't that nice. Is this something you want to do?"

"Absolutely," I said.

"Well, I think that sounds great! Should I bring anything?"

"I don't know, Mom. You can call them if you want."

"I should at least bring a bottle of wine or a salad, I could bring a salad. Even I can't mess up a salad." Mom was getting lost in her thoughts, so I placed my hand on her shoulder returning her attention back to me.

"Mom."

"What? Has something happened?" she asked, looking all around us.

"No, Mom, calm down. We're totally safe," I said smiling in hopes to lighten the mood. "Come on, let's go for a walk." I looped my arm through hers and led her away from the festival and towards the water. "There's a really great path that runs through the marshes."

"All right."

We reached the path just as a large flock of loudly squawking geese flew overhead in a perfect V formation.

"You know whenever I hear geese flying overhead like that, it always reminds me of a group of old ladies out shopping. Blah blah blah blah honk honk honk honk," she said, mimicking their cacophony. As if in response, the geese got louder. "Must be quite a sale," she said with a straight face.

"You're awesome, Mom. A little strange at times, but awesome." I put my arm around her shoulders. "So, I've been having some interesting experiences lately."

"Really?" my mother asked reservedly.

"This past week, since my birthday to be exact, I have been seeing things a little differently."

"What do you mean?" she said, looking at me earnestly.

"Well, at first I thought it was just the fluorescent lights in school." My mother slowly nodded. "But it became stronger and more apparent."

"What did? What are you seeing Lucas?"

"I can see who the dark ones and the light ones are. Their lightness, or darkness, I can see it swirling around them." My mother dropped her coffee.

"Shoot!" she said, looking down. "I'm sorry, Luke."

"Don't worry about it." I picked up the now empty cup.

"You can see them. You can see everyone?"

"Well, not exactly everyone. Some don't have anything around them at all."

"The grays," my mother answered. I took a deep breath, loving the feeling of telling someone everything.

"I thought maybe that's what it was."

"Lucas, we have to find your father and tell him what has happened. Things are progressing far faster than we ever could have imagined."

"But there's more." She stopped dead in her tracks.

"More?"

THE UNDECIDED

"When they touch me, or if I touch them, I can feel them. I can almost *hear* them, their hopes, fears, desires, even their depravity."

"Oh Lucas."

"And sometimes, I can communicate with them. On a subconscious level, they can't hear me, at least I don't think they can, but I can change the light surrounding them. I'm still trying to figure that one out."

My mother took the empty coffee cup from my hand. "Come on, we need to talk to your dad. This may have just been thrown out of our hands."

"What do you mean?"

"I mean that I can't answer any of your questions. I don't understand any of this anymore than you do, but there is someone who can."

"There is? Who?"

"I've never met him. He came to me in a dream and told me that you would be needing him soon." We approached a trashcan, and she threw the cup in. "This is really wild."

"Is there anything else, Lucas? Anything else that you haven't told me?"

I thought about the dreams where I held back the darkness, and the strange way some people like Mr. Kenzie, the lunch lady, and Captain Bob look and talk to me as if they knew me. I thought of how everyone's light changed after I played on John's guitar, and I let out a big sigh.

"I think we had better wait until we find Dad." My mother nodded, and we both started walking a little faster.

CHAPTER FIFTEEN

I filled them in on everything and watched as they attempted to mask their stunned expressions. It was almost humorous. My mother was wringing her hands and my dad sat still as a statue, deep in thought.

"I know this is a lot to take in. Maybe I should have told you sooner, but I wasn't sure if it was really happening or all in my head."

"You did the right thing, Luke. But the time has come for us to take the next step." My mother nodded in agreement.

"Next step?"

"In seven days someone from the council will meet with you," my father explained. "They are going to help you understand what exactly is happening to you, and more importantly, why."

"We don't know much about this meeting, all we know is that you must go alone," my mother added.

"Okay. So you drop me off, I meet with this council guy, and he tells me what the heck's going on, right? Sounds good to me, but why seven days? Why can't we go now?"

"I don't know, Lucas. All I know is what I was told. Seven days."

"Where?" I asked.

"I'm afraid I don't know that either. The location will come before you are scheduled to meet."

I rubbed my hands through my hair in frustration.

"I hope you guys realize how really crazy all this sounds. Right?" I looked from one to the other. "You agree this is not normal, even for being abnormal, this is starting to sound pretty whacked."

"Lucas, nothing has been normal for a long time as far as we're concerned," answered my dad.

***

THE UNDECIDED

Sunday night quickly arrived, and we headed to the Rossi's for dinner. We pulled into their driveway approximately ten minutes later. Their house glowed warmly, and the amazing aroma of our future meal struck me half way up the walkway.

The front door opened with a quick jerk, and Mare stood there with a welcoming smile, her auburn hair flowing about her shoulders. The light from the dining room created a halo around her entire form, and I stood mesmerized.

"Lucas, you made it! Come in, please." She stood aside allowing us to file into the foyer. Her father appeared from one room and her mother scuttled in from another. Introductions were made all around, and before we knew it, we were standing in the living room, my parents holding glasses of red wine and laughing as if they had known each other for years, not minutes.

"I'm not sure what's for dinner, but you have to know that this is the most amazing smell I think I have ever encountered," I told Mare.

"Wait until you taste it. It's eggplant parmesan. I promise, you've never tasted anything like it."

"I believe you," I said. "Where's Grace?" I asked, looking around.

"She's in her room. She's not feeling very well today," Mare answered, looking at the ground.

"Is she okay?" I asked.

"She's just tired, that's all. She has good days and bad days. I guess this turned into a bad day," Mare answered with a shrug of her shoulders. She picked up a tray of fresh mozzarella, basil and tomato and offered it to my parents. Just as I was about to pluck one of those colorful concoctions off of the tray, someone sang my name.

"Lucas!"

Grace stood in the hallway wearing a faded yellow nightgown and a bright pink handkerchief around her head.

"Hi Grace." I couldn't help but smile, because the light that was shining all around her was blinding. She was so beautiful, and so frail. Her parents both rose off of the couch at the same time rushing to her side.

"I'm fine," she whispered. "I promise, Daddy. I just wanted to see Lucas." Her parents stood straighter and accepted what she said with reservation. They looked to me and then back at Grace.

"Well, just for a little while, you need your rest Gracie," her mother said.

"I understand," she told her mother. Then she looked at her father. "I'm okay, Daddy." Then she looked at me. "I'm better now."

Grace floated across the room to me, and I thought that the only thing missing was a pair of wings. She took my hand looking at my wrist. It was softly glowing. She smiled and entwined her fingers with mine.

"Wanna see my room?" she asked. I looked to her parents who nodded an approval and told her that I would love nothing better.

She opened her bedroom door and led me inside to one very pink room. Lace curtains hung in the window and Disney Princess decals were scattered along the walls. A long white dresser and the frame around the mirror were covered in greeting cards. There was a desk covered with prescription medicine bottles alongside a gray plastic pitcher. Her floor was lined with every stuffed animal imaginable.

"This has got to be the coolest room I have ever seen. Well, for a girl's room, anyway." She giggled and squeezed my hand.

"Come here." She led me to the window. I struggled not to step on any of her animal friends and ran into her bed. She laughed at my clumsiness, and I was shaken to realize that her bed was a hospital bed complete with rails and hydraulics. I glanced at Mare who was staring at the bed with hatred.

"Look. Out there, see them?" Grace asked pointing out the window into the dark night.

"Um, what exactly am I supposed to be seeing?"

"Wait! There's one! See, over there! A firefly!" She dropped my hand placing hers on the windowpane.

"Fireflies? Isn't firefly season over?" I asked Mare who walked up beside me.

THE UNDECIDED

"For the most part, but sometimes you can still spot them through September, depending on how cold it is."

"Aren't they beautiful?" Grace asked. "I pretend they're angels flying around our house protecting us from bad things."

"Angels, huh?" Mare rolled her eyes and walked away. "They always reminded me of light bulbs."

"Light bulbs!" Grace said through a loud bellowing laugh.

"Yes, light bulbs! I used to think that every time a firefly lit up, someone was having a great idea."

"What does a light bulb have to do with an idea?"

"You know, like in Looney Tunes."

"Looney Tunes, what's that?" she asked. I grabbed my chest in despair.

"Mare, don't tell me your sister has never heard of Looney Tunes." Mare was straightening the bed sheets. I looked back to Grace. "You know, Bugs Bunny, Sylvester the Cat, Yo Sammity Sam?"

"I know who Bugs Bunny is."

"Oh boy. Tell you what. Next time I come over I'll bring my best of the Looney Tunes DVD. I promise, after you watch it, you will never look at a firefly the same way again." She laughed looking back out the window.

"I used to catch them and sneak them inside, you know."

"I don't think you're the first kid to ever try that one," I answered with a wink.

"I'm not allowed to catch them anymore." She longingly watched the sporadic flashes outside, and before I could ask her why, she answered me. "They're afraid I might fall cause it's so dark outside. My bones aren't very strong anymore, and I can't run anymore, not really. I don't think I'd be able to catch even one."

I grabbed her hand and a peaceful calm washed over me. Smiling, she looked down at my wrist, then up to my face.

"I can feel you," she said.

"I can feel you too," I whispered. She smiled and looked back out the window.

ROBIN DONARUMA

"Maybe it's better that I don't catch them anymore, that way they will always be out there to protect me."

"Maybe you're right," I answered as Mare approached. "What are you two whispering about?"

"Our next date."

"Oh really?" she asked, looking pointedly at Grace.

"It's okay Mare, you can come too," she said teasingly.

"Well thank you, your highness," she said with a royal bow. Grace laughed and called her silly just as her right leg gave out. I grabbed her before she fell. Mare sobered instantly.

"Gracie?"

"I'm fine Mare, I promise. I think maybe I'm ready to lay down now, though." She looked at me. "I get tired pretty fast."

Mare helped her into bed and tucked her in. Grace pulled the blankets up around her and she seemed to all but disappear into the mammoth bed.

"That's better. Wait. Where's Hairy?" she asked, looking around the room. Assuming she was referring to one of her stuffed animals I picked up a furry rabbit.

"Is this it?"

"No, silly," she laughed. "Hairy isn't a toy, he's my cat." As if waiting for his cue, a dark blur jumped onto the bed and let out the loudest meow I had ever heard. It looked at me, and I stumbled back hitting the dresser and knocking several cards onto the floor because standing in front of me was the strangest and ugliest creature I had ever seen.

"What—is—that?" I hesitantly asked. They both laughed.

"That's my cat, Hairy!" Grace said as she petted the mutated formation purring in front of her.

"I know what cats look like, and that is no cat." Mare picked up the bony gray and white mass.

"Oh Lucas, don't be such a baby. This is Hairy. Hairy, this is Lucas," she whispered to the cat. "Don't mind him, he's probably a dog person."

"Hairy? That cat doesn't have any hair." I took a step closer, still weary of the beady green eyes protruding from the narrow face that was watching me intently.

THE UNDECIDED

"Exactly! Hairy is a hairless cat. We got it for Gracie after her first Chemo treatment." And then the light bulb went off, and I felt like an idiot. Well, it was still creepy looking. I walked closer and petted it. I can't say that it was a good experience. It was like petting warm bones.

"See? He likes you!" Grace proudly stated. "I knew he would, of course, but he doesn't always like everybody. He's a little shy sometimes," she whispered.

"I bet I know why," I said, referring to his appearance. Mare kicked me.

"I think he's perfect," Grace said with stars in her eyes. Mare put Hairy on the bed, and he walked to Grace and licked her face before walking towards me. He gave me a large, mournful meow and then leaped into my arms. I caught him and stood there helpless as he rubbed his head against me purring louder than any cat I had ever heard.

"Is there anyone or anything that doesn't like you?" Mare asked smiling.

"Of course not," Grace answered, watching the two of us (meaning me and the cat) with unadorned pleasure. Mare looked at me and then at Grace and shook her head as if she'd given up.

"I don't know what's going on, and right now, I don't care, I'm hungry. I'm going to go see if I can help Mom with dinner and let her know you're in bed, okay brat?" Grace removed her attention from Hairy and me and nodded.

"You coming, Lucas, or are you and Hairy working out your engagement?"

I tried to put Hairy down, but he moved further up my shoulder.

"I'll be right there. I think." Mare stifled a laugh and walked out of the room. I moved towards Grace, hoping that Hairy would come to his senses and hop down. "Okay boy, it's been fun, but I've gotta go." As if understanding, he jumped onto the bed. After circling a couple of times, Hairy curled himself up against Grace's arm. He started licking his paw and I had to repress a tiny shiver. What was he actually washing? Certainly not any fur. Hairy stopped, looked at me with those saucer-like green eyes and meowed. Time to go.

"You get some rest, Grace, I'll see you again, real soon." She reached out and grabbed my hand.

"Promise?" She closed her eyes and smiled.

"I promise." She was so fragile, and yet her light was the strongest I had ever encountered. She squeezed my hand and opened her eyes, looking at my wrist.

"Are you an angel?" she whispered.

"No," I whispered back. I looked at my glowing wrist.

"I think you're an angel," she said sleepily.

"That's funny, I was just thinking the same thing about you."

"You're funny, Lucas. I can't wait for our date," she said through half closed eyelids. I gave her hand a slight squeeze and let go just as her mom came in.

"I see you met Hairy," Mrs. Rossi said, tucking the covers in closer around Grace.

"Yes. He's quite a, uh, looker."

"You could say that," She said, watching Hairy stretch out beside Grace who was fast asleep.

"I'll go see if Mare needs any help." I turned to go, but she caught my hand.

"Lucas, I know this sounds crazy. And maybe it is. Lord knows we've been feeling kind of crazy around here lately." She looked at Grace. "There is something between you and Grace. Ever since she met you yesterday, she has been different. Almost hopeful." Tears rimmed her eyes, and I could feel her fears, her worst fear. It made me sick. No one should have to live in such turmoil. "I don't know what it is. And really, I don't care," she continued. "I just wanted to thank you. And to let you know that if there is anything you or your family ever needs, please don't hesitate to ask."

I was taken aback at her sincerity. I gave her hand a short squeeze and glanced to Grace.

"Thank you Mrs. Rossi. I will remember that." The Rossi's pain ran very deep. Watching Grace deteriorate in front of their eyes put a big toll on this family, and while the parents keep going, Mare seemed to be stuck in her own bitter war with reality.

CHAPTER SIXTEEN

Dinner went off without a hitch. Everyone laughed a lot and the food was out of this world. We said our goodbyes a short while after eating a generous portion of tiramisu and were walking through our own front door by ten o'clock. My parents were unusually quiet on the way home, but I was too full to care. All I wanted to do was crash on my bed; however, my parents had other plans.

"Lucas, we want to talk with you for a couple minutes, do you mind?" my dad asked. I love it when Dad pretends to give me an option when we both know I don't have one.

"Sure, Dad." I plopped down on the couch and threw my feet onto the ottoman. "What's up?"

"The Rossi's are nice people," my mother started.

"They definitely can cook, that's for sure." My dad looked at me and rubbed his stomach appreciatively.

"Okay, enough boys. I'll be more than happy to make that for you. Kathy gave me the recipe." My dad and I exchanged glances. We both knew that the day my mother produced a meal like that out of our kitchen would be the day that pink, curly tailed pigs would fly past our windows.

"We wanted to talk to you about Grace," Dad began.

"Grace is sick," I flatly stated.

"Yes, we know. When you were in her room, her parents gave us a brief rundown. She has AML."

"What's AML?"

"Acute Myeloid Leukemia. She was in remission for a while, but it has come back."

It was one thing knowing she was sick, but putting a name on it made it more real.

"What exactly does that mean for Grace?" I asked.

"They can't know for sure, but the statistics for reoccurrences aren't usually very good ones."

I nodded my head not knowing what to say.

"But what we're curious about, Luke, is this connection that you two seem to have," my father said as he moved closer to my mother.

"We could sense it as soon as she walked in the room," my mother stated.

"And the Rossi's told us when you met at the festival yesterday, it was like pulling teeth to separate her from you," my father finished.

I touched my necklace. It was warm.

"I know that Grace is sick. Now, I know how sick. But when I first met her, well not even met her. When I first saw her," I looked to my dad, "it was the brightest, purest light that I had ever seen. I was drawn to her like a moth to a flame. And I think she can sense that something is different about me."

"You think she sees light too?" my mother asked.

"Not exactly. She noticed my birthmark right away, but when she took my hand she asked me *who I was*."

"Well, had she met you before?" my father asked.

"No, but it wasn't like that. She told me I was beautiful. She definitely sees something in me."

"Well, that would explain why she seems so fixated on you I suppose. But what could she be seeing? Do you know?"

"No. I don't. But tonight, when we were in her room, she told me that she could *feel* me." My mother inhaled and my father sat back against the pillows.

"What does that mean?" my mother whispered.

"Mean? How do I know what it means?" I stood up. "Do you think I understand what any of this means? Do you think any of this makes sense to me? Because believe me, it doesn't. I don't know what anything means anymore."

My mother walked to me and held me tightly.

"Of course you don't. I meant it as more of a rhetorical question, I guess. I know this can't be easy for you. What we need to remember is that whatever is happening to you, it's good. It's all for the good." My mother pulled back to look at my face. "And we'll be with you every step of the way, Lucas." My father got up and joined the hug fest.

THE UNDECIDED

"Every step," my father said. Their love poured out of them as fast and furious as Niagara Falls and a calmness washed over me allowing me to actually believe them.

***

Monday morning, I approached school with a mission. Talking to my parents about what was going on took a lot of weight off my shoulders. I was meeting with someone from the Council in a few days, but until then, I decided to start keeping notes of who were white, dark, and of course, gray.

British Lit. was uneventful; however, I did notice that the grays were bouncing in between both light and dark energies while the white and the darks gravitated purely amongst their own. I started writing down my observations in a spiral notebook so I wouldn't forget them when Mr. Holland called me out.

"Mr. Aarons. My, my, aren't you the wordsmith today?" He slowly walked to my desk. "I know that I encourage copious note taking, but I dare not think it necessary during my recitations." I closed my notebook as he neared. "My words fly up, my thoughts remain below: words without thoughts never to heaven go."

He moved my book onto my closed notebook, winked, and then addressed the class who was giggling at the scene.

"Hamlet, Act III. And *that* you may write down, young friends."

The rest of class breezed by, and I made sure that the rest of my notes were mental ones. Before I walked out of class, Mr. Holland stopped me.

"Lucas, I leave you with one important point that you may write down at your leisure," he said, smiling slyly.

"Yes, Mr. Holland?"

"Well, actually, they're the wise words of Mark Twain. You do know him do you not?" I nodded that I did. "Good. He once said that he made it a point to never let his schooling interfere with his education." I just stared at him. Was this supposed to mean something to me?

"Okay, thanks Mr. Holland." I headed out the door.

ROBIN DONARUMA

"Just think about it Lucas. It will all make sense soon." I looked back at him with question. He tilted his head slightly in acknowledgement. I took a step towards him, but he ushered a student into the classroom and closed the door just as the tardy bell rang. Great. Now I was slightly freaked out and late.

Music was playing through the closed door of Music Theory. I opened it slowly and squeezed through the opening hoping to make it to my seat without being noticed. Not a chance.

"Ah, it seems Mr. Aarons found my class worthy of attending after all," Mr. Kenzie yelled to the class, raising his voice above the music. Was that N'Sync? Oh boy. Maybe I should have just skipped class altogether.

"Sorry Mr. Kenzie. I was talking with Mr. Holland after class." I rushed back to my seat with my head held down, hoping no one noticed my embarrassment.

"Holland, huh? What do you have to talk with him about? His definition of music is anything that has a Beatle performing in it. He even likes Yoko Ono for the love of God."

I stared at him, not really sure if he wanted me to respond or not. He decided to let it go. I sat down.

"Well, Mr. Aarons, before you so rudely interrupted us, we were listening to Crystal's song that she chose as the most influential in her life." He pointed to a cheerleader type girl who waved to the class and then exclaimed. "N'Sync is totally awesome! I like so had a crush on Lance Bass." Some of the other girls sitting around her agreed and they all began talking about posters they used to own.

"All right girls. Apparently, none of you keep up on N'Sync news today else you would have chosen a different member to fall in love with. But enough of that, on to John Brown's pick."

I looked at John who gave me a thumbs-up sign

"Don't worry dude, you'll totally dig."

"I don't doubt it for a minute, man," I said. Mr. Kenzie inserted a CD into the player and read from John's paper.

"John first heard this song when he was ten years old hanging out with his older cousin, Ryan. From the first note, to the last, John writes that he was instantly hooked

THE UNDECIDED

and has never listened to music quite the same ever again. Ladies and gentlemen, Rush's 'Tom Sawyer.'"

I signaled to John that I approved of his choice, then sat back and enjoyed, glad that John had chosen one of their shorter songs since Rush rarely produced a song under five minutes. As the song reached its final verse, Mr. Kenzie lowered the volume.

"Look at the difference between Crystal's song and John's song. Two totally different sounds, two different genres, different instruments, very little about those two songs have anything in common. But to each of them, it holds a special place right in here." He tapped his heart. "That is the beauty of music. You don't have to like everything you hear, and I promise you, you won't. If you don't believe me, go ask Mr. Holland for his Yoko Ono record. But what *is* important, is that you take the time to listen to all types of music and develop an appreciation for them, whether you personally want to ever listen to it again, or not." He walked over and popped out the CD, replacing it with another one. "You never know, what you end up liking, and it might even surprise you. Take our tardy Lucas Aarons, for example, his choice is totally different in every way from the first two, not better, not worse. Different. Music is as individual as the human soul." He started the CD. "Kids, this is Johnny Cash. The song's called 'Hurt.'" He turned it up and let the melancholy words and simple guitar strains fill the class.

"When a man considers himself contradictory and troubled, a devout but troubled Christian, a lover of the very things in life that threaten to take life away from you such as drugs and alcohol. When a man like that meets a pure, honest, and peaceful moment amid all of that turmoil, the result is truth. Honesty. When Johnny Cash sings, I feel him not just singing from his lips, but from his soul. I was walking into the garage to bring my father some iced tea (he was working on the brakes of our old car) when this song came on our little transistor radio with one working speaker sitting on top of a metal vice on the tool bench. I stopped in my tracks and was drawn to the radio, to Johnny's voice, as if he had busted an arm through that one working speaker and reached across the garage and grabbed my heart. Grabbed my soul. It was the moment that I felt the power of music and a moment that forever changed me." He put my paper down and let the song play on for a few more beats before turning it down.

"I don't know about you guys, but that's pretty damn cool. Nice job Aarons." He gave me a salute and switched another CD into the player. For the next forty-five minutes, we listened to excerpts from everything from Bon Jovi to the Jonas Brothers. There was a little snickering over the Jonas Brothers, and "Memory" from the Broadway show *CATS*, but overall, everyone was really digging this class and all of the music.

When class was over, I attempted to apologize for being late, but Mr. Kenzie beat me to the punch.

"'Hurt' huh?" he asked me. "I've got to admit, I was a little surprised. Thought for sure you were more of a Foo Fighters kid," he said with a wink.

"Well, actually, I love the Foo Fighters, but that wasn't what the assignment was. It was that first..."

"I know, I know. Can't you tell when I'm yanking your chain? Incidentally, did you know that Johnny Cash was a Biblical scholar and yet he called himself the biggest sinner of them all?"

"Well, I'm sure he's not the only one with that title. Excuse me, Mr. Kenzie, I better run, I don't want to be late for my next class. Teachers don't seem to like that too much." I could still hear him laughing as I turned the corner.

CHAPTER SEVENTEEN

All I could think about was meeting someone from the Council at the end of the week. Thursday night Mom received word on the when and where of it. I was to meet at the docks, across from Stony Creek Market, this Sunday morning at 8:00 a.m. I thought it would be a lot easier and make more sense if this guy came over for pizza, but I didn't have much choice in the matter. As far as I was concerned, Sunday couldn't come fast enough.

Around five o'clock on Saturday I threw a couple of things into my canvas bag, including a DVD of *The Best of the Looney Toons,* and headed over to Stony Creek. Mare was working until five-thirty and we agreed to meet there then walk to her house for my date with Grace. I arrived at the market at five-twenty. Mare was wiping down the counter as I walked in.

"I've still got five minutes," she said apologetically. There was a streak of flour across her forehead, and I bent over the counter to wipe it off.

"I'll wait for you. Believe me." Her cheeks blushed and white sparks lit around her like small firecrackers.

"What's with the bag?" she asked, breaking the moment.

"Ah, things for my date. Top secret." She rolled her eyes as she whipped off her apron. Judy and Trudy both exploded into the room walking in unison, of course.

"Lucas!" they both cried.

"Ladies," I answered.

"So, Lucas. We hear that you're like a totally awesome guitar player," Trudy stated.

"Really? Sounds like a bunch of gossip to me."

"No, I swear. Becca told us. She said that you played at the puppet house and totally rocked," Judy said.

"Yeah, totally rocked," Trudy echoed.

"She was probably thinking of John."

"No, it was definitely you."

"Definitely."

"So we were thinking, like, maybe you can give us some lessons?"

"Yeah, we think the guitar is killer."

"You two play?" I asked.

"Well, no Lucas, like that's why we would need some lessons," Trudy rolled her eyes at me.

"Don't worry, Daddy said he'll buy us both like the best guitars there are."

"It will be so awesome," Trudy said to Judy.

"We could be like famous guitar players," Judy answered.

"Totally famous," Trudy responded as they both became lost in their daydreams of becoming famous musicians.

"So what do you say?" They both turned to me and asked simultaneously. That always freaks me out.

"Wow. Well, I'm not sure if I..."

"Ready?" Mare asked, saving me from making any hasty promises.

"Oh yeah."

"We better go, don't want to be late. Bye Trudy, Judy," Mare said, grabbing my arm and ushering me to the door.

"Well, call us Lucas!" they yelled as I was pulled out of the door.

"Wow. Thanks."

"No problem. They're really harmless, but between the two of them, they have a memory like a steel trap. Once you commit, that's it."

"I understand and owe you for this one." We walked towards her house enjoying the setting sun.

"I can't believe that it's barely six o'clock and it's starting to get dark already."

"Just wait. In another month, it will be dark before we even get out of school."

"That's depressing."

"Totally. You can tell that the season is starting to change, not just because of the lack of sun, but the sounds of the bugs change too."

"The sound of bugs?"

THE UNDECIDED

"Yeah, you know, the frogs, crickets, cicadas. You will start to hear them less and less the cooler it gets."

"Wow. I've never lived in seasons before. Florida is kind of like living in a house where your lights are always turned on. Nothing ever really stops, and the bugs are always there. And frogs."

"Well, you're not in Florida anymore, Luke," she said as we reached her front porch.

"That is for sure," I answered. Mare stopped and looked at me, concerned.

"Do you miss Florida?" she asked.

"Well, I miss my friends, of course. And I miss the beach. A lot. But as far as living there, and living here?" I took her hand and looked into her eyes. "I can't imagine being anywhere else." I stepped closer to her, not really knowing what I intended to do, but wanting to be as close to her as I could. She looked up at me expectantly, and her front door opened.

"Lucas!" Mrs. Rossi exclaimed with a smile stretching across her face.

I exchanged Mare's hand for Mrs. Rossi's.

"Hi Mrs. Rossi." She gave me a quick, yet firm hug before ushering us inside.

"Please, please, come in. Are you hungry? Can I get you something to eat or something to drink?" she asked, closing the door.

"No thanks, maybe in a little bit though. I would hate to keep my date waiting."

"Oh of course, I understand!" she replied smiling. "You just let me know. Grace has been looking forward to this all week. It's all she's been talking about. Lucas this, Lucas that."

"Well, she's not the only one. Is she in her room?" I asked.

"Yes. She's in bed. She's just been a little more tired than usual these days, sometimes the medicine will do that to you."

"I'll bet it does. May I?" Gesturing towards her bedroom.

"Please, of course. You just let me know if you need anything. Anything at all."

"Okay,

ROBIN DONARUMA

Mom," Mare said. "We get it."

The pink glow from her room met me as I rounded the hallway. She was sitting in her bed dressed in a pink dress with pink sequence sewn in a swirling pattern and a pink kerchief with the same matching sequenced pattern on her head. She was sound asleep with Hairy curled up beside her. The cat perked up as soon as we entered her room, which made Grace open her eyes.

"Lucas!" she said sleepily. "You came."

"Of course I did. Wait. You weren't going to cancel our date on me, were you? Cause if you want me to leave." I pretended to leave.

"No! Of course not!" she half screamed. She reached for the bed remote and adjusted the height of the bed, which helped her sit up straighter. Hairy walked over to me and meowed. I shuddered.

"Hello Hairy."

"He wants you to pet him, silly."

"Pet what?" I whispered to Mare who shoved me closer to the cat. "Okay. Hi Hairy. Good to see you too." He meowed that long, mournful cry again.

"Boy, he really likes you," Grace said giggling.

"Lucky me," I mumbled under my breath.

"Okay. I'm going to go wash the wonderful aroma of Stony Pizza off of me. Do you think you two can behave yourselves?" I lifted up my left hand and put my right hand over my heart.

"Scout's honor," I promised. With a quick roll of her eyes, she left the room.

"I thought she'd never leave!" Grace exclaimed, which caught me so off guard I burst into laughter.

"I can tell this is going to be one awesome date." I was completely mesmerized by how bright she was. She seemed brighter than before, if that was even possible.

"What's in your bag?" She asked pointing to the bag that was still hanging off my shoulder.

"Oh, nothing much. Just a DVD, a couple of Hershey bars, and your present."

"Present?" she said at the same time Hairy meowed that awful meow. I looked at the cat and at Grace.

"Now that was creepy," I said.

"Oh, he's just excited. What did you bring me? Can I see it?" she asked, clapping her hands together.

"Okay, but you have to promise me something."

"Anything," she said, practically jumping up and down in her bed.

"You have to promise me that you will never lose that smile."

"Lucas that's a silly thing to promise. But okay, I will never lose my smile. Now can I see it?"

I gently put the bag down and after a few minutes of prolonging the giving, much to Grace's chagrin, I took out a small brown paper bag.

"Oops, I forgot." I walked to her dresser and turned on the small pink lamp sitting on top of it and turned the main overhead light off. "There. That's better." I gently sat on one side of her bed and placed the paper bag in her lap.

"What is it? Can I open it?" Hairy inspected the bag.

"Absolutely."

Grace slowly unraveled the top of the paper and carefully peeked inside. She looked up at me with a puzzled expression.

"You got me jelly?" she giggled.

"Ah, ye of little faith." I took the bag from her and reached my hand inside. "A jelly jar, perhaps, but not jelly." I took out the large glass container.

"Fireflies!" she whispered. She reached for the jar.

"Not so fast," I stated.

"I want to hold them, please."

"Oh, you will." I unscrewed the top of the jelly jar and within seconds fireflies were flying around her room. Grace inhaled deeply.

"Oh, Lucas. They're everywhere!" I looked into her watery eyes and the joy that I saw humbled me. She held out her hand and gently cupped a firefly. "Look! I did it! I caught one!" One landed on her kerchief as others danced around her. It was the most magical moment I had ever witnessed. "My angels," she whispered. "My little angels."

I didn't hear Mare or her parents enter the room. Mare came up beside me and kissed my cheek. I looked to her and then to her parents who all mirrored the same emotion that was rolling inside of me. Mr. Rossi began catching fireflies with Grace. Mrs. Rossi looked at me and touched her heart.

"Can you believe it mama? Lucas brought me my very own fireflies!"

"So I see," she said, trying to sound stern.

"Well, I thought a puppy might not fare so well with Hairy."

"A puppy." She looked up summoning strength from heaven as she clasped the silver cross around her neck. "Lord help whoever dares bring a dog into this house."

Mr. Rossi placed his hand on my shoulder and gave it a warm, tight squeeze.

"Thank you for making my little girl smile," he whispered so no one could hear him. I could feel his emotions and the gratitude and happiness he was feeling at that moment was so powerful that I felt as though I were intruding. I watched Mare help Grace catch fireflies. A soft glow formed around Mare's hair. The energy in the room, the love, was palpable.

After a few more minutes, the parents excused themselves and I popped in the DVD and passed out Hershey bars. I couldn't concentrate on the cartoon. All I was able to see was Grace and her luminescence. She was glowing.

Around ten o'clock, well after Grace fell asleep, we propped open her window so the fireflies could escape if they wanted to, and I said my goodbyes.

"Thanks for tonight, Lucas."

"No problem. It was really great."

"You have no idea how great. Not only to see Gracie so happy, but my parents." Tears welled in her eyes, and she looked towards the hydrangea bushes. "We used to be a happy family. Now, we hardly laugh at all. So tonight. Tonight was a big deal. For all of us." I pulled her towards me and hugged her tightly.

"I know. Things will get better. One way or another, believe me," I said into her hair, loving the way it smelled, a mixture of rosemary and mint.

"I wish I could believe you. I want to."

"So do it."

THE UNDECIDED

"It's so easy to believe you." She pulled away and looked up at me. "Every doctor that we've seen, well, what they tell us is not the kind of stuff that you want to hear." I nodded. "Facts are facts, you know?" She pulled away and started to walk towards the street. I followed until she stopped and turned back to me. "But whenever you're with her, she seems so different, like she used to be. And so when you tell me everything will get better, I actually almost believe you." She laughed. "It's as if you cast some magical spell over everyone you meet."

"You're not starting that again, are you? Are you still jealous about the lunch lady?" I teased.

"You pretend like you don't know what I'm talking about, but I know there is something about you Lucas Aarons. I haven't quite got my finger on it yet, but I will."

"Well, I guess you had better make sure you spend a lot of time with me so you don't miss anything." I stepped closer and grabbed both of her hands.

"No, I wouldn't want to miss anything." The closer I moved to Mare the smaller the world and my surroundings became. I was drawn to her and helpless to let go.

"Lucas," she whispered.

"Mare," I whispered back.

"Lucas," she whispered again.

"Mare!" her father hollered from the front door. And like a bucket of cold water being dumped over my head, I was snapped back to reality. I dropped her hands and backed up two solid steps.

"I guess I had better go," I said to her. I waved to her dad who waved back before exiting the still opened door.

"I guess so," she snickered. "See you tomorrow?" she asked.

"Ah, tomorrow I can't. I sort of have this thing in the morning." She looked at me questioningly. "With my mom. I have to go with my mom to meet this guy. I'm not sure how long it's going to take."

"All day?"

"I doubt it."

"Cool. Well, a bunch of us are meeting down at Lenny's around six. You know where that is?"

ROBIN DONARUMA

"I think so. If not, I'm sure I can find it. One thing about Branford is that nothing is very far away."
"That's for sure." The porch lights flicked off and on.
"And that's my cue. Thanks again for tonight, Luke."
"Anytime. See you tomorrow at six." I headed home, turning back once to catch a flash of auburn hair just as the front door closed.

CHAPTER EIGHTEEN

At seven-thirty on Sunday morning I walked into the kitchen to find both my parents whispering frantically over their steaming mugs of coffee.

"Good morning," I announced. It was comical to watch how fast they stopped talking, pulling away from each other as if they had been caught.

"Good morning, Lucas. Are you hungry? We don't have much time, but you really should eat something," my mother said walking to the fridge.

"I'll just grab a banana," I said. My mother put down her coffee cup and began wringing her hands together, never a good sign.

"Oh, okay, if you're sure. We're supposed to be there at eight, so we should probably leave in what Joey? Ten minutes?"

"Yeah, ten minutes will give us plenty of time." I don't think I've ever seen my dad this nervous.

"Do you want to bring a sweater? It's chilly in the mornings now," my mother asked me.

"Mom, I'm fine. Just relax. This is a good thing, right?" I looked to my dad for help.

"He'll be fine, Mary. You know he will. There is nothing to worry about." My mother let out a big breath and looked up so the tears that were perched on her eyelids wouldn't roll down her cheeks.

"I know, I know. I just feel so helpless in all of this, the not knowing. It's not something I'm very good at."

"Hey, preaching to the choir, Mom."

"I suppose so. Okay, let's just go."

My dad jingled his keys and ushered my mother and me through the garage door. Exactly eight minutes later we pulled into a small graveled lot adjacent to the docks across from Stony Creek Market. We got out of the car and walked to the dock where several small boats were moored.

ROBIN DONARUMA

The water was smooth, but there was a dense fog hovering above the water line making the Thimble Islands difficult to see. My mother was checking her watch every ten seconds while my father slowly scanned our surroundings.

"It's one minute until eight. I don't see anyone. Joey, what do you think?" my mother frantically whispered.

"Patience, Mary. Patience," he answered, continuing to scan the docks like the Terminator.

"It's eight," my mother announced just as a small motorboat slipped through the fog heading right towards us.

"Well, you've got to give him something for punctuality," my dad said smoothly, moving my mother and me closer to him.

There was one person in the boat, but before I could get a decent look at him, he swung the boat around backing it into the dock.

The motor stopped and a large knotted rope sailed over a pylon. In a single movement that was surprisingly spry for someone his size, he jumped out of the boat and reached into his pocket, his back still to us. A puff of gray smoke wafted above his covered head and a feeling of familiarity lightly tapped me on the shoulder. He had pulled out a pipe. It was Captain Bob.

"Ahoy there!" he cheerfully greeted us. I stood staring at him with my mouth wide open. My mother relaxed immediately, and my father approached him with his hand out stretched. "Mr. Aarons," he said, grasping my father's hand and heartily shaking it. "And you must be the missus." My mother extended her hand.

"Mary. And you are?"

Captain Bob took off his hat tucking it under his arm.

"Excuse me, ma'am. This fog does something awful to my senses these days. Name's Robert Sariel, but most folks round here call me Captain Bob, ain't that right, Lucas?" he said to me.

"You know him, Lucas?" my mother asked.

"I met him at the festival. Mare introduced him to me."

My father scanned the docks once more. "Well, it's nice to meet you Robert, er, Captain Bob. I'm afraid we mistook you for someone else."

THE UNDECIDED

"We're waiting for someone," Mom interjected.

"You don't say." He placed his pipe in his mouth. "What's this feller look like?"

"I'm afraid I'm not really sure," my mother answered.

"He got a name?"

"Not one that I'm aware of."

"So you folks are standing here on a Sunday morning waiting for some feller you never seen nor heard of?" He shook his head and put his hat back on top of his unruly white hair. "So, how do you know I'm not him?" he asked with a twinkle in his eye.

"Well, I um," my mother stuttered as my father pushed his way in front of us.

"Are you who we're supposed to meet? Captain Bob?"

"Aye." He looked to me. "I bet you knew that though, didn't you Luke." All eyes turned to me now.

"Um, well, the thought did cross my mind." With that, Captain Bob slapped his knee with his free hand and announced.

"Alright, then let's get a move on. This fog isn't getting any thinner."

My mother stepped up. "So you, you're from the Council?" she whispered, and he responded with a hearty laugh.

"Me? Oh no Missus. But I thank ye for the compliment. I'm just the water taxi. I'm here to take Lucas to see Urim."

"Where exactly are you taking him?" my father asked.

"Can't we go with him? I thought that we would be able to go," my mother started.

Captain Bob held up his pipe in a gesture to silence my parents who were starting to talk over each other.

"Now, now Aarons, one question at a time. I'm not as young as I used to be." He winked at me, put his pipe back in his mouth and addressed my parents' questions. "I am taking him just yonder, not too far from here to a small island some folks call Roger's Island. If you look real good, you can just make out the tip. That's where Urim is. Now as to you going with our young Lucas here, that won't be necessary." My mother bristled at this news. "You know the way it works Mary. The council requested Lucas only.

ROBIN DONARUMA

This goes beyond what you or I want. Trust me, you won't even know he's gone. He'll be back before you know it."

My mother looked to my dad, who was staring at Captain Bob with a level of intensity that I've never seen before. In two solid movements my father exhaled and gave one curt nod of his head.

"Tell you what Mary," my father said lightly. "How about we run across the street and get some coffee and one of those bagel sandwiches Lucas is always talking about."

"Bialys, Dad."

"Right. Bialys."

"We don't want to be late Mary. I'm afraid we must leave now."

My mother looked at me, at Captain Bob, then back to me. Tears were in her eyes, and she began wringing her hands. I hugged her whispering in her ear.

"I'll be fine, Mom. Trust me. I need to do this. Please."

My mother pulled back pasting a plastic smile on her face.

"I know, of course. I know. You go. Go with Mr. Bob, we'll be right here if you need us, okay?"

I kissed her on her head.

"I never doubted that you wouldn't be. Love you." I turned to my dad and hugged him. "Go get her some coffee, would you?" Just when I would have pulled back from the hug, he held on for a second more.

"We will be here waiting for you."

"I know." I pulled back, turning to Captain Bob. "Let's roll."

"Aye, aye! Right this way young Aarons." He pointed to the small boat and I hopped in finding a seat beside a salt encrusted net. Captain Bob jumped into the boat taking off the rope in one swift movement. Before I knew it, the motor had started, and we were headed towards the misty wall. I gave my parents a reassuring wave and watched my father kiss my mother on the cheek and walk across the street to the market. My mother didn't move, she just stoically watched as I disappeared into the mist, not even bothering to wipe away the tears that were pouring down her cheeks. I knew I was safe, but physically leaving my parents for the unknown was something I had never experienced. I swallowed the lump in my throat reminding myself that I wanted this. I forced myself to turn from my mother's diminishing figure and steer my attention towards the approaching island. It looked like a brown iceberg.

"Ready, son?"

"Absolutely," I answered.

"Right answer." Just like he did at Stony Creek, he whipped the boat around and threw out a rope, securing it to a dock.

"We're here!" he announced.

I waited for him to get out of the boat first, but he didn't budge.

"Well, what are you waiting for, son?"

"Um. What?"

"Go on." He motioned for me to get out of the boat. "Go on now."

"Aren't you coming?" I meekly asked.

"Like I told your mama, Luke. This don't include us. Now go on, I'll be here when it comes time to head back."

"But where am I going?"

"Just walk down the dock 'til you see a path leading up to the main house. Can't miss it."

I got out of the boat and saw the path, but had no idea who I was supposed to meet. How would I know who they were? I turned to Captain Bob to ask as much, but he was gone. Captain Bob and the boat. Not only didn't I hear the motor, there wasn't any wake in the water either. It was as if he disappeared into thin air, or thick fog.

"That's just great," I mumbled, trying not to recall every horror movie I had ever seen. The path led up to a rocky slope, and I ascended the slight incline looking back every ten feet or so. I could no longer see the water because of the fog. At the top of the path a large structure became visible. Not having a whole lot of choices, I started towards it. The closer I got to the house, the lighter and warmer the air became. Splotches of color popped out of the grayness, and the large structure turned into a huge, looming mansion.

"Hey!" someone yelled. I jumped and ducked at the same time.

"Hey! Lucas, heads up!" I whirled around looking for the source of the voice and was hit from behind by

something very hard in the middle of my back. I fell to the ground and lay there wondering if I should make a run for it, or play dead.
"I see you made it," came a voice above me. I slowly rolled over landing on top of whatever just hit me. I reached under my back and grabbed the source of my pain. A large, wet ball. I looked at the man looming above me.
"I assume this is yours."
"Mine? Nope. That's not mine. But Millie will be mighty glad you found it for her," he answered then whistled the loudest, shrillest sound I had ever heard. I sat up and instantly wished I hadn't, for out of nowhere came a white Polar Bear and it was headed straight for me.
"There she is. See? What did I tell you?" said the unhelpful stranger.
Before I was able to stand, I was trampled by the white beast. It wrestled the ball from my grip and licked my face before removing herself from my prone form.
"I told you she'd be appreciative." He picked up the ball that Millie dropped at his feet and threw it. The ball sailed through the air, but I never saw or heard it land. Millie, forgetting me in an instant, was off, and I can't say that I was too sad to see her go.
"Let me help you up, son." I took his hand and was surprised by his strength as he single handedly hoisted me onto my feet.
"Thanks," I said, looking around making sure that Millie was still entertained elsewhere. "That's some dog you have there."
"That she is, son. She's a Great Pyrenees, or as some call them, a livestock guardian dog. Though the only livestock we've got 'round here is a bucket of tennis balls. But I suppose you've figured that out already?"
"I suppose I have. Um, listen, I'm supposed to meet someone here."
"Well, looks like you already did," he said with a casual and knowing smile.
"Yes, I did. But I think I'm supposed to meet someone else here." I paused allowing him the opportunity to offer

THE UNDECIDED

up any information he might have. "A Captain Bob dropped me off?"

I wondered if he was the one I was supposed to meet, but he didn't look like what I imagined a member from the Council would look like. This guy looked like someone pulled him out of a Western movie, minus the cowboy hat. His mustache covering his upper lip and his scruffy beard were much lighter than his salt and pepper hair. His clothes hung loosely off of his body making him look as if he'd been sleeping outside for the past two nights.

"Ah, Bobby dropped you off? Tell me something, is he still smoking that old pipe?"

"Yeah, he smokes a pipe."

"He keeps telling me he's gonna quit," he added to himself. "Oh well, I guess that figures. Some things never change," he said smiling then looked at me. "You remember that. Now come on. You hungry?"

"But I'm supposed to..."

"Supposed to meet someone?"

"Right."

"Well, seeing as how I'm the only soul on this rock, I'd say you already did. Now come on, I've got blueberry pancakes hot off the griddle." He lazily sauntered towards the huge house.

"Are you from the Council?" He stopped, turning to look first at my wrist then necklace.

"You are exactly where you need to be right now, Lucas Aarons." He moved towards me and his eyes took on a serious gleam that wasn't there before. "They are coming Lucas, and they are coming faster than we imagined. You must listen and not question, feel and not think. It is in the moments of silence that the most wisdom is gained. Remember this, and you will be ready for what is to come." He stepped back and smiled brightly. "Now, how 'bout those hotcakes?"

CHAPTER NINETEEN

The house, which wasn't really a house, but more of a mansion, was amazing. Even using the word amazing is lame, but I don't know how else to describe it. The closer we got, the bigger it became. The landscaping alone was more elaborate than any I had ever seen and the flowers and trees were in full bloom despite it being the middle of September.

"Right this way, Luke," he said, opening one of the biggest doors I had ever seen. He stepped aside allowing me to enter first. I walked in and was struck speechless. It felt like *Alice in Wonderland* when she ate that cookie, or drank that potion, I don't remember which one, and shrunk down to the size of a mouse. Everything was huge.

"Well, what do you think?"

"I like a house you can land a plane in," I answered. He laughed an affectionate, slow laugh. He watched me kind of like the way my grandfather used to watch me play in the yard.

"Well, no planes will be landing in here today. Come on, kitchen's this way."

As huge as the house was, the kitchen turned out to be warm and comforting. Don't get me wrong, it was huge too, but not in an intimidating way. One wall was completely made up of windows overlooking the ocean. Sun poured in through the multitude of glass and skylights giving the illusion of being outside. On the kitchen counter, just as promised, was a huge plate filled with steaming stacks of blueberry pancakes.

"Sit down," he said, piling pancakes onto a plate. He sat the plate in front of me and added a smaller dish of bacon, a bottle of warmed maple syrup, and a tall glass of milk.

"That good for now?" he asked as I began digging in.

"This is awesome," I said with my mouth full, meaning every syllable. "Aren't you going to have any?"

THE UNDECIDED

"Nah, you go ahead," he said as he pulled out a chair and sat beside me. "I've never been a big fan of breakfast."

I shrugged my shoulders piercing the last bite of pancake on my plate with my fork sopping up the last of the syrup. I followed that bite with a gulp of milk and sat back in my chair, completely sated.

"Had enough?" he asked.

"Definitely. Thank you."

"No thanks needed Lucas, but they are appreciated." He stood up and walked to one of the windows overlooking the water.

"So you *are* from the Council?" I meekly asked. He turned and looked at me with that same affectionate smile.

"That I am, Lucas, that I am. Name's Ethan." He held his hand out for me to shake. I grabbed his hand and tried to listen to him but got nothing. I gave his hand two firm shakes. He softly chuckled and clapped his hand on my shoulder.

"Not yet son. You're not quite ready."

"Why not?"

He looked at me thoughtfully then exhaled a deep breath. "Come on. Follow me. Millie's gotta have found her ball by now." We walked into the back yard and Ethan whispered Millie's name. Between the crashing shore surrounding us on the island, the birds, wind, and every other outdoor noise, I found it curious as to why he was whispering.

"Would you like me to whistle for her?" I asked.

"Nope. She heard me."

"I barely heard you. How in the world could she?" Before I finished my sentence a white flash shot past me, landing in front of Ethan.

"Good girl," Ethan said as he petted her. He walked towards the edge of the yard, which bled into a rocky decline towards the ocean. I followed him.

"Branford treating you alright?"

"Yeah, it's pretty cool."

"I thought you'd like it there. It was between Branford or Mesquite." He looked at me and answered the question before I could even ask it. "A small town outside of Las Vegas."

"Why? Why Branford or Mesquite?"

"I thought your mama filled you in on some of this."

"Well, kind of." He looked at me expectantly. I guess I wasn't done talking. "She told me about a White Army and a Dark Army."

"Mmmhmm," he mumbled, his silence encouraging me to continue.

"And the gray ones."

"Yup."

"And that I am supposed to be some sort of leader of the White Army." He kept staring at me, not adding to the conversation, so I continued. "And that we moved to Branford to help fight the war."

"Sounds about right to me," he answered looking out to the ocean. "And how do you feel about all of this? Sound like a bunch of mumbo jumbo to you?"

"Well, honestly, at first I really thought my mom had lost it. That maybe she was a little touched in the head I guess. But it also kind of explained a lot of stuff that was going on with me."

"Like your dreams."

"Exactly! I mean, I knew that they were just dreams, but they always felt like so much more than that. So then we moved, and other stuff started happening with me."

"By the way, a belated happy birthday." He looked at my necklace.

"Thanks." I paused trying to get a grip as to where this conversation, this one-sided conversation was heading. "You know, it seems to me that you already know all this stuff that I'm telling you. I thought that I was here so you could tell me stuff."

"On the first day of class does your teacher start teaching you a new calculus problem as soon as you walk in the door?"

"What does that have to do with any…" his expression made me stop. "No."

"No, of course not. First you take a test to see what you already know, that way they know where to start."

"Okay. But can you at least answer one question? Why me?"

"Why not?"

"That's not an answer."

"Maybe not a very good one. But your question wasn't a very good one either. I sometimes think that if everyone would just stop wasting so much time asking why this or why that, and just accept what is theirs to accept, everything would run a little more smoothly around here."

"Well, it's not like I'm asking you why I don't have blonde hair, I'm asking you why I have to be the leader of this White Army? Who am I? I'm no one."

"Are you? Do you think it's normal to know what other people are feeling or hiding deep in their souls? You know any other kids doing that these days?" He started walking across the yard. "You like tennis?"

"Tennis? Yeah, sure I guess."

"Come on. I haven't played in years."

After two games of tennis, two games in which Ethan totally kicked my butt, we headed back to the house. Ethan was quite happy about himself, and I was sweaty and utterly confused as to why I was there.

"Help yourself to whatever's in the fridge, I'm gonna go clean up. I almost worked up a sweat," he said slyly as he walked out of the kitchen.

"Funny guy." I mumbled opening the refrigerator. Inside were several pre-made sandwiches along with bottled water and every kind of fruit imaginable. I grabbed a roast beef sandwich and a bottle of water and sat down at the table. Millie was standing in the corner of the kitchen tracking my every move. I tore off a piece of my bread and held it towards her.

"Hungry?" I asked. She responded with a low 'woof' and wagged her tail but didn't move from her spot.

"Suit yourself," I said popping it into my mouth. Looking around, nothing seemed otherworldly. It was a house, just like any other, albeit much larger. Ethan definitely had some quirks, but came across as human as everyone else. I finished my sandwich and stood. It was time to get this powwow started. It was already afternoon and I wasn't sure how long this was supposed to take, but if I was going to be home by dinner, it was time to get things rolling. I walked to Millie and as crazy as it sounds, asked her where Ethan was. With a soft woof Millie stood up and walked towards the glass door. Nothing was truly surprising me at this point, at least not too much, so I followed and didn't skip a beat when I saw Ethan sitting outside looking out at the ocean.

"Thanks, Millie," I said giving her a quick pat on the head. Ethan had changed into a soft yellow linen shirt that was being tousled by the wind. His face was lifted towards the sun and his eyes were closed. I was wondering how to let my presence be known when he spoke.

"Get enough to eat?" he asked without moving.

"Yeah. Thanks." I waited for him to open up a conversation, but he seemed quite content to continue resting in the sun. "Um, so listen, I was thinking that we could maybe get started with whatever we're supposed to get started doing? It's afternoon already and if I'm going to get home before it gets dark, don't you think we should start?"

He opened one eye and looked at me.

"Start?" He asked.

"Yeah, start talking about what's going on with me."

"Oh, that." He shut his eye again and leaned back in his chair. "Humor me for a moment and lean back in that chair of yours. Close your eyes."

He opened one eye again. "Go on. Just lean back and close your eyes. Tell me, Luke, what do hear?"

"The ocean?" I answered.

"Be more specific."

"The waves hitting the shore."

"That's better. What else?"

"I hear the wind blowing through the trees."

"Specifically."

"The leaves hitting each other and branches creaking in the wind. Birds singing. A cricket, I think?"

"And what do you feel?"

"I feel the warmth from the sun. The breeze blowing through my hair, on my face."

"What else?"

I sighed in frustration at his litany of pointless questions.

"I feel the hard wood from this chair, and it's not exactly pleasant."

THE UNDECIDED

"Point taken," he said with a soft chuckle. "Continue."

"The grass in between my toes is soft and warm. I just felt the shadow of a bird flying over us."

"What else are your senses showing you?"

"Smell. I can smell the ocean water, a salty, fishy aroma. I also smell the grass and the peonies growing along the path behind us. I smell warmth. Maybe it's just the humid air, but it definitely has a smell. My mother used to call it the smell of summer."

"Now put all of those senses together. Layer them on top of one another."

I did and completely relaxed. A little rest shouldn't take up too much time. Maybe he needed a little down time after playing tennis. I kept my eyes closed and layered my senses starting with the sounds of the water hitting the shore just beyond where we were sitting. I continued to add every other sound, smell, and feeling that I could conjure up. I was in a complete state of relaxation, and it was amazing. Everything around me was thrumming with life and energy. I felt it pulsating around me, through me, above, and below me. Like a rock in the middle of a stream, it flowed over and around me. I was witness to the most beautiful symphony of all, life. The more I listened, the more I heard. I heard not just birds singing, but I heard different birds calling and answering each other. Frogs, crickets, everything seemed to be awake and active. Where I once walked down this path as clueless as a deaf man, I now sat keenly aware of my surroundings.

The warmth of the sun eventually faded and a chill ran up my arms rousing me from my sedated state. I slowly opened my eyes and felt refreshed and energized. I smiled at the sight of the sun slowly drifting towards the horizon until the realization hit me upside the head causing me to bolt out of my chair. I looked at my cell phone. It was six o'clock. The chair beside me was empty. I must have fallen asleep!

This guy is really starting to get on my nerves. This whole trip was turning into one big joke. I looked towards the house and saw lights on in the kitchen. I started back with heavy footsteps pounding my frustration into the Earth. I don't care if he's from the Council or planet

ROBIN DONARUMA

Vulcan, this guy's whacked, and I'm outta here. I whipped open the kitchen door with my exit speech perched on the edge of my tongue. Ethan entered the kitchen carrying a huge platter in front of him.
"I hope you like tacos," he cheerily stated.

CHAPTER TWENTY

"Tacos? You let me fall asleep out there!" I hotly replied.

"Were you asleep? I thought you were in more of a meditative state," he answered, placing a bowl of Spanish rice on the table. "I bet you're hungry."

"I'm not hungry, I'm angry! This has all been a colossal waste of time. What is this some kind of joke to you?"

"No Lucas, this is many things, but not a joke. Far from it," Ethan said. "You will understand everything soon enough."

"Soon enough? The day's over! I've got to leave now, and I haven't learned anything except how to take a nap!" I grabbed a taco and headed for the door. "Later." I followed the same path that led me to the house earlier in the day and found the dock just as I left it, empty. I wiped the taco grease on my jeans wishing that I had grabbed two of them and pulled out my iPod. It was six twenty-six, the sun was sinking with a vengeance, and there was no sign of Captain Bob. I put in my ear buds and hit shuffle. "Black and White Army" by Sting and the Police came on. Cool song, but the whole black and white thing was a little sore right now. Forward. "White Room" by Cream. Forward. "Black and White" by Three Dog Night. Forward. "Black Dog" by Led Zeppelin. Forward. "White" by the Cult.

I ripped off the earphones and turned the iPod off. I checked my phone for a signal. No go.

"Come on Bob." I mumbled walking to the end of the dock. It was almost totally dark now. "Great," I said, watching the sun disappear below the ocean's horizon. I turned back towards the house. Millie was sitting at the top end of the dock. *Woof.* I rubbed my hands through my hair trying to stop the headache that was creeping in. *Woof.*

"Millie? He's not coming, is he?" I asked her. *Woof.* "I don't know what's worse. My being stuck on this island with some strange guy or the fact that I'm actually talking to a dog." "*Woof,*" she responded, wagging her tail happily. She stood up and turned towards the house waiting for me to follow. "I don't suppose I have much of a choice here, do I?" She wagged her tail, and I followed her back up to the house that was aglow with lights.

Entering through the kitchen I have to admit that I was happy to see the food still on the table. There was no sign of Ethan. Millie walked to the table and offered a subtle bark, gaining my attention. There was a note.

Lucas,
Please help yourself to more dinner, as I'm sure you are pretty hungry right about now. Your bedroom is the second door off of the kitchen. Sleep well, more to come tomorrow.

Ethan

P.S. Don't worry about your parents as they are aware of where you are and when you are to return home.

"That's just great. How about filling me in?" I threw the note on the table and Millie voiced her concern with a groan and a cock of her head. "I suppose you knew about this too, huh?" She wagged her tail and licked her lips either in guilt or temptation from the food. In defeat, I sat down and started filling my plate with tacos and rice. If I were stuck on this island in the middle of nowhere with a guy who kept disappearing and a dog that communicates, I guess I had better keep up my strength.

CHAPTER TWENTY-ONE

Ethan never came back that night. My room was, just as he had written, right off of the kitchen and was nicely appointed minus a television.

After checking my cell phone for service one more time (to no avail) I laid down on the bed and found that I was more tired than I realized. I could hear Millie just outside my door and in a strange way felt that comforting. I took out my iPod, but after the black and white concert down on the dock, thought that maybe getting some sleep would be a better way to go. Before closing my eyes, I promised myself that I would get some answers tomorrow or start swimming. Within five minutes I was fast asleep.

The grass was cool and soft. I breathed deeply, closed my eyes taking in the heady, unique aroma that surrounded me. It was ocean, air, and earth all at once. Birds sailed above, and I watched their dance, laughing at their antics. I wished I could join them. The sun warmed my skin. I held out my hands and tilted my face absorbing as much as it would allow. I was free here. I was alone, yet part of everything. Connected. Energy rushed through my veins as I watched the birds in flight. Power coursed through my body with each crash of the waves below. The sun nourished me. I walked to the edge of the grass and looked out to the endless ocean before me. A seagull landed at my feet. I reached out to touch the downy white feathers and was thrilled when it didn't immediately fly away. It blinked its ebony eyes before taking flight. Watching it ascend fed me with great joy.

Its white wings flapped until it became one with the sun, and I could stare no more. Daring one more glimpse towards the blazing sun, my smile faded. The sun was falling from the sky. Nature quieted. It became cold. I no longer felt happy and strong, instead I felt vulnerable and afraid. The ocean became a black, ominous entity. I backed away from it. I was disconnected and alone.

A pinprick of light across the ocean glowed in the distance. It grew upwards from the water morphing into a large wall of light. My heart fluttered.

A sphere appeared in the center of the light wall and rotated slowly. Blues and Greens swirled inside of the massive globe until settling into small blobs. Earth! Landmasses appeared through the white swirling clouds and millions of brilliant, sparkling lights scattered themselves around the globe. It was stunning. I stood in awe of its magnificence and felt humbled to be witness. The Earth stopped its rotation with North America facing me. The eastern part of America became enlarged, magnifying the diamond-like entities that danced overtop the landmass. The New England area grew larger than the rest of the Eastern Seaboard and Connecticut, the largest. Branford was elevated from the rest of Connecticut, and the sparkling light entities were dancing and moving around much like fireflies, but brighter and faster. I held out my hand to them and they rushed towards me, landing on my arm. I could feel them, each and every one of them, all at once. I felt their happiness and their love. I laughed with a free heart full of joy, and I loved each of them back. I walked closer, and they enveloped me. There was barely any sound, only a small fluttering noise, which echoed my own heartbeat. I scooped a handful of the sparkling lights into my hand and poured them into my other never wanting this moment to end.

Several of the lights flew back to the landmass, seeming as if they had been drawn back by a magnet. I was sad to see them go, but reveled in the ones that remained behind. Many more followed, some back to Branford and some beyond the map. I watched helplessly as they began to leave me. I tried to stop them, but could not. The fluttering stopped, and I was no longer bathed in their magnificence. I was alone again, standing on the edge of the cliff left to watch them dance without me. I longed to be with them, I held my arm out once more, but they wouldn't come to me. My heart broke.

THE UNDECIDED

Then I saw it. A dark, oily mass moving towards them. It crept across the map consuming the lights as it spanned across the state. "No!" I shallowly screamed. I watched helplessly as the sparkling entities were devoured by the cold darkness. Tears pooled in my eyes and began to stream down my face as I stood perilously close to the edge of the cliff. "No!" I voiced a little louder this time. The darkness quickened its consumption and I held out my hand and yelled as loud as I was able "Stop!"

It stopped. I released the breath I had been holding and backed away from the scene with relief. The darkness shifted its direction and began to ooze towards me. I backed up a few steps unable to look away as it spanned above the map and reached towards me. I was powerless to stop it. I felt drained and desolate, cold and alone. Its liquid dance mesmerized me and the darkness started to become inviting. I stared into the faceless creature and was hit with waves of horror and fear. Not just mine, but of others before me who were consumed by this monster. Whispers of poisoned promises washed around my head, filling it with lies and temptations. There was nowhere to run, no one to turn to for help. The whispers became screams pounding into my head. I covered my ears to muffle the sound. My breath became shallow. My hope was gone. It was coming for me. My hands slid from ears to my neck as I gasped for the air that no longer freely came to me. I felt something hard and warm under my shirt and pulled it free from the faded cotton. My necklace. I grasped it with my left hand and closed my eyes. A tingling sensation moved up my arm and through my body. A blast of cool air rushed into my lungs waking me from my reverie. White light bled through my fingers and shot out from where I stood like rays of sunlight. The darkness stopped. I held my arms up by my side and looked into the shrinking mass. "No," I grumbled. It surged upwards again, trying to find a way around me. "No!" I repeated, much louder this time. I held my hands up higher and the entity retreated. The whispering calmed as its hold on me was released. In one fluid motion, it shrank back to the map allowing the dancing lights to once again shine. My heart soared, and I stepped towards them. So did the darkness. I reached out my hands, beckoning them to *come to me, and the darkness sank its own tentacle towards them. I moved, the darkness moved. It was toying with me. Anger flooded my senses and I rushed towards the mass swinging my arms wildly as if shooing away a stray dog. Sparks of light shot all around me as I growled with frustration. It recoiled, and just as I thought, I had defeated the mass; it rose up taking on the form of a large face. With its mouth agape, it stared into me and made the most unhuman, evil sound imaginable. I watched helplessly as in one motion it devoured all of the light entities. Before I could react, it turned to me and attacked.*

I woke up screaming, tears streaming down my face. I didn't recognize where I was, and I jumped out of bed. Something was scratching the door. A shadow slowly moved along the door's edge and fear rooted me to the floor. A muted woof vibrated through the door and thankfully shook me back to reality. I sat on the bed with a heavy, exhausted sigh. "Millie," I whispered. "Woof," she replied. I took another few seconds to compose myself, then, opened the door. She stood there with her tail wagging looking just as I had left her last night. I patted her head and asked out loud "What time is it?" half expecting her to answer me.

"Just past six," Ethan hollered from the kitchen. Ethan was back, once again, arranging food on the table.

"Glad to see you're an early riser. I never understood people that sleep half their days away. Seems a shame to me, and a bit of a waste." He placed a platter of French toast on the table. "Ready to eat?"

I sat as he artfully placed every type of breakfast food that I could ever want on the table.

"You look different," I said, watching him.

"Different?" He stopped and looked at me. "Different how?"

"Yeah, I don't know. Something is different." I couldn't put my finger on it. "I don't know, maybe it's your clothes."

"Maybe," he said.

"So where did you go last night? Why did you take off?"

"I was here the whole time, Luke," he said as he sat down at the table beside me. "I'm not as young as I used to

THE UNDECIDED

be. You can't expect me to keep up late hours like a teenager."

"Late hours? It was six-thirty!"

"I take it you got my note?"

"Yeah, I got your note. It would have been nice if you had told me that I was staying here yourself. And why didn't my parents tell me? You say they know about this?"

"They do."

"Then why didn't they tell me? Why didn't I pack any clothes or my toothbrush?"

"Because it's already here."

"What? My clothes are here?"

"Yup. You gonna eat?"

With an exasperated sigh I piled food on my plate finding myself much hungrier than I would have believed.

"Well, as long as I make that boat tonight. I have plans," I said between mouthfuls.

"Your plans will still be there when you get back. Meanwhile, we have work to do."

"You say that like I'm not going back today."

"Mmmhmmm," he said, feeding Millie a piece of bacon.

"Well, when exactly am I going back?"

"When we're done with what we came here to do."

"Which is?"

"Tell me something, Luke. How did you sleep last night?" he pointedly asked. I put down my fork, having promptly lost my appetite. He looked into my eyes with a knowing gleam. "Time to get to work, son." He stood up and walked to the back door, Millie at his heel. "You finish up in here, then meet me out back." He left, and I quickly finished what was on my plate. It was time to get this show on the road.

Ethan was playing fetch with Millie. He threw a ball across the yard into the greenery, and Millie was off in a shot. Ethan turned his attention towards me.

"Luke, you have a cell phone?"

"Yeah, but good luck getting a signal out here." I took it from my pocket and put it in his outstretched hand. He looked at it, turning it back and forth as if he had never seen one before.

"Do you have your, oh what do you call it now, your Pod with you?"

"My pod? Do you mean my iPod?" I took it out of another pocket and showed it to him. "This?"

"Yes, that's it. Your iPod." He held out his other hand and I placed it in his outstretched palm. "These things really fit in your ears?" he asked looking at the ear buds.

"Yeah. Wanna try it out?"

"Oh no, thank you, Lucas. I had something else in mind."

Ethan walked to the edge of the cliff and in one fell swoop threw both my iPod and cell phone into the ocean.

"Hey! What are you crazy?" He had a serene smile pasted across his face. I did not. "Why did you do that?"

"If you ever take the time to look around you when you're at school, or a store, even walking down a street you'd notice how many people walk around with those things stuck in their ears."

"So what?"

"They walk around like robots feeding on noise that is constantly assaulting their brains. It robs them of their chance to actually listen. Nobody listens anymore, Lucas."

"We're *listening* to music!"

"Yes, and I don't mean to imply that music isn't a wonderful gift, it is indeed. But it's like chocolate cake."

"What?"

"Chocolate cake can be a wonderful treat. Eating a slice of cake now and again won't make you fat or clog your arteries if you eat it in moderation. But if you were to eat cake for breakfast, lunch, and dinner, and maybe even for a snack here or there, you would poison your body. Water is essential for life, but if you drink too much, too fast, you will end your life because of it."

"There's no such thing as too much music," I countered, and he paused thoughtfully.

"Point taken. Perhaps my analogy was a bit off. It's not the music that is harmful, but more the constant barrage of information into one source." He tapped his ears.

"Fine, that's all fine and good, but why did you have to throw my iPod in the ocean?"

"So you can start listening Lucas."

THE UNDECIDED

"Listen? I listen. I've been waiting for you to say something worth listening to since yesterday."

"Let me rephrase that. So that you can start *learning* how to listen."

"No problem. Picked that one up pretty much right out of the womb."

"If that was true, you wouldn't be here with me. There's more than one way to listen, Luke. You're more than just a walking pair of ears. Remember yesterday when we were sitting just over there?" He pointed to two white Adirondack chairs.

"Yeah, that's where you let me fall asleep."

"Perhaps. But before that, were you not more aware of your surroundings than ever before?"

"I guess so."

"The more that you listen, with *all* of your senses and right here," he tapped his chest right above his heart, "the more that will be revealed to you. The answers surround you, if you would only take the time to listen."

"No offense, but isn't that what you're here for? To tell me answers?"

Ethan smiled a knowing smile, reminding me again of a younger version of my grandfather. "I could tell you how to play a game of baseball. I could explain all of the rules and strategies, but until you actually get out on the field and start swinging the bat, you're never really going to understand the game. Everything you need to know has always been with you, only you can know what that is."

"How?"

"By listening with all of your senses, your heart, your mind, and your spirit. Your dream last night, remember how you felt when the light came to you?"

"How did you know?"

"That feeling, that openness is where your answers lie. Seek the truth. Seek the truth, and your spirit will be set free."

"How did you know about my dream?"

"You're asking the wrong questions, Luke. See that basket over there?" He pointed to the greenery where Millie previously disappeared.

"Yeah."

"Go grab it, and meet me on the other side of that green wall."

"Okay." I picked up the ordinary brown woven basket and walked around the hedge. Behind the ordinary green bush was the most amazing assortment of flowers I had ever seen. I looked around in wonderment.

"Beautiful, isn't it?"

"This is amazing," I answered, walking through the flowers. "There's so many of them." Ethan clipped several flowers and placed them in the basket I was holding.

"You have a favorite?" he asked.

"A favorite?" I asked looking around me. "I don't see how that would even be possible. There are just too many to choose from. They're all cool."

"So is ice cream, but you won't catch me eating anchovy and garlic flavor. And yes, before you ask, that is an actual flavor."

"Well, that's different. You can't compare ice cream with flowers. And that's disgusting, anchovy and garlic? Gross."

"Again, you don't like my analogy, huh?"

"Well, yeah. Choosing between chocolate and anchovy ice cream is a no brainer."

"Okay, how about vanilla and chocolate. Which do you prefer?"

"Chocolate, of course."

"Ah-ha! And these?" Ethan asked, holding up a stem of purple heather and a white daisy. "Which do you prefer?"

"I don't know. They're too different to compare."

"And if I add this red rose?" he said as he clipped a fully bloomed red rose and held it beside the daisy and heather.

"Everyone likes roses." I shrugged my shoulders.

"And you?"

"I don't know. I like them all. I like them all together, not just one in particular."

"Good answer, Luke." Ethan warmly smiled and handed me the clippers. "Finish up for me, will you? When the basket is full, meet me inside the kitchen." Ethan took off his gardening gloves and handed them to me before walking back towards the hedge. Just before he disappeared from sight, he turned back once more. "You know, it's interesting when you think about it. Each flower is unique to the other in size, shape, and color and yet only when they are all put together does their true beauty really shine." Before I could blink, he was gone.

    I turned back to the garden and breathed in the heady aroma that no perfume manufacturer could ever dream of duplicating. I clipped every different type of flower that I could find until my basket was overflowing. Sticking the pruners in my back pocket, I headed back to the house with my bounty feeling rejuvenated. I placed the flowers on the counter next to another note from Ethan.

> Lucas,
> Meet me out by the fence in the back about one hundred yards from the tennis court. Help yourself to a sandwich if you're hungry, I left one in the icebox for you.
>
>   Ethan

"What's with this guy and notes?" I asked myself, walking to the refrigerator. "At least he knows how to make a mean sandwich."

CHAPTER TWENTY-TWO

Ethan was standing by a long wooden fence dressed in all white.

"Hey, you changed, huh?" I asked him.

"No," he said smiling.

"Your clothes. You're wearing all white," I said pointing to his linen shirt that was blowing in the wind.

"No. But I do have something for you to change into." He tossed a white cloth at me.

"A shirt? What for?" I asked, holding it up. It was white, like Ethan's, but not as refined.

"To put on, of course. Go ahead." He walked around me and picked up a can of paint and a paintbrush. The shirt fit me perfectly.

"Okay. What now?"

"Start east and work west." He handed me the paintbrush setting the paint can down by the first plank of the fence.

"You've got to be kidding me, right?"

"Solid strokes. Same motion. It will go on smoother."

"You're serious." I stared at him incredulously.

"I'm always serious, Luke."

"No," I stated.

"No?"

"No. I think you've watched The Karate Kid one too many times, E." I tossed the paintbrush next to the paint can. "But I'm no Daniel-san and you're certainly no Miyagi."

"The Karate Kid?"

"Yeah, you know, the movie where he learns karate from washing cars and *painting fences*!" I hit the fence for dramatic emphasis.

"Oh, I think I saw that one. That was good. Daniel was quite impatient and frustrated at the beginning but then went on to win the tournament, right?"

"Yeah," I said weakly.

Ethan picked the paintbrush off of the grass and handed it to me. "Remember, solid strokes up and down." He walked away.

"Wait!"

Ethan turned around lifting one eyebrow in question. I was tempted to throw the paintbrush again, but I couldn't seem to let go of it.

"So, what color?"

"White, of course," he said as he walked back to the house.

"Of course." I opened the can and sat down in the grass dipping the bristles into the paint. "This really stinks."

"Woof!"

Startled, I dropped the paintbrush onto the grass and turned to find Millie sitting directly behind me.

"Geeze! A little notice next time would be nice, Millie. The last thing I need is to have a heart attack on this rock. So, are you here to make sure I'm following orders or keep me company?"

"Woof," she replied moving closer to me.

"Maybe a little bit of both, huh?" I said, scratching behind her ears. "Alright, let's get this over with. It's not like I have anything else to do."

The sun was directly above me without a cloud in the sky. There was a constant breeze so the heat never became too unbearable. The glare off of the newly painted planks of fencing was blindingly bright, but other than that, I found that I was actually enjoying myself. Millie had fallen asleep and was breathing rhythmically behind me. I painted without thinking about what I was doing. Two strokes up and two down pretty much did the job. I thought about what Ethan had said about not listening and was determined to prove him wrong. I listened, all the time. I closed my eyes and everything glowed behind my eyelids from the brightness of the sun. The wind ruffled my hair, and I listened as seagulls flew overhead. I dropped the paintbrush and lay down beside Millie placing one hand on her warm fur. I was completely relaxed. I turned towards Millie lazily opening my eyes. Light was swirling all around Millie's prone form. I lifted my hand off of her belly, and the light came with me, shifting around my every move. I sat up and placed both hands on her and became enveloped in her light. I stood and stepped away from her wishing that she would wake up. And then she did.

"Woof," she said as usual. "It's about time, Luke," she said, not quite as usual. I jumped back.

"What the?"

"What?" the soft female voice echoed in my head. Or was it a woof? That's it. Maybe I inhaled too many paint fumes. Maybe I was still asleep.

"Okay, wait, did you say what or woof?" I rubbed my hands over my head that was starting to ache. "Oh my God, I'm losing it, I'm totally losing it. I'm talking to a dog, no I'm hearing a dog talk to me. I've got to get out of here."

"Calm down Lucas, you're not losing anything."

"No?" I dropped my hands and looked at her. "Then why am I hearing a dog talk? Your lips aren't even moving! What am I saying, you don't even have any lips!"

"No, I don't. You're hearing my thoughts. And I must say it's about time. Ethan and I were starting to wonder how long this was going to take."

"You're saying Ethan can hear you too?"

"Of course," she said with a hint of laughter. "Come on, Ethan is waiting for us." She started back towards the house. "Oh, and I'm sorry for running into you when you first arrived. I really love tennis balls."

"No problem," I said weakly. "So, you're really a dog, right? You're not like going to morph into a person or anything are you?"

"Of course not. I am a dog, just as you see."

"Then why can I all of a sudden hear you?"

"Because the veil is thinning, Lucas. You are starting to break through the limitations that you have imposed upon yourself."

"Limitations? What are you talking about?" I asked with a shift of an eyebrow. The irony of my question didn't elude me.

"The limitations that one creates from the environment that they live in. If one doesn't learn to stop and listen, they will never hear. You are starting to listen, Lucas, and this pleases the Council greatly."

"But how do I know what to listen for?"

"Your touchstone inside hears truth, and it is then that you simply know without knowing why."

"My touchstone?"

"By getting out of yourself, you will indeed find yourself, Lucas Aarons. In that you must have faith. You must learn to let go that which you believe to be true and open your mind and your heart so that you may be shown what truly is. Let Ethan lead you so that you may one day lead those who so desperately run from darkness."

"This has got to be the strangest day yet."

"I wish that were true, but much is yet to come, friend Lucas," Millie said and then licked my hand and gave me one final woof before she trotted over to Ethan who was, much to my surprise, a few feet away.

"Whoa!" I said, looking him up and down. He was still wearing all white, but what struck me was his hair. It still had the same flowing shoulder length style, but now instead of being salt and pepper, it was totally white. "Your hair. Your hair is white!"

He looked at me with a knowing smile and nodded once.

"As it has always been, Lucas."

"Come on. I know I'm hearing dogs talk now, but I'm not crazy. When I got here, you had dark hair, and now you're Colonel Sanders white!"

"A wise friend of mine once said that when the student is ready, the teacher will appear."

"What?" I uttered tiredly, not quite sure that I wanted any answers.

"Perhaps it is not I who have changed, but you Lucas. You saw me as you wanted to see me. You heard Millie only as a dog, because that is how you saw her, as a dog. The more layers that you peel away from your person, the clearer all will become. You see me now as I truly am, not because I have changed, but because you have, Lucas. Your transformation has begun." He looked at my wrist then turned towards the house. It was glowing brighter than it ever had before. I touched it and a tingling sensation rushed through my body. I spread my hands before me noticing a subtle light emanating around me.

ROBIN DONARUMA

"Whoa," I whispered to myself just before tracing Ethan's footsteps towards the house.

CHAPTER TWENTY-THREE

Ethan was in the kitchen holding a glass of iced water. He handed it to me, and I gratefully accepted it drinking it greedily as he talked.

"Milton once wrote." He paused. "You do know of John Milton, don't you?"

"Isn't he a poet?"

"Yes. English to be precise. He once wrote that the mind is its own place, and can make a heaven of hell, or a hell of heaven. You see, it is all in how we perceive our surroundings and our reaction to them. Of course, that defines who we are and what we will become. What you have been up until now; your life requires a new definition."

"A new definition?"

"You must learn to listen with more than your ears, speak with much more than your voice, and feel with every fiber of your being—and more. You, Lucas are the leader of the White Army. You are a light in a lonely, dark desert for many, many souls. In many ways, life as you know it, depends solely upon you."

"Okay, luckily, that's not the first time I've heard that, though I must say you win the award for most dramatic. So what am I supposed to do? Throw my textbooks at them? I'm a senior in high school. I only got my driver's license last year. I live with my parents, my mother still does my laundry, I don't even have a job, so what exactly am I supposed to do and to who? How do I even know who members of the Dark Army are?"

Ethan looked at me with a slight edge of disappointment and then walked out onto the deck just off of the eating area. I followed.

"Okay, I mean, I can see darkness around some people, I guess they're part of the dark team, but what am I supposed to do about it?"

"If a room is bathed in darkness, what is the logical action to take in order to see?"

"Turn on a light," I said, shrugging my shoulders at such a simple question. Ethan turned and looked directly into my eyes nailing me to the floor with his intensity.

"You're that light, Lucas." He grabbed my wrist. "You will help lead the *push* against the dark."

"By?"

"By turning on as many lights as possible."

"Can dark entities be changed?"

"Sometimes, yes," he answered thoughtfully. "But that is a dangerous road to tackle. Most resist, and the result is oftentimes death or worse. No morality, you see. Not exactly a fair playing field."

"Okay, so if I'm not supposed to change the dark entities to light, how are we supposed to win this war?"

"You forget. There is a third player in this game."

"The grays."

"Precisely. The undecided."

"I can't hear or see anything with grays," I said, immediately thinking of Mare.

"The grays are the hardest to track and the most unstable of all the players in this game. They could go to either side at any time and we are powerless to stop them. This area of Branford has one of the largest gray contingencies that we have yet to see. You must help them choose the path of light."

"How?"

"This is for you to determine. You have felt the power of the light and its wonder." I nodded that I had. "You must now become one with it. Only when you and the light are one and the same at all times will you be ready for the war."

"War. That sounds so, I don't know, something that the Dark Army would say. I mean, you have to admit, war isn't exactly a feel good subject."

"War is dispirited, defense is requisite. We have no choice but to defend our own preservation. You must show others how to live by being an example for them. They will follow you."

"How can you be so sure?"

THE UNDECIDED

"Because you have the mark." He pointed to my wrist. "And because it is written as thus."

I looked at my wrist and felt like a bowling ball just fell from my esophagus into my stomach. After all, it's not every day a kid learns that the fate of the world is sitting on his shoulders, and believes it.

"All the answers are surrounding you, Lucas. All will unfold exactly as it should. It has already begun. I know that you feel it." He looked to me for confirmation, and I nodded willingly. "Turn your power outward, not inward, and the light will shine around you like a beacon for all to see. I give you my word, when you leave here, you will be ready."

"So I guess what you're saying is that I'm not going home tonight, either, huh?" I asked resignedly.

"No son, not until you're ready."

"I suppose my parents know about this."

"Yes."

"Great. Well, there goes any shot with Mare. There's nothing like standing a girl up on your first date. A girl who is one of the *undecided*, by the way. Could have worked a little white magic on her, so to speak, if you weren't keeping me stuck on this rock like a prisoner."

"Opportunities are never lost, just rearranged a bit here and there. Now if you look in your room, you'll see that something arrived for you this morning."

"Really?" I walked to my very tidy guest room, and there like the Holy Grail on an altar was Layla. "Excellent." I began to play. "How did she get here? I never saw a boat."

"There are various modes of delivery, some apparent, and some not quite as much."

"Well, however she got here, thank you." I stopped strumming and held Layla tightly against my chest. "Wait a minute, you don't plan on throwing her into the ocean too, do you?"

"No, of course not. Music is part of your gift, Lucas. And that is something that no one, not even I, can ever dispose of."

"You like music?" I asked him as we made our way back out onto the deck.

"Oh most definitely. Probably not all of the same types of music that you listen to, but I do enjoy music."

"You probably like Mozart and Bach, huh?"

"Yes, I do, and many others, some of which you haven't heard of and some that have yet to be heard."

"I won't even ask what that means." My spirits were much brighter now that I had some form of familiarity in my hands. "So what bands do you like that I would know?"

"That's a tougher question than it seems. Well, there is one band that is very popular with the council that we all enjoy."

"Really? Who?"

"U2."

"U2? Excellent. Definitely one of my top ten." I started playing "One." "You know, this song is one of the most played songs at weddings, but it's not a love song, it's actually about splitting up. It's not about oneness, it's actually about differences. Pretty powerful stuff and very cool. So why U2?" Ethan was watching me closely. I was beginning to relax and open up, from the inside out. My wrist was glowing, so I bet that the rest of me was pretty much following suit.

"Simple. They're a band with a lot of soul."

Ethan left but wherever he was headed, I wasn't too concerned, besides, he'd probably write me a note anyway.

THE UNDECIDED

CHAPTER TWENTY-FOUR

    Over a week had gone by since arriving on the island. Ethan and I, and even Millie, had formed a routine, of sorts, and moved around each other quite naturally. Mornings consisted of what Ethan termed a time of reflection, a time when I'm supposed to tap into my surroundings and become one with them. Unfortunately, it's not as easy as it sounds, but Ethan assures me that each day I'm *getting stronger and closer to the path that I need to walk upon* (Ethan's words, not mine). I've got to admit, it was really cool talking with Millie. I've never thought of life from a dog's perspective, or any animal for that matter, but talking with Millie has really made me a little more conscious of all of our little furry friends.
    Afternoons consisted of me helping Ethan with various things around the house, always outside, never inside. Occasionally, we would play a game of tennis (Ethan really loved tennis) and sometimes swim in the pool, talking the whole time. Well, mostly Ethan would talk, and I would listen. Our nightly routine after dinner was usually me playing Layla out on the back deck until bed, or until Ethan pulled his disappearing act, which he did on numerous occasions.
    I thought about my parents and Mare, who I hoped would still be speaking to me after my return. I thought about school and wondered how my parents were explaining my absence. I definitely wasn't looking forward to catching up on all of the homework that I have undoubtedly missed, but a bigger part of me just really didn't care. I didn't care that I was missing school, or dates, or family dinners. At this point, I'm not even sure when I'm going to be going home, but I also didn't care. I was settling into a sense of calm and peace that I had never experienced before. I became as familiar with every

shrub, flower, tree, and rock on this land as if it were my own, and I had lived here my entire existence.

I was growing stronger and more confident, but I still feared the unknown. My dreams were clear and free from darkness, and I slept better here than I ever did at home.

"There you are," Ethan said, stealthily walking up behind me.

"Here I am, Obi-Wan. Star Wars." He stared at me blankly. "Never mind. What's up?"

"Another movie?" I nodded and followed him to the flower garden. "Millie tells me that you have many questions forming inside."

"She does? How would she know that? I never told her anything. Don't tell me that she can read my mind too?"

"No, no, at least, not in the sense that you speak of. Dogs can intuit many situations: unease, ill health, fright, concern; in you she feels unrest and uncertainty."

"Well, I'm sure that can't exactly come as a surprise to you."

"No. I've been waiting for your questions. I cannot answer a question that hasn't been asked."

"Sometimes I don't even know the question myself, I just know that I feel like I'm missing something. A big something." Ethan nodded slowly as we turned into the beautiful array of multi-colored flowers that never ceased to amaze me. I breathed deeply. "Amazing."

"Yes, quite," he answered quietly.

"Why can't I just tell everyone that they should choose good over evil. Isn't that kind of a no-brainer? And it would save a whole lot of time."

"And how do you propose to do that?"

"I don't know. Talk about good things, start a club or something. I've seen gray's get light sparks surrounding them before, I know it can..."

"When?" Ethan turned sharply. "When did you see this change occur?"

"A bunch of us were hanging out one day. We were playing music, and I noticed that Mare, you know the one I stood up, had some light dancing around her after a song."

"And tell me Lucas, was it you playing this song?"

THE UNDECIDED

"Um, yeah, actually it was. Queensryche, "Silent Lucidity", ever heard of it?"

"No."

"Didn't think so. It's pretty awesome. I'll play it for you tonight. Great lyrics."

"Yes, you must play it for me. And her light, did it remain?"

"For a while, until she saw her little sister, Grace. Grace is really sick, and as soon as she saw her, it faded. But what I'm trying to say is that we should get a whole bunch of them in one area and show them that they need to choose."

"Kind of like a big church rally?"

"Yes! Well, no, not exactly."

"You're forgetting one important element here, Lucas. They aren't cattle to be herded and branded. They are each individuals with their own thoughts, beliefs, and experiences. What may be right for one is not necessarily going to be right for them all."

"But choosing good over evil is pretty, pardon the pun, black and white. You are either in or you're out."

"Perhaps, eventually. But consider your group of friends much like a class of Algebra. When learning, do you all learn the same, at the same speed, and with the same mental capacity?"

"No," I said deflated. Ethan picked up two baskets, the large one that I use to collect the clipped stems and one about half its size.

"Hold these two baskets for me, will you?"

"Sure." I held one on each arm and followed him as he clipped flowers taking turns placing them in each basket.

"Everyone is so impatient these days. I think a lot of that is associated with all of those electronic gadgets. I appreciate your wanting to expedite the process of turning those to the light, but the human soul is not as easily manipulated as one might imagine."

"I didn't mean to manipulate everyone, not exactly, I was just thinking that if we rationally talked about what was really happening, and what could happen—people are smart and have a survival instinct, so why not tap into that right off the bat and get them on our side right out of the gate?"

"Because what may seem logical and instinctual to one individual, may seem underhanded and devious to another. You mustn't think to speak only to their minds, you must learn to speak to their hearts, their touchstones within. Look at the baskets." Ethan took the small basket, which was overflowing with vibrant flowers and placed it on the ground. "This basket is completely full, I don't think I can fit another flower into it, do you agree?"

"Yeah, but there's plenty of room in this one still." I handed him the large basket, which was barely filled halfway.

"Ah yes, a much larger capacity in this one." He placed the large basket beside the smaller one. "Both began this walk with us empty, fully prepared to hold the flowers that we collected. This smaller basket is now full and is content to be placed upon the ground, while the larger basket is still ready to continue our walk with us, ready to hold more flowers. At the end of our walk in the garden, both baskets will be filled. Because our smaller basket did not continue as far on our walk as the larger basket, does that mean that it is any less full?"

"Well, there's more in the larger basket, but they're both full."

"Precisely. And it is the same with each soul. Some are content with small baskets, while others require large ones. When the small baskets are filled and they happily sit down in the grass, it does not make them any less than the larger baskets that continue down the road. Eventually, both will be filled, just in their own time. There are no short cuts here, Lucas, we wish that there were."

"Somehow, I kind of thought you'd say that."

"The longest and hardest road you will ever travel upon is the one from your head to your heart." Ethan touched my head and then my chest, and I felt a jolt of power at each touch. "You must learn to listen to your heart and be clear enough of mind to decipher what it is telling you. It is not an easy journey, but once travelled upon successfully, a power which you can only dream of awaits you."

THE UNDECIDED

"I'm trying, Ethan, I really am. I just don't know what else I can do!" Frustration brought moisture to my eyes, and I looked away before he saw me.

"Remember one thing Lucas. It is the step after step that is hard, not the whole of the journey itself. You are the chosen one, and all will happen as it should, when it should."

"Do you really believe that I can do this?" I whispered.

"Again, you are asking the wrong questions. What I believe is of no consequence to you. It is what you believe here that holds the truth." He tapped my heart again with his index finger, and a powerful wave of love washed through. "I look forward to hearing that song tonight." He walked away.

I brushed away the tears that were now streaming down my face and looked at the two baskets filled with flowers. I emptied the smaller into the larger basket as his love swirled around me. With the large basket around my arm, I walked back towards the house.

CHAPTER TWENTY-FIVE

 I stopped tracking the days I'd been away from home. It just didn't matter anymore. My hair was longer, and a shadow of facial hair surrounded my jaw line and upper lip. Occasionally, I looked into a mirror if I happened to pass one by, but I never stopped to contemplate my appearance. It just simply didn't matter.
 I cherished my mornings of reflection. Where once they were a hassle, they were now vital to my existence. It was like plugging into life each day. I grew stronger in my manipulation of the light. Many afternoons Ethan would bring me wilted flowers or a small flying insect, like a dragonfly, and show me how to intertwine our energies. By doing so, I could direct the dragonfly to fly in whichever direction I chose. It was my own remote control dragonfly. With a wilted flower, usually just cut from the garden, there was very little light to tap into, so I practiced transferring my own into it prolonging its life for a little longer. It never ceased to amaze me, nor make me feel empowered. The more I practiced and manipulated elements of life, the more I became a true part of it, and that humbled me. I never took without giving back. It was harmony in the truest sense of the word.
 My communication with Millie had also improved. I was now able to talk with her using only my mind. I thought about my first few days on the island, and it seemed like a lifetime ago. I thought about my reactions to Ethan in the beginning and felt ashamed. So much had changed. I was still the same Lucas Aarons as I ever was with the same likes and dislikes, but it's kind of like I got an upgrade. Lucas version 2.0.
 I lifted my face up to the warm sunshine and drank in all that surrounded me. My hair, just touching my shoulders, danced in the wind. I held my hands out and celebrated the life that danced in my palm and wove

THE UNDECIDED

through my spread fingers. A warm, wet tongue stirred me from my reverie, and I looked down to see the smiling face I had so come to love.

"Ready for our game, Lucas?" Millie asked, wagging her tail excitedly. She picked up a tennis ball and walked towards the open, grassy area.

"Of course I am, Millie. Lead the way." I was following her through the hedges when she stopped suddenly and dropped her ball.

"Oh no," she said whining.

"What is it Millie?"

"Distress. Pain," she said making her way over to a large tree. She whined and stomped her front paws nervously. "Here, Lucas. Here."

I ran the short distance between us and saw in front of her a black bird with red and yellow splotches on its wings. Its wing was obviously broken and the small, young bird was gasping for breath. I bent down and looked up from where it was lying. There was a nest several feet up in the tree.

"It must have fallen from its nest," I said.

"His light is fading Lucas, you must help him."

Millie began whimpering again.

"We can take him back to the house, but I don't think he's going to make it, Millie. I'm not a vet, there's not a whole lot I can do."

"You can do everything Lucas. Have you learned nothing? You are the one."

Tears welled behind my eyes, and I closed them in frustration.

"This is a bird, Millie, not a wilted flower. What do you expect me to do?"

"Woof!" Millie yelled in frustration.

"Stop thinking Lucas and start feeling!"

Closing my eyes I took two deep breaths listening to the energy around me. Millie vibrated as if she was on fire. The distress of this small bird was weighing heavily upon her. I added myself, my own energy, to the mix. The slight bird was breathing even more shallowly. His light was dim. I carefully picked him up, trying not to cause any pain to his broken wing and our energies melded. My left arm ached echoing the pain from his left wing, and I felt a tremor in my chest that I equated with fear, but other than that, there didn't seem to be any other damage to him.

"Shhh, it's okay little guy, you'll be okay." I stroked his downy head and sang to him, much like my mother used to pacify me. "It's okay," I sang over and over. His small black eyes watched me intently, and I felt his heart begin to slow. My light fed him.

The pain in my arm subsided, and my chest quieted. The bird struggled to stand up in my hands. I laughed joyously.

"There, see? I told you you'd be okay." Millie walked over and sniffed the bird as it flapped his wings defensively. Millie licked him and then stood back, not wanting to scare him.

"You did it Lucas! I knew you could do it!"

I stood and opened my hands allowing the bird to leave. He clumsily flew to a low branch in the nearby tree, and the reality of what had just happened started to sink in.

"Millie?" I asked aloud, trying to keep the nervousness out of my voice.

"Ethan is here, Lucas," she said excitedly, before letting out a loud woof and licking my hand. "You have done well, my friend. We will play our game another time." Then she was gone. I could sense Ethan behind me, but I was still too stunned to turn around and acknowledge him.

"Did what I think happen, just happen?" I asked quietly.

"It did."

"But how?" I looked down at my hands.

"Because you are the chosen one."

"The wing. I fixed it?"

"You did."

"It was dying, I saw it."

"Yes."

"I brought it back to life?"

"Sort of."

"What do you mean, sort of?" I turned around sharply.

"Come, let's walk. His mother is waiting for us to leave so that she may tend to him." We moved towards the Adirondack chairs overlooking the ocean. "That young bird was dying and had a broken wing, and you successfully transferred your light to his. Kind of like stoking a fire, you might say."

"But his wing..."

"Henry Ford once said that whether you believe you can do a thing or not, you are right."

"Henry Ford, the car guy?"

"Yes, and then some. The point he was trying to make, as am I, is that if you believe that you can do something, you will. If you believe that you cannot, you will not. The mind inevitably will always win, no matter the battle. This is what I have been trying to teach you Lucas, to let go. Let go with your mind and listen to your heart. Connect the two and miraculous events will occur. Today, you stopped thinking and reacted. The result was life." I stared at Ethan, not sure how to respond. "The right words spoken at the right time is as beautiful as gold apples in a silver bowl."

"So, are you saying that I have the power to bring the dead back to life? To heal people and animals and..."

"Mmm, yes and no."

"Can you please, for once, just give me a straight answer? I'm kind of freaking out here!"

"Okay. Yes, you have the ability to manipulate the life force of another living entity, if you are able to maintain the head and heart connection, of course."

"Of course."

"You just did as much. However, the life force of a small bird and that of a human being are two different, what would you say, balls of wax."

"Balls of wax?"

"A mountain versus a sand dune, if you will. Perhaps made out of similar sources, but very different in formation and purpose."

"Okay..."

"Do you know what the primary difference is between animals and humans?"

"Well, aside from the obvious ones?"

"Yes."

ROBIN DONARUMA

"Well, if you had asked me that a few weeks ago, I would have answered that we're different because we have souls and animals don't. But that was before I met Millie."

"And yet you are correct. Well, so to speak. We are all part of the same life force, the same spirit, and that is what you tap into. Perhaps you can effect a change on a person's emotional state and sometimes their physical states as well, but remember that what humans hold unique to animals is their right of free will."

"Free will."

"A unique gift that allows, even many times, demands that each person think for themselves and determine their own answers instead of falling into the trap of following others. Intellectual choices are theirs, while animals react instinctively without rational thought."

"I don't understand."

"Just like your U2 song stating that *we are one, but we're not the same*. Life is one energy force that we all share, and must in turn respect, but the individual life forces are not the same. Laws that apply to that small bird will not apply to your mother or father."

I stared at him thoughtfully letting all that had just happened and all that I was hearing sink in. I felt as though I was just catapulted from high school into a post-doctorate class. I stared down at my hands and my birth marked wrist that was still aglow.

"You can feel it within you, can you not?"

"I can. I just can't believe it."

"Understood. You are becoming one with the law of sensitive dependence on initial conditions."

"Come again."

"The butterfly effect. You've heard of this?"

"Yeah, of course. That's where a butterfly flaps its wings over here and there's like a tsunami in China, right?"

"Because of the molecules set in motion from the action of that butterfly's wings, yes. This notion used to be widely ridiculed until it finally was proven by scientists and given the official name of the law of sensitive dependence on initial conditions."

"Okay."

THE UNDECIDED

"What that law really means, what it means to you is that *everything* you do, and *everything* you don't do, matters. The act of doing or not doing will have an impact on the rest of the world, not just Branford. I will leave you here to think about all that has transpired. You have grown, Lucas, and though it may not always seem so to you, know that you are ready."

I whipped my head around to face him.

"Ready? I'm ready? To go home?"

"Yes, son. It is time."

I looked around me, shocked by the idea of leaving all of what I had come to love.

"I'm not ready," I firmly stated.

"You have manipulated the light on your own, I can teach you nothing more."

"But, but who will help you with the flowers, and how is Millie going to get her exercise if I'm not here to throw the ball with her?" I asked desperately.

"We too shall move on, Lucas. We will go home also. There is much that we need to prepare for."

I ran my hands through my shaggy, long hair and felt the stubble that spread across my chin.

"I don't want to leave you," I whispered. Ethan stepped closer and put his hand on my shoulder. Love poured from him into me, and my emotion became evident as tears rolled down my face. "I'm scared."

"I know. But you are ready, and I can keep you here no longer. Do you even know how long you have been apart from your loved ones?"

"Three weeks maybe?" I shrugged. "Honestly, I stopped counting." He nodded knowingly.

"Forty days, Lucas."

"Forty days!" I was shocked.

"When you leave here, we will guide you. When you sleep, we will watch over you. When you wake, we will speak to you. There are others in Branford that will protect you as much as they are able."

"Who?"

"They will become known to you when needed."

"But..."

"No more questions. Now is a time for reflection. Millie will come to you when it is time to leave the island."

I looked out to the ocean hoping that words would be floating out there for me to grab and speak, for my mind was whirling at such a speed I wasn't sure of anything right now. I turned to utter as much to Ethan, but he was gone. I plopped down into the white wooden chair probably for the last time. I rubbed the arms with my hands loving every knot, splinter and smooth painted patch. I kicked off my shoes and dug my toes into the Earth. Would I take these feelings with me? I was afraid that by leaving the island, I was leaving behind a crucial part of myself, and that terrified me.

Forty days. How did that happen? I leaned my head back against the chair and called to the wind to cleanse me and for the sun to warm me. A cloud sailed away from the sun and bolts of sunshine shot into me. I smiled in thanks and calmed. I heard birds overhead and thought of my little black bird. I recalled the feel of its slight body responding to mine. The power and beauty of that act made me realize that the power didn't come from me, it came through me. That realization rocked me to my core and rightly humbled me. A smile spread across my lips as the truth sunk in. I wasn't alone. Something much bigger was pushing the buttons, and I just happened to be one of those buttons. I grabbed my necklace, and heat shot through my fingers and throughout my body. White light exploded in my mind. I was weightless and free. Love swirled around me, and music filled the air. Millions of tiny, sparkling lights danced around me. I held out my arms and offered my love. They clung to me and gave me theirs in return. The lights retreated, and I awoke to a familiar, moist greeting from my best friend.

"Millie," I said, patting her head as I stretched and stood up.

"It's time to go home, Lucas."

"I know," I said without emotion. Though a part of me wished that I could stay here forever, I knew that it was time to go.

"I will miss playing tennis balls with you, friend Lucas."

THE UNDECIDED

I stooped down and gave Millie a big hug around her fluffy white neck.

"And I will miss you, friend Millie. Thank you. For everything."

She wagged her tail, licked my face, and then trotted to the path leading down to the dock.

Ethan was standing there holding Layla. He appeared as nothing more than a splash of flowing white against a hard, dark background. He smiled lovingly as I approached. He started to hand my guitar to me then stopped.

"You spoke of groups earlier, Lucas. Teaching in groups to, I believe you said, *save time*?"

"Yeah," I responded wearily.

"I was thinking. A very, very wise friend of mine once found himself in a very similar situation that you find yourself in today, this need to get across to many people. This wise friend found that by speaking in a language that they could all understand, his point was better received. For instance, you wouldn't speak in Latin to a group of Russians, right?"

"I'm pretty sure we all speak the same language in Branford, Ethan."

"Yes, yes. Drop the literal meaning, Lucas. What my friend chose to do was instead of standing up on a box and teaching his large groups what he wanted them to know, he made up stories, parables. Stories that allowed each person to relate their lessons, in whatever manner they desired, to their own lives. This provided a much greater understanding to the masses."

"You're not saying that I should make up stories are you?"

"Of course not, Lucas." Ethan handed me my guitar looking into my eyes with intent. "Even musical instruments like this guitar, though it is lifeless, can be used as a voice. If the notes are played clearly, they will recognize the melody. I have always said that music is a gift. With you, it becomes much more. You are truly at your strongest when you give yourself to music. It is a time when you connect your head and your heart. Music is the key to your success. If you lose your way, music will bring you back. Remember this."

I stared at my guitar with renewed interest. Ethan turned towards the dock.

"Ah, there he is."

Captain Bob was standing at the foot of the dock smoking his pipe.

"Robert. Very good to see you again," Ethan greeted him kindly.

"Ethan," he acknowledged, lifting his pipe. "Is he ready?"

"Yes," Ethan responded without hesitation. I wasn't sure in what respect that question was asked, but either way I took it to be a good sign. With one final rub of Millie's head, I walked onto the dock.

"Lucas, remember that it is impossible to defeat the Dark Army, we look only to overcome them. Darkness is meant to be here, it has been since the beginning of time, it was just never meant to progress to such numbers."

"I think I understand."

"Don't look for a path to follow, be that path for others to walk upon. They will follow you, Lucas."

"How do I find you?"

"This was to be our only time together."

"But..."

"I'm sorry, that is what is written."

Captain Bob looked at a brewing storm in the sky. The wind picked up and his beard swayed with each gust.

"You feel that, E?" Captain Bob asked.

"Yes." Ethan laid a hand on my arm. "It is time, Lucas. You must go now. The Dark Army has sensed your presence. You were only safe from them while you were here, with me."

"What exactly does that mean?"

"The war has begun. You must go now."

Before I realized what had happened, I was seated in the boat, and Captain Bob was revving the motor.

"Ethan, I just wanted to say thanks. Thanks for putting up with me."

"It was an honor, Lucas. Now, you must go. Go in peace."

THE UNDECIDED

We took off from the dock like a bolt, and I had to grip Layla to keep her from flying overboard. I looked back to the shore where Millie and Ethan stood watching us disappear into the fog surrounding the island. Just as they disappeared from my sight, Millie howled a lone, sad howl. In my mind, I howled too hoping that she could still hear me.

Captain Bob didn't say a word the entire trip back, which was fine with me. I closed my eyes as we sailed through the thick fog bank heading back to reality. The further we got from the island, the more confident I felt. I felt peaceful and was struck with a keen sense of clarity. Suddenly everything that I had experienced and learned on the island made sense. It was like I had just aged twenty years, but in a good way. I was confident and filled with hope. I missed my parents. I was eager to see them and tell them the good news. When I opened my eyes, Captain Bob was staring at me with his mouth wide open, his pipe barely hanging on to his moist bottom lip.

"I'll be damned. It is you." His pipe fell, and I reached over to pick it up.

With newly found confidence I responded with one final word. "Yes." I handed him his pipe, and he awkwardly closed his mouth and directed his attention to the approaching shoreline.

"Thank God," he quietly uttered to himself.

The sun was beginning to glow on the horizon as we quickly approached Stony Creek. My parents' car was already there, waiting for me. My heart beat a little faster, and suddenly I couldn't wait to jump out of the boat and grab onto my parents. My mom was reaching into the car through the backseat window as my dad walked back from the market carrying two cups. My mother's head spun around as Captain Bob effortlessly docked the small boat against the wharf.

"Lucas?" she asked with surprise in her voice. I gracefully got out of the boat and walked to my mother.

"I knew you'd be back. You forgot these in the back of the car, and I know that you wouldn't be able to survive without them." My mother held up my iPod and cell phone, the same ones that Ethan had thrown into the ocean. I

laughed. "Very cool, Ethan." I walked to my mother and was about to take them from her hand, but she dropped them to the ground.
"Lucas?"
"Hi, Mom." I knew that my dad had reached the car because of the sound of two cups being dropped onto the graveled walk. I turned to him. "Hi, Dad."
"Lucas?" he asked in the same exact way as my mother. They both sounded confused.
"What? Don't I even get a hug after being gone for so long?" I took my mother in my arms and hugged her tightly. Love enveloped us, and I felt happy. My dad put his hand on my shoulder, and I let go of my mother and hugged my father. My mother stroked my hair.
"Lucas, your hair, it's so long." She brushed my stubbled cheek. "I don't understand. You've only been gone for a few minutes."
"A few minutes? I've been gone for forty days."
"Lucas," my dad interjected, "I'm not exactly sure what's happening here, but you just got on that boat," he pointed to Captain Bob's boat that was no longer there, "no more than fifteen minutes ago."
I took a minute to absorb what they were saying, and I suddenly was overtaken with laughter. The whole time I was gone, it was as if time here had stopped. I looked back to see if Captain Bob was anywhere in sight, but no luck there.
"Wow," I said, trying to stifle my humor. "Well, I guess I didn't stand up Mare after all," I said to myself.
"How about we all go home and discuss exactly what just happened here, or there, or wherever you were," my dad suggested, opening the car door.
"There is something very different about you, Luke. Something has changed, hasn't it?" my mother asked me.
"Yes," I stated. "Something wonderful." I grabbed my mother's hand and sent her some of the love that was overflowing in me. She looked down to our hands and tears fell down her cheeks and dropped onto my fingers. "It has begun," I told her. I slowly dropped her hand and looked at my father. "I'm not quite ready to go home yet. I think I'll walk for a while, if that's okay with you."

THE UNDECIDED

My father was watching me intently and responded only with one curt nod of his head.

"I'll be home soon, I promise," I said walking down the dock.

"Lucas! Wait! Don't you want these?" My mother held up my cell phone and iPod again.

"No thanks," I said with a sly smile thinking of my dear friends Ethan and Millie. "I don't need them."

"Lucas! Don't be too late, okay?" my mother desperately added.

"Don't worry, Mom, I won't be late, I've got a date tonight."

CHAPTER TWENTY-SIX

I walked without a destination in mind. I felt as if I had been reborn and was seeing things for the first time. Stores were beginning to open up for the day, and life was slowly starting to come alive in downtown Branford. The church in the town green rang its bells as families with beautifully clad children filed through the large white doors. Most that approached the church were surrounded by white light, as I expected, but was surprised to witness dark energies walking through the doors as well.

Ahead of me a woman pushing a stroller was scolding her son for not tucking in his shirt. The baby cried when she stopped walking to fix his shirttails. As I passed by, I discreetly touched a little foot that was sticking out of the stroller. *Peace*, I thought. The crying stopped. I continued on and so did the mother with the quieted baby and disgruntled little boy.

Energy ebbed and flowed around me as I headed away from the green and down to the trolley tracks leading to the marshes. Following one of the well-worn paths running parallel along the river, I enjoyed every noise, subtle and not so subtle that I heard while deeply breathing in the briny, moist air.

I stepped off of the path and headed towards a large rock formation that appeared to be floating among the golden reeds. I climbed on top of the largest one.

"Awesome," I said aloud. A hawk flew overhead as a small ant crawled across my hand. A rustling noise behind me caught my attention. It was two deer staring at me looking as surprised to see me as I was to see them. I held my hand out, silently calling to them. I felt their trepidation and intense desire to continue down their path. "Come," I whispered. They walked towards me until they were close enough to touch. They were so beautiful. I wanted to reach out to them, but dared not ruin the moment. "Go in peace."

THE UNDECIDED

I dropped my hand, and in the blink of an eye, they were gone. I laughed with joy and laid back on the rock, soaking up the sun that so generously poured upon me.

I knew that I had better start home, but I was reluctant to leave the peace that I had just found. I closed my eyes giving myself another ten minutes.

I sat up on the rock surprised that I had fallen asleep so easily. I jumped into the reeds brushing my right hand across my body. The wind shifted and parted the reeds allowing me to find my way back to the path. Just ahead of me something was sticking out of the reeds. As I approached, a sense of dread fell over me. It was the leg of a deer. Pushing the grass to the side I saw what the reeds attempted to hide from me, two eviscerated deer. Their throats and bellies had been split open leaving blood and entrails littering the peaceful surroundings. I backed away looking around me for their killer. The birds stopped singing as a gray cloud slowly moved in front of the sun. A chill ran down my spine, and I waited for what I knew was to come.

"Lucas," my name hissed all around me, making it impossible for me to tell the direction of its source. "Lucas, you've been a very naughty boy hiding from me all this time."

"Where are you?" I demanded, becoming more angry than scared. "Show yourself!" I screamed, turning in circles.

"But you can't hide from me anymore, Lucas. You can feel me all around you, can't you? A cold breeze ruffled my hair.

I enveloped myself with white light.

"You've learned some new tricks I see," the voice mocked me. "So have I."

The leg of the deer corpse moved. My light faltered as I watched in horror as the bloody flesh stood on its broken legs. I backed away from the beast that stared at me with hatred. It awkwardly moved towards me baring its small teeth, its intestines dragging beneath it.

"Come here, Lucas, it won't hurt a bit. I swear," said the deer approaching me with increasing speed. I stood frozen and barely noticed the white flash that rushed from behind me toppling the dead beast to the ground.

ROBIN DONARUMA

"Millie!" I whispered. Millie had her mouth around the neck of the deer, breaking it for the second time. The cloud drifted away from the sun allowing warmth and light to cover us once again. Millie was licking the blood off of her white paws.

"Millie, what are you doing here? I thought that..."

"I don't have much time, friend Lucas. You need to go home now." Millie walked closer to me and nuzzled my hand.

"How did you?"

"I am now your watcher, Lucas. I always will be."

"So you get to stay with me?"

"On this realm only."

"What realm?" I asked.

"The in-between. The place where your mind and spirit go when your body rests."

"You mean that I'm asleep right now? This isn't real? It never happened?"

"Oh it very much happened. But yes, you are asleep, and you must wake up now so that you can go home." Then she bit me. "Wake up, Lucas!"

I shot up from the rock. "Whoa." My hand held the impression of Millie's teeth. I jumped off of the rock and made my way through the reeds and onto the main path that would lead me home. But not after first timidly peering into the brush to make sure it was free from anything resembling a deer.

CHAPTER TWENTY-SEVEN

    I walked faster than normal fueled by a sense of foreboding. I reached our street and forced myself to slow down. Everything appeared as it should, birds were singing, kids were playing, lawnmowers echoing through the air. Nothing felt out of the ordinary. I scratched my head, trying to clear out the cobwebs wondering if I would have enough time for a haircut before meeting Mare at Lenny's tonight.
    My house came into view, and I slowly exhaled. Everything looked normal, with the exception of a moving van parked in front of the house next to us. Both my parents were standing in the street talking with another couple. I slowed. My breath caught in my throat, and the smile slid from my lips. Something wasn't right.
    My mother laughed at something the couple had said. I tapped into the energy surrounding me and felt chilled to the bone. They weren't dark energies, but a very dark shade of gray, darker than I had ever seen. It reminded me of the thick, dark smoke that funnels out of burning buildings.
    "Is this why I had to come home, Millie?" I softly asked.
    "Lucas!" my mother yelled excitedly. "Come here, I want to introduce you to our new neighbors!"
    Sensing my hesitation, my father walked over to me clapping me on the shoulder.
    "Come on, I don't think they bite," my dad said jovially.
    "Well, not today anyway, we just had a big lunch," the man said, attempting to join in the jest. "Chad Donahue." He stuck out his hand, and I firmly grasped it trying to see if I could read him. Nothing. His vibe was as murky as the energy surrounding him.
    "Pleased to meet you, Mr. Donahue."

"Please, call me Chad. And this little filly to my left is my beautiful bride, Brittney," he said enthusiastically. She dutifully stepped forward and presented her hand.

"But you can call me Brit, everyone does. My goodness, you have the most beautiful eyes I think I've ever seen!" she said, letting go of my hand.

They looked like they had just finished golfing eighteen holes at the country club. They appeared completely harmless, but the pit in the bottom of my stomach kept warning me that something was very off.

"Thank you," I replied, hoping to make my exit. Not so lucky.

"I just can't wait for you to meet our son, Devin. You two will get along great, I just know it! He'll be starting school tomorrow."

Alarms went off with every fiber of my being.

"Is he here, I'd love to meet him," I heard myself answering.

"No, unfortunately he went into town, something about guitar strings, I don't know. To be honest, once he starts talking about music it's like it's in one ear and out the other, you know what I mean?" Brit chummily asked my mother.

"I sure do. Lucas plays guitar too."

"You're kidding!" Brit exclaimed, clapping as enthusiastically as a high school cheerleader. "Oh this is just perfect Chad! Did you hear that? Lucas plays guitar too!"

"Of course I heard it, the whole street heard it Brit," he lovingly chided his wife, then looked at me. "We've been living overseas for the past couple of years, so Dev and his sister, Mindy, haven't exactly had a bevy of friends to choose from."

"Where overseas?" I asked.

"Southeast Asia, mostly. A lot of small villages that hardly anyone has heard of."

"Mr. Donahue works for Yale, Lucas," my mother explained. "He was working on a research project studying economic growth, is that right Chad?"

"Perfectly," he responded with a huge smile.

THE UNDECIDED

"That couldn't have been too easy on the kids," my dad chimed in.

"Well, actually, the kids really loved it for the first year and a half, but then you could tell they were really itching to be back on home turf."

"Devin was so homesick that he even threatened to move back by himself. Can you believe that?" Mrs. Donahue said, shaking her head.

"Dad!"

"Out here, Mindy," Mr. Donahue responded. "Come here, there's someone I want you to meet." Out of the garage came a small, petite blonde who was absolutely stunning. I smiled appreciatively until I saw the wave of blackness that followed directly behind her. Enveloping her like a cloak once she stopped.

"Hi, she said sweetly to my mother who introduced herself. I watched the darkness crawl onto my mother's skin as if tasting her, and it took all of my strength to not reach over and rip her hand from Mindy's. Instead, I gripped my mother's shoulder and Mindy quickly withdrew her hand.

"Mindy, this is Lucas, Lucas, Mindy." I kept one hand on my mother and stuck the other in my pocket. She looked at me and her smile wavered. She made no move to shake my hand. She cocked her head slightly to one side and pasted on a smile that put teenage pageant contestants to shame.

"Mindy and Devin are what you'd call Irish Twins," her dad said, ruffling her perfectly straight hair. "Eleven months apart."

"Oh my goodness," my mother said. "Are you a senior too?"

"Yes, ma'am. When we were in Cambodia I was able to take some online courses that let me move up so I could be with Devin."

"She and Devin are very close," Mrs. Donahue explained.

"Sometimes it's like we're the same person," she said, looking directly at me. "Nice necklace."

"Thanks. Well, nice to meet you all, I had better get going."

"Luke's got a big date tonight," my dad offered in hushed tones.

"Pleasure's all ours, Lucas," Mr. Donahue said with a perfect smile.

"I know Devin will be so anxious to meet you. Maybe you'll have some classes together?" Mrs. Donahue offered. I glanced at Mindy who was watching me with interest.

"I certainly hope so, Mrs. Donahue. I'll look for him in school tomorrow."

"Wonderful!" she responded as I walked up our driveway. "Have fun on your date!"

I concentrated on keeping my pace casual, but it was all I could do to not run into the house.

There was a lot that I still wasn't sure of, but there were three things that I would bet my life on. One, the darkness had finally found me. Two, the war between the dark and the light had begun, and three, the name of the leader of the Dark Army was Devin Donahue, my new neighbor.

CHAPTER TWENTY-EIGHT

I was waiting for my parents at the kitchen table. They finally came in about ten minutes later grinning from ear to ear.

"Lucas, aren't they wonderful? I think this is going to be a great year! To think that they have a son exactly your age who plays guitar too!" my mother joyfully announced.

"Well, just because they both play guitar doesn't mean that they're going to become best friends and college roommates, Mary."

"Oh I know, but boy that Mindy sure is a knockout, don't you think so, Lucas?"

I was patiently watching their interaction, waiting for a moment when I knew I had both of their undivided attentions. And by the look on my mother's face when she turned to me, I'd say that I had it.

"Lucas? What's wrong?" My mother's new found excitement vanished, and all eyes were now focused on me.

"Not everything is as it seems," I said.

"Come again?" my dad said, walking closer to me.

"The Donahues. You must stay away from them, far away from them."

"Lucas, I don't understand. They're the nicest people we've met in a long time."

"A little too nice. A little too perfect, maybe," my dad interjected. "What do you know, Luke?"

"That they have chosen their side in this war and it is not with us."

"They're dark?"

I stood up and towered over my mother hoping that the seriousness of this next statement would sink in.

"Yes. But it's more than that. I believe that their son, Devin, is the leader of the Dark Army just as I am the leader of the White."

"Impossible," my mother stammered.

"Impossible for him, but not for me?"
"Well, I mean, oh Joe, what if Lucas is right?"
"I don't think *if* fits into this equation Mary. If Lucas says it is so, then it is."
"Then what do we do? We have to move!"
"No," I stated. "It's time for the push. It's time for us to fight. And to win."
My mother walked to me and placed her hand on my cheek.
"What happened to you on that island?" she whispered. "You're so, so grown-up, so wise."
I smiled lovingly into her eyes placing my hand over hers.
"I learned how to listen." I kissed her on the forehead and nodded at my father. "Now, if you'll excuse me, I've been waiting for this date for a really long time."
I left my parents standing in the kitchen, grasping each other's hands. I considered staying home and not going to meet Mare. After all, this new development was kind of important and left a lot to think about, but sitting in my room all night wasn't going to accomplish anything.
I took a quick shower, brushed my teeth and threw on an old pair of jeans and a plain, faded green tee shirt. I grabbed my keys and was out the door before my parent's distressed looks could sway me to stay. I hopped into my Saab and flew out of our driveway noting that the moving truck was gone, and made my way to Lenny's Indian Head Inn, the hangout for Branford High seniors.

***

If I hadn't been looking for it, I would have driven right past it. It was a small, rustic building hidden by the dozens of cars parked in front of it. I opted for a much roomier parking place across the street. Music echoed from the back deck overlooking the marshes. Laughter and warm yellow light poured out of the open windows along with the intoxicating aroma of deep fried food.
I entered through a large wooden door with a porthole window and was greeted by an older woman with long white hair.

THE UNDECIDED

"You made it!" she said, possessively grabbing my right arm.

"Yes, I made it," I replied, wondering who was squeezing the life out of my arm.

"Mare and the girls told me you might be coming, and I said that I'd look out for you." I forgot about my arm.

"Mare's here?" I asked, scouring the dining room.

"Oh, she's here as well as about half of the senior class! Out back, that is. You're just as cute as she described. Actually, maybe even cuter," she said with a wink.

"Thank you," I said blushing. "Well, it was nice to meet you, I had better go find everyone."

"I'll help you find them, don't you worry. They're all out back. And you're in luck, it's open mic night tonight."

"You don't say."

"There she is, standing near the railing. See?"

I had seen her before she mentioned where she was. She drew me in like a moth to a flame. "Absolutely," I answered. I tried to pry my arm from my escort and make my way over to her, but her grip tightened.

"Remember, Lucas, your music is the key. It always has been." She winked, let go of my arm, and walked back into the restaurant. I stared after her and noticed an image of a small white dog on the back of her tee shirt.

"Millie?" I whispered to myself just before everything went dark.

"Guess who!" a familiar voice asked, pulling my head down.

"Someone short," I answered, prying the fingers off of my face. "Hi, Becca," I said hugging her. It really was great to see everyone. It had been a long time since I had talked much less seen any friends.

"Ha ha. I'm so glad you made it!" she said with her ever present smile and glowing energy. "And I'm not the only one," she coyly sang gesturing to Mare who was walking towards us. I began walking too, and before we knew it we were face to face. She was looking at me questioningly.

"Hi."

"Hi."

"I know I just saw you like two days ago, but you look different."

"Do I?" I couldn't stop staring into her eyes.
"Your hair looks different, I think. Does it? I don't know. It doesn't matter. I'm glad you're here."
"Me too." I grabbed her hand and pulled her into me, hugging her tightly. I inhaled the unique fragrance that was Mare. "I missed you," I whispered, pulling away.
"Oh, Lucas, you're funny. Come on, I saved you a seat." She held onto one of my hands and dragged me to a table with two empty seats. Becca and Scott or Jeff, one of the football players, I can never get them straight, were already sitting down. Looking around, there were a lot of familiar faces from school, some I knew, some I didn't. I noticed Peter sitting just inside the restaurant with his parents looking longingly outside at the rest of us.
"Isn't it great out here?" Mare asked me, shaking me out of my reverie.
"It's perfect," I said and meant it. The weather was perfectly warm and calm, and the sounds of the water could still be heard just over the din of the crowd. I was relieved to see that there was a lot of light energy here. Jeff joined the table, or Scott, whichever one he was, and I watched with interest as their gray energies became flecked with light sitting next to Becca. There were some dark entities here too, but they remained either inside the restaurant or across the deck in their own group. Mare still held my hand, and I picked it up and softly kissed her knuckles.
"Thanks for asking me to come tonight," I said, watching her cheeks blush and her grayness explode with light sparks.
"Thanks for coming."
We were interrupted by a huge plate of fried everything.
"Whoa."
"The Fisherman's Platter. Trust me, after eating this you won't eat fried food for like a year, or at least not until next week. It's so good! Here, taste the scallop."
It was the best thing I think I had ever put in my mouth, okay so I was really hungry and sitting next to the perfect girl, but it was amazing. We barely finished the platter, and I was totally full. The once aromatic aroma of fried fish now sat like a lump at the bottom of my stomach.

THE UNDECIDED

After this meal, I think I could never eat fried food again and be okay.

"This is like my fourth napkin. It's quite a love hate relationship with fried food, isn't it?" Mare asked, wiping grease from her fingers.

"Definitely. I'll go get some wet wipes. I don't think these napkins are cutting it."

"Oh, that would be great. I think I'm too full to move."

I gave her a peck on her cheek and walked into the restaurant in search of wet wipes. The restaurant was filled with students from school too, most of them with their parents. I stopped at Peter's table.

"Hi, Peter, remember me?" I asked, nodding a hello to his parents.

"Yeah, of course. Lucas," he answered shyly.

"I know you're out with your parents, but maybe next week, if you want, you can come hang with us out there?" I suggested pointing out the window to the crowd behind him. Peter looked as if he was going to pass out.

"Sure," he squeaked. His mother nudged him with her elbow and his father was grinning from ear to ear. "Thanks," he shyly added.

"See you at school tomorrow."

I walked near the bar area that was standing room only due to a football game blaring from two large screen plasmas. Energy was ebbing and flowing all around me. I grabbed the wipes and headed back noticing how the dark energies gravitated away from me as the white energies moved towards me.

I placed the wipes in the center of the table, keeping one for myself.

"You're just in time!" Mare smiled. "It's open mic night tonight," she said, pointing to a small stage built onto the deck. There was a small drum kit, a keyboard, one acoustic, a bass, and an electric guitar.

"Excellent," I said, moving out of the way for the waitress, who seemed to be standing unnaturally close to me. I moved to the other side of the table, and she unwittingly followed me. Eventually, her tray was filled, and she left.

"Did you see that?" Mare laughed. "She was totally stalking you."
"I don't think so."
"She totally was."
"Hey, there's John," I said, glad to change the subject. Across the deck John was in deep conversation with three other kids from school that I recognized but didn't know their names. He saw me and mimicked the peace sign.
"Lucas!" he yelled then pointed to the stage.
"Looks like John's ready."
"Yeah, he usually is," Mare responded. "His band is a regular; they're really good."
I spotted a group of girls beside John that were a pale gray and decided that would be a good place to watch the performance.
"Well then, let's watch. Come on." I pulled Mare alongside me as I made my way over there. John and his buddies began checking the levels, and Mare and I found a table near the front. Before we knew it, Becca, Jeff, Scott, and about fifty other seniors had followed our lead and were standing around us.
"Doesn't it seem like everyone just followed us over here?"
"Best seat in the house," I said putting my arm around her shoulder.
"No, really. Look around, everyone is literally right here beside us." She looked around, and I was grateful to hear John's band start playing.
"Zeppelin," I said with a huge grin. "Excellent." Everyone scrambled to find something to wave in the air as the sultry sounds of "Stairway to Heaven" began to unfold. "They're good," I said and meant it. Sure, there were some logistical elements and mimicking Plant's voice was never going to happen, but they were having a great time, and so was everyone else. I closed my eyes and let myself into the music feeling that familiar sense of peace that I reveled in on the island.
"Lucas?" Mare brushed my hair back behind one of my ears. I opened my eyes and looked at her with a soft smile. "I thought maybe you fell asleep," she mused.

THE UNDECIDED

"John is rather fond of lengthy music, but no I wasn't sleeping, just listening."

Mare looked around and then chewed on her bottom lip as if she wasn't sure what to say.

"You okay?" I said, sitting up a little taller in my wooden seat.

"I was just wondering something."

"What?"

"Well, when you went inside to get those wet naps I saw you talking to that boy from school, I don't even know his name."

"Peter?"

"Peter, yeah that's right."

"And?"

"Well, I guess I was just wondering why. What did you say to him?"

"Don't you have a class with Peter?"

"Yeah, he's in my Physics class."

"And yet you didn't know his name and have never talked with him?"

"Well, it's not as bad as you're making it sound. It's not like I purposely ignore him every day, it's just that we travel in different circles."

"Maybe it's time to stop walking in circles and start walking straight," I said with a smile. "I invited Peter to come outside and join us next time instead of looking out a window and wondering what it would be like to have a friend."

Mare stared at me as if she had never seen me before.

"You can't be real," she whispered out loud.

"Are you okay?"

"Yeah, I'm fine. It's just that, I don't really know how to put this."

I could see that she had questions dying to be let out. I put my hand over her fidgeting ones and poured my light into her. She looked into my eyes and took a deep breath.

"I feel like I'm addicted to you."

Not what I expected to hear. I raised my eyebrows in shock.

"That didn't come out right. I know we don't know each other that well, or for that long really, but when I'm around you—you make me feel happy. And I want to feel happy all the time."

"You make me feel happy too, Mare," I answered quickly.

"I do?"

"Absolutely. I love being with you." I put my hand on her cheek and moved towards her. Lightly, I brushed my lips against hers and felt our energies merge. She kissed me back, and I was weightless until she pulled away.

"Lucas."

"Yes?" I answered in a daze.

"Don't you hear that?"

"No."

"They're chanting your name," she said laughing.

"What?" I pulled myself back down to reality and looked at John still on stage. He had finished his song and was chanting my name over the microphone, and apparently, everyone else had joined him.

"He lives and breathes ladies and gentlemen!" John said, pointing to me. A few people in the crowd whistled having witnessed my private moment. I stood up and pointed to John implying that I would get him back for this.

"Lucas, come on man, you're up!" John took the electric guitar off of his shoulder and held it out to me.

"No, man, you keep going, I'm a little busy," I said with a hint of humor. The crowd began wooing us and John began chanting my name once again.

"Go on, Lucas, I don't think you have a choice." Mare said, smiling her brilliant smile. I looked to the crowd and noticed the hostess standing in the doorway of the restaurant. She was absolutely beaming. She mouthed for me to "go on," and before I realized it I was standing on the stage.

"Okay John, I'll play but only if you and your guys back me up," I said, putting the guitar around my neck.

"Excellent!" John answered.

"Okay, grab the acoustic and follow my lead, John. Paul, right?" I asked the keyboardist. "Try this out." I played a series of eight notes. "Loop that until you want to do something else. You guys will know when to come in

THE UNDECIDED

and when you do, just do whatever makes you happy," I said and then walked to the microphone.

"Hi, my name's Lucas." Everyone began to cheer, which made me laugh. "Thank you, thank you very much." I looked back at John who gave me thumbs up. "I'm kind of new here, so I don't know all of you yet, but I've gotta say that I think Branford is pretty cool." Everyone started cheering again including Mare who was whistling with two fingers. "I made a good friend recently named Ethan. I don't know when I'll be seeing him again, but I know that wherever he is, he can hear me. This song is for you Ethan." I began shredding a chord in sync with Paul's keyboard. The cheering became louder as everyone caught on to the tune, and John and the drummer, Kyle, joined in.

I fell away from myself with every note played and word sung. I chose the classic U2 song, "City of Blinding Lights" and dedicated it to Ethan who I really missed, but I didn't realize quite how much. Just as the powerful lyrics say, I used to think that I knew so much until Ethan showed me that I knew nothing at all. I looked at Mare. White light was mixing with her grayness. Everyone was singing along, and several people from the restaurant even came out onto the deck.

When the last chord was played, the house went wild. John, Paul, and Kyle were high fiving each other, and the crowd rushed the platform. It was definitely cool to get so much positive attention from playing my music, but what was amazing was how bright it had become outside, and it wasn't from the lights. Everyone was buzzing with a white, shimmering vibration. It was wild. There wasn't a dark entity in sight. In the restaurant, three tables of gray energies were there and curiously watching us through the window, but there wasn't another dark entity that I could see. Mare bounced over to me.

"Lucas, that was amazing! Do you hear everyone?" Becca joined her and jumped on me.

"You're so awesome! You're like going to be famous one day, I know it!" Jeff and Scott were by her side and also totally surrounded by white light. I thought about what Ethan had told me, my music was the key.

"Thanks," I told everyone. Questions were being thrown at me, but all I could think about was what was happening. "I'll be right back," I told everyone. I walked into the restaurant and to the bar where I saw dark energies earlier. They were gone.

"When the power of love overcomes the love of power, the world will know peace."

I spun around to find the hostess smiling at me. She took my hand.

"What? Jimi Hendrix said that. There's a car with the bumper sticker out in the parking lot. I thought it kind of catchy and rather appropriate, don't you think?" the hostess answered beaming.

"Who are you?"

"A friend of a friend."

"Ethan?"

"You are not alone, Lucas. You have many watchers on this realm as well. They will reveal themselves when needed."

"Hey, here you are." Mare walked into the bar and looked at my hand still in the clutches of the hostess.

"What's your name?"

"Barbara. But you can call me Barb." She winked at me then let go of my hand. "Everyone does. Well, I had better go help clean up, a lot of people left quite a mess out there when they left."

"Barb?"

"Yes?" She turned back towards me.

"Is Ethan here?" I asked hopefully.

"No dear." She was about to speak and then looked at Mare whom I had forgotten was standing beside us. "Ethan isn't able to travel this far right now, but don't worry, there will be a time when your paths will once again cross." And then she was gone.

"Um, hello? Earth to Lucas," Mare said, snapping her fingers in front of my face.

"I'm sorry," I said and hugged her tightly. "I was just thinking of something."

"What's going on Lucas?" She pulled away and grabbed both of my hands. "You can tell me. You can tell me

THE UNDECIDED

anything." I looked around to the bartender who was busily wiping down the bar.

"How about we get out of here?" I asked, not waiting for an answer. I held on to one of her hands and pulled her out of the restaurant. I took a moment to inhale the fresh evening air, and it calmed my senses. We walked through the packed parking lot and down to a dirt path running parallel with the marsh. Lenny's was still alive with Branford High seniors and music was still being played on the stage. We walked until the sounds of the frogs and crickets overpowered the sounds coming from the restaurant. I sat on a large rock, pulling Mare down beside me. She was waiting for me to say something, but I didn't know what to say.

"Are you okay, Lucas?"

"I've never been better in my life." I looked at her. "I know that you have questions, and I know that I come off as a little strange at times maybe, but I'm not sure what I'm supposed to say."

"How about the truth?"

"The truth," I repeated smiling. "I could tell you anything I wanted to, how would you know what was true and what wasn't?"

"Because I know that you would never lie to me." She took my hand. "And for the record, you've never come off as strange, it's other people."

"Other people?"

"The way people act around you, at school, at the festival, here at Lenny's, even at my house with Grace. There is something about you that is different. I can feel it when you touch me, when you sing, when you walk up to a boy that no one has ever even cared existed and invite him to join us. I just don't know what it is. Tell me. Trust me."

"Okay." I looked at her and wiped any humor from my face. "I'm a vampire."

"Lucas! Stop it," she said laughingly.

"Come on, I was appealing to your *Twilight* sensibilities. You have to admit that was a little funny, and I think you almost believed me for like a millisecond."

"Hardly. You're one funny boy Lucas, but I'm serious."

ROBIN DONARUMA

"Hey, I'm just a normal kid trying to get through my last year of high school, just like everyone else, but lately, ever since I turned eighteen, I've been sort of seeing things differently."

"What do you mean?"

I took a deep breath and looked out over the marsh.

"I can see the energy that surrounds people."

"You mean like their auras? What are you like psychic or something?"

"No, nothing like that. Well, sort of like that I guess. It's a little more black and white than that, pardon the pun." I said into the ether.

"So you're not psychic?"

"No, I'm not psychic, Mare. The truth is that I see energies as either dark or white. Good or bad. Simple as that."

"I don't understand."

"I don't blame you, I'm still getting used to it myself."

"So you can tell if someone is good or if someone is bad? Well, isn't that kind of obvious by how they act? Are you sure it's not some sort of eye problem?"

"Do you remember that serial killer Ted Bundy?"

"Yeah, he was the one that killed all of those girls at Florida State, right?"

"On the outside he looked and acted, for the most part, like an upstanding citizen. Smart, good looking, well dressed. But on the inside, he was pure evil. Everyone is not always what they seem."

"So, you can see everyone's true nature."

"Yes."

She stood beside me and looked back to Lenny's where a lot of the people were starting to leave.

"And that woman? Who was she to you?"

"I'm not really sure, that was the first time I've ever seen her, but she is a friend of a friend of mine."

"She's good."

"Oh, yes. It doesn't get much better," I said smiling.

"What about Becca? You can see her?"

"What do you think?"

"I love Becca, she's my best friend. I think I would know if she was evil. She's not, right?"

THE UNDECIDED

"No, she's surrounded by white light." Mare exhaled a deep breath. "Trust your instincts, Mare, I may see them easily enough, but human nature has a built in alarm systems. You never doubted that Becca was anything but good."

"No, she's too happy all the time to be evil." I laughed out loud, grabbed her hand and began to walk. She stopped.

"What about me? What do you see when you look at me?"

"Beauty. Goodness." I took her face in my hands. "In you, I see everything." I leaned in closer to her lips. She pulled back.

"That wasn't an answer. What do you see, white or black? That's a simple enough question." I dropped my hands. This wasn't going to be as easy as I thought.

"Don't you know who you are? You don't need me to tell you."

"But that's just it. Maybe I don't. I know I'm a good person, but sometimes I don't want to be."

"What do you mean?"

"Well, it's not like I want to go rob a bank or hurt anyone or anything, but sometimes I just get so angry..."

I watched the light drain away and the gray return.

"Mad at what?"

"At God. At my parents. At myself."

"Grace," I said softly. Tears began falling from her eyes, and she roughly wiped them away.

"Grace," she repeated. "Why would God do that to someone so young? Make someone so sick? It's so hard to watch her suffer and not be able to do anything about it." I pulled her into my arms and tried to comfort her, but she pulled away. "And the good person that I am, when I'm not cursing God, I'm busy feeling sorry for myself. We were a happy family until Gracie got sick, then I just ceased to exist. Sometimes I feel like I'm one of their tenants, working for room and board. They never ask me about school or work, or college, or boyfriends." She looked at me coyly. "It's always about Grace, and sometimes I hate her for it. So look at me now Lucas and tell me what you see, I think that I already know."

ROBIN DONARUMA

    This time I grabbed her and wouldn't let her go. I held her tightly until I felt her tension release and her breathing return to a calmer cadence.

"There's a small caveat to my visions," I said. She pulled back to look up at me. I wiped her tears from her cheeks, glad to see that they finally stopped falling.

"What?" she asked gruffly.

"There is another shade that I can see. Gray."

"Gray?"

"The undecided."

"Undecided in what? You mean like me? I'm gray?"

"Yes."

"I'm not dark?"

"No. You are exactly as you described to me, someone who is stuck between two worlds. We have within us the gift of free will. It is your choice to turn to the light or follow the dark path. You will choose the right one; I'll make sure of it." I leaned down to kiss her. She relaxed in my arms, and I knew that telling her was the right thing to do. I wasn't going to tell her about my supersonic trip to the Thimble Islands or how if I listen to music I light up like a nuclear plant, or any of the little things like me being the leader of the White Army, but it did feel good to talk about it to her. That, and it gave me a pretty awesome excuse to kiss her again.

THE UNDECIDED

CHAPTER TWENTY-NINE

I woke from a dreamless sleep feeling energetic and excited to get back to school. Now that Mare knew something about what was going on with me, I didn't feel quite so alone.

Outside, a car door slammed. The Donahues. I thought of Mindy, and my stomach reeled. I knew that they played a vital role in this war, and until I met Devin, I wouldn't know just how vital that role actually was. From my window, I watched a car back out of their driveway and shoot off down the street. I couldn't see who was in it, but the further the car got from my house, the better I felt. I let the curtain fall back against the sill, and I finished getting dressed.

I walked into school prepared for something, but not really sure what. Everything seemed normal. I walked towards my first hour class and noticed how many more people seemed to know my name than last Friday. I guess hanging out at Lenny's helped expand my friend ratio. Cool. Dark entities took pains to avoid me, and the ones surrounded by light walked nearer to me. The more light entities that were in one place, the less there were dark ones. The push had begun.

I reached British Lit. just as Mr. Holland was about to shut the door.

"Ah! Good timing Mr. Aarons, by the skin of your teeth some might say."

"Good morning Mr. Holland." The bell rang as I crossed the threshold, and Mr. Holland shut the door directly behind me. I squeezed Mare's shoulder before sitting in my seat watching as light flecks danced around her.

"I trust you all had a long fun filled weekend these days past? Ah good, well they're good and done now, so let's get to work, shall we?" The classroom door opened.

ROBIN DONARUMA

Pain shot through my head, and I felt sick to my stomach. I dropped my pencil and Mare picked it up for me.

"Are you okay?" she mouthed. I nodded and looked up trying to force a smile onto my face. My smile faded as I watched Devin Donahue walk through the opened door. Like his own personal entourage, a wave of darkness, darker and larger than I had ever seen, followed him into the room enveloping him once he stopped moving. The class began talking in hushed tones, taking advantage of the preoccupation of Mr. Holland. Girls were sizing him up and from looking at their smiles and furtive glances I'd say they liked what they saw. Even Mare was watching Devin with a glimmer of appreciation. He handed a paper to Mr. Holland and waited while he fumbled to find a syllabus for him. Unlike his sister's smooth blonde hair, Devin's hair was jet black and curled riotously around his head. His skin, which had an olive tone to it, offset his eyes, which were the brightest shade of blue that I had ever seen.

I closed my eyes and focused on the white light. I surrounded myself with it and pushed it out to those around me. My headache subsided, and I opened my eyes feeling much stronger. He was watching me. Smiling with teeth as white and perfect as any I'd ever seen; I felt as though the cold hand of a witch was scratching down my back. I sat up straighter in my desk and grabbed my necklace, smiling back at him. His smile faded, and he took a step back.

"Ladies and Gentlemen, I have the distinguished honor of introducing you to your new classmate, Devin Donahue. Mr. Donahue just made his way here from the South of Asia of all places." He gestured to an open seat and Devin took his place, on the other side of the classroom, parallel to my desk. "Okay, now, where were we? Ah yes..."

I couldn't really say what class was about, but it felt like it went on forever. My mind was reeling wondering what I should do. I knew, without a doubt, that Devin was as important to the Dark Army as I was to the White. I wished that I could talk with Ethan.

The bell finally rang, and I shot out of my seat, ready to be out of this room that now felt sick with stale air.

THE UNDECIDED

"See you at lunch?" Mare asked me.

"You bet." I attempted a smile.

"Are you sure you're okay?"

"Never better," I said, smiling much brighter. This seemed to appease her as she squeezed my arm and made her way to the door with Becca who was patiently waiting for her.

Devin approached the door at the same time that Mare and Becca did. He dropped a book and Mare immediately stooped down to pick it up. I couldn't hear exactly what was said, but whatever it was made her laugh. Becca continued out to the hall while Devin and Mare talked. My heart sank as I watched her light flecks fade.

Mare left the classroom, and Devin looked at me. I grabbed my books and walked towards him. He waited for me. Just as I was about to approach him, Mr. Holland interrupted.

"Devin, would you mind coming over here for a moment? I have a reading list that I think you will find most helpful."

Devin's smile faded as he walked over to the desk.

"Sure, Mr. Holland," he responded, dropping eye contact with me.

"It won't take but a moment," Mr. Holland said as he was looking at me. "It is not in the stars to hold our destiny, but in ourselves." He dropped his gaze and handed Devin a piece of paper. I left the room, my mind whirling.

Walking into Music Theory, I was assaulted by applause from the class. I looked behind me. Did I miss something here?

"Mr. Aarons, I heard that you were quite the virtuoso this weekend?" Mr. Kenzie said with a half-smile.

"He rocked!" someone yelled out.

My cheeks heated as I beelined for my seat.

"Well, then I've got some good or possibly great news for everyone." He leaned over his desk and grabbed a rolled up poster. "The brass at Branford High has finally stopped listening to all those old ladies who work in the library and started listening to me. So it is with great pleasure that I announce to you Branford High's first official Battle of the Bands competition."

Mr. Kenzie held up the poster, and the class went wild.
"So start polishing your tubas folks, it's in a *very short* three weeks."
"Three weeks?" John exclaimed.
"Yeah, yeah, I know, I tried to buy some more time, but the old ladies got their hooks into the rest of the year with their bake sales or some other crap. Hey, you take whatever you can get, right?"
The entire class was humming with excitement.
"This is so awesome," John said to me excitedly.
"You're signing up aren't you?" I asked.
"Absolutely! Pink Zeppelin shall rock the house," John said, playing air guitar.
"*Pink Zeppelin?*"
"Too much?" He dropped his pretend guitar. "I told Paul it was lame. What do you think about the Wizards of Odd? No? The Rock Dogs?"
"You've really put some thought into this, huh?"
"You have no idea. We have come up with like a million names, but we never agree on any of them. I think it holds us back artistically."
"I think you're doing all right, name or not," I told him, trying not to laugh.
"Thanks man. You're signing up too, right?"
"I don't know. Definitely something to think about."
"Dude, you've got to. You're like amazing! Hey, I can talk with the boys, maybe you can play with us?"
"No, you've definitely got your own thing going on, you don't need me. But thanks."
"You have to sign up, Dude," he said, pointing at me. "Seriously."
"I'll think about it. Seriously," I said while moving his finger from in front of my face.
"Okay, okay, settle down. I know it's the most exciting news you've heard since hearing Justin Beiber shaved his head, but I actually have a class to teach here."
"Justin Beiber shaved his head?" A girl in the front row cried, clutching her throat in shock.
"No, I made that up, but I swear if I don't stop hearing that damn song of his or seeing his be-dimpled little face on another magazine cover, I'm going to find out where he

THE UNDECIDED

lives, drive to his house in the middle of the night, crawl through his window with a pair of clippers, and personally shave it off for him."

Half of the class applauded while the small group of girls in the front sat there with their mouths wide open, afraid to say anything else. One of the girls even pulled her hair back and stuffed it inside her jacket.

"Okay, let's start this." Mr. Kenzie walked to the chalkboard and began drawing various types of musical notes. He was talking about quarter notes when the door opened. Pain shot through my head and my stomach soured. Devin. Blackness crept into the room swirling around Devin as he casually sauntered in and handed Mr. Kenzie a paper.

"It appears that we have a new addition to our class. Ladies and gentlemen, meet Devin Donahue." Mr. Kenzie announced to the class. "Where did you move here from, Devin?"

"My family and I have been living in Southeast Asia, sir."

"No kidding?"

"My dad was doing research for the university."

"Yale, I suppose?"

"Yes, sir."

"I'm a Princeton man, myself, but I won't hold it against you."

"Thank you, sir." The girls began excitedly whispering amongst each other. I bet I could guess about what.

"You like music, Mr. Donahue?"

"Absolutely. It's my life."

"Really? What kind or kinds do you prefer?"

"Metal."

"Metal? How hard?"

"The harder the better. Slayer, Tool, and Slipknot are cool."

"Ew, gross. Aren't they the ones that wear like those mutilated masks with stringy hair?" said a girl from the front row.

"Yeah, all they do is scream into the microphone. You can't even tell what they're saying. They're scary," said her

ROBIN DONARUMA

friend. Devin didn't seem to mind, instead his smile grew wider, and he walked closer to them.

"I also have been getting into a lot of Norwegian Black Metal lately. Maybe you'd like them better? I could bring some in for you to listen to?"

She blushed and battered her eyelashes. She thought he was being nice, maybe even flirting with her, but in reality he was making fun of her right to her face. Music didn't get any darker than Norwegian Black Metal, and he knew it. Everything about them was dark, not just their music. With corpse painted faces and blood-splattered bodies black metal bands are the antithesis of anything good.

"Sure," she sweetly answered. "I didn't mean to offend you, I just don't get how you can call that music?"

"Music, like many things in life is subjective. Raindrops hitting a metal trash can in my backyard is music to me, but to someone else, just an annoying noise outside their window."

"I guess," she said, twirling her hair.

"Listening to Taylor Swift makes me want to hang myself, but I don't judge other people who like her music."

"Well, look at that, we got a lesson in anyway," said Mr. Kenzie. "And a great one at that. Now, if you please, Mr. Donahue, I believe there is a desk with your name on it up there and to the right."

"You got it," he winked at the girl on his way up to the desk, which was parallel to mine.

Class continued much like British Lit. It was all a blur, and before I knew it, the bell rang. I hurried to the front, ready to meet my new neighbor, but Mr. Kenzie called him over to his desk before I could reach him.

"Mr. Donahue, if I could have a moment of your time, sir?" He looked at me but addressed the class that was scrambling to exit through the small door. "Remember, three weeks."

"So what do you think of our new student? He's into some pretty hard core music," John said out in the hallway.

"He's actually my neighbor."

"Really?"

THE UNDECIDED

"I haven't met him yet, only his parents, and his sister."

"Well, I don't really dig metal myself, at least not the hard core stuff, so not judging anyone here, he could be the nicest guy on the planet, but damn, he didn't have to dis Taylor Swift. That was just wrong." John turned down the hallway shaking his head. I headed towards my next class praying that it would be Devin free.

***

I headed to the lunchroom with a much clearer head. I hadn't seen Devin since Music Theory and it helped me refocus my thoughts on other things. Mare was waiting for me in the front of the cafeteria. "Did you hear about the Battle of the Bands contest?" she asked excitedly.

"Yeah, Mr. Kenzie mentioned it in class." I picked up a tray and started piling on the food.

"Well? You're signing up, right?"

"I don't know. I haven't really thought about it."

"Lucas, you have to, you're the best singer I've ever heard. I swear!"

"Thanks Mare," I said, stroking her hair. "There's just kind of a lot going on right now, and I don't know that I'll have the time to do it."

"It's not for three weeks, that's plenty of time!" We approached Muriel, the lunch lady, who was waiting for us with a friendly smile.

"She's right, you know, Luke," she said, taking my money. "You have to sign up." She placed change into my hand and looked into my eyes. "I'll be there," she said with a wink. We walked to our usual table.

"Ah, Lucas and his groupies. So tell me," Mare asked in a lowered voice, "does she have white around her?"

"Most definitely." We sat down, and I bit into my turkey wrap just as a sharp pain shot through my head. I dropped the sandwich onto my tray and pressed my palm against the pain.

"You okay Lucas?" Mare asked.

"Oh look, there's Devin, he's new, have you guys met him?" Becca asked Jeff and Scott. Both of them shook their head.

ROBIN DONARUMA

"No, but I wouldn't mind getting to know his friend," Jeff answered, motioning towards the cafeteria doors. I didn't have to turn around to know whom he was talking about.

"I think that's his sister," Mare answered.

"His sister? Don't you think they're kind of friendly with each other? Like not brother and sister friendly?" Mare turned to look, and out of the corner of my eye I could see them walking amid their black smoky clouds holding hands and whispering in each other's ears.

"I don't know, I think it's kind of nice that they're a close family."

"If that was my sister, you can bet that I'd be close to her too."

"Ew, gross Jeff," said Becca, wrinkling her nose. "I don't know, I'm sure he's nice and all, but there's something about him that's sort of, I don't know, something just seems kind of off."

"Yeah, well, you're like the only girl in the school that thinks that," Mare responded. "You don't think he's cute?"

"I guess so. I don't know, I can't explain it, never mind." Becca dismissed the subject and returned to her food. Mare looked at me.

"Do you have a headache?"

"Yeah, something like that." I pushed my tray away and stood up.

"Where are you going?" Mare asked.

"To meet my new neighbor."

THE UNDECIDED

CHAPTER THIRTY

His back was towards me. It was his sister, Mindy, that noticed me first. With a familiar whisper into his ear, Devin slowly turned.

"Lucas, right?" Devin innocently asked. "I wanted to introduce myself to you in class this morning, but you know how first days can be."

"Hi Mindy," I said, acknowledging his sister. "I was wondering if we would run into each other today, I'm glad to finally meet you."

"Branford is turning out to be quite an interesting little town. Lots of friendly locals." He looked at Mare standing just behind me. "Mare, right? This is my sister, Mindy. Maybe you wouldn't mind taking her under your wing and showing her around sometime?"

Mare looked at me then back to Mindy.

"Sure, that sounds great. Anytime."

"Cool. Thanks," Mindy responded, walking closer to Mare, but staying clear from me.

It was like talking through a glass wall. We could see and hear each other clearly, but we both maintained our own defenses. The air was thick and cold, and the tension was palpable. Of course, to everyone else, it looked as if we were carrying on an innocent conversation, but we both knew differently. I could feel the shifting of energies in the lunchroom. The white energies were moving to my side of the cafeteria while the dark ones chose tables closer to Devin. The grays remained peppered throughout.

"Lucas, you forgot your folder!" Muriel hurried towards me waving a green folder. I didn't have a green folder and was about to say as much when I noticed an image of a white dog on the cover. I looked at Muriel, who had a knowing gleam in her eye. "You had better get going to class before you're late," she said, walking away. "And don't forget to sign up for that contest!" she yelled, sitting back down on her cushioned seat at the head of the lunch line. I looked down at the folder and knew that Millie was there, somewhere, looking after me. I smiled and looked at Devin whose own smile now wavered. Mindy walked back to stand beside Devin.

"Muriel's probably right, I had better get to class."

"No problem. Hey, I'll just see you at home, right?"

I nodded curtly and grabbed Mare's hand as we walked towards the door.

"Hey Lucas," Devin hollered. "You're signing up for the Battle of the Bands?"

"I don't know."

"Too bad. I signed up. I was hoping maybe you'd give me a little competition." He smiled triumphantly, and it really annoyed me.

"Maybe I will, Devin. Lately, I've been feeling up for a good fight."

I turned around and walked out the door, pulling Mare alongside me.

"Well, that was weird."

"What do you mean?"

"You and Devin."

"Do you know that they just moved in next door to my house?"

"Really? So you've met him before then?"

"No, just his sister and his parents."

Mare stopped walking and moved closer speaking in a hushed whisper.

"Lucas, can you see him? What do you see when you look at him."

"Mare, we really don't have time to get into this right now, how about I come over later?"

"I have to work until eight."

"Then I'll meet you at Stony Creek, we'll talk then."

"Okay," she said with a smile. "See you tonight." I grabbed her hand before she was able to walk away and pulled her close. "Wait." I kissed her softly on her lips then moved my way to her forehead and then her ear.

"Just promise me one thing," I whispered into her ear. "Promise me you'll stay away from Devin." She pulled back surprised.

THE UNDECIDED

"Lucas?"

"Promise me."

"Okay, fine, I promise."

"See you at eight." She headed off to class, and I looked down at the folder that Muriel had given me and opened it. Inside was an application for the Battle of the Bands completely filled out with my name on top.

"Okay, I give up," I said smiling. "Battle of the Bands it is." I closed the folder and swear that I heard a muted "Woof."

CHAPTER THIRTY-ONE

I arrived at Stony Creek Market just before eight o'clock. I hopped up the stairs to the deck trying to figure out how I was going to convince Mare to steer clear of Devin without sounding like a lunatic. I couldn't tell her everything, but I did need to tell her something to strengthen my case.

I reached the front door, and as I was about to pull it open, someone called my name. A plume of smoke drifted out of the darkness.

"Captain Bob," I said, feeling oddly pleased to see him.

"Lucas." He curtly nodded placing his pipe in his mouth. He stepped into the light. "Ethan has a message for you."

"Ethan?" I moved towards Captain Bob, my eyes darting behind him.

"You know he can't come here."

"I know." I felt deflated.

"But he is still with you. The Council watches all that you do. They have watchers planted here to help you if you need it."

"Muriel?" I asked.

"Yes, she is one of many."

"Who else?" I asked.

"That's not for me to say, Lucas. I came here, because Ethan is concerned."

"Concerned about what?"

"The push has begun, and the darkness is moving faster than we thought possible. It is stronger than we imagined."

"So what, are you here to freak me out more than I already am? Because let me tell you something, not only is the darkness here, it's living next door to me, and they look like the freaking Cleavers," I said exasperated.

"Cleavers? Never mind." He took the pipe out of his mouth and looked at me earnestly. "You cannot afford to doubt your abilities. The dark is strong, but you are stronger. Focus on what you need to do, not on what it could do. If you don't believe in yourself, you will fail."

"I do, I will," I said.

"You are the chosen one for a reason, Lucas." He paused to take a deep drag from his pipe. "Do you know what makes moments in our lives truly amazing? It's those moments when the supernatural meets the natural. When those two elements collide, miracles happen. Tap into your supernatural, Luke." He put the pipe back in his mouth.

"That's Ethan's message for me?"

"Yup." He started to walk away, then turned back. "Oh, and one other thing, make sure you sign up for that Battle of the Bands competition."

I threw my head back and laughed.

"Of course he did. Did he also tell me what to..." He was gone. "Well that's just great. Goodbye to you too." I looked at my watch, which now read eight o'clock. I walked into the market smiling at the familiar chime that rang as I opened the door. My smile quickly fell when I saw Devin and Mindy talking with Mare.

"Lucas, there you are! I was just finishing up," Mare said taking off her apron and shoving it behind the counter. "Be right back." She disappeared behind the kitchen door.

"Lucas, your mom was telling us what great pizza they have here, so we thought we'd come check it out." Mindy sweetly said.

"We couldn't believe it when we walked through the door and actually saw a familiar face. Branford is a lot smaller than we thought," Devin said mimicking his sister's smile.

"Aside from Pepe's up in New Haven, this is the best pizza around," I said, struggling to maintain a nonchalance that I definitely did not feel.

"Can't wait to take a bite and try it out myself," Devin retorted.

As if on cue, Mare came out of the kitchen holding a large pizza box.

ROBIN DONARUMA

"Here you go, one meat lover's special." She handed the box to Devin as she rounded the counter.

"Thanks Mare, I'm sure we're going to love it," he said, staring directly into her eyes. Mare was transfixed until Mindy came up and hugged her.

"I can't wait until tomorrow. It's been so long since I've had a real girlfriend to hang out with." It was all I could do to not rip her arms off of her. What appeared as a casual, friendly hug to everyone else looked like a brutal attack to me. Her darkness enveloped Mare and swirled around her, tasting her. When she pulled back, bits of blackness remained swirling around the gray. I unclenched my teeth before looking back to Devin. Unfortunately, he noticed my unease and was taking much pleasure from it.

"Well, we had better get this home, don't want to keep Mom and Dad waiting, Min. See you tomorrow at school, Mare. Lucas."

"Bye guys," Mare said. We both watched as Mindy looped her arm through one of Devin's and sauntered out of the market into the blackness outside.

"Before you say a word, I'm hanging out with Mindy, not Devin. And I can't control who orders pizza, so don't go there," she said defensively.

"Hey, I wasn't going to say a word, come here." I held her tightly and infused my light into her, trying to eradicate the left over darkness. I felt her relax and her defensiveness diminished.

"You done here?" I asked, wanting to get outside into the fresh air more than anything.

"Yeah, just let me grab my purse," she said smiling and looking almost relieved. She kissed my cheek. "Thanks, Lucas."

"For what?" I asked.

"I don't know. For coming here, for making me feel happy." She bent over the counter and whipped out a small bag that she slung over one shoulder.

"Good night Mr. Hotchkiss, I'm leaving now," she yelled to the back of the restaurant. A faint *good night* was returned, and we both left through the front door. I led her to my car that was parked alongside the restaurant but paused before opening the door.

196

THE UNDECIDED

"How about walking? Do you mind?" I asked her.

"No, that sounds great. It's so beautiful out tonight, it's really starting to feel like fall," she said as we walked hand in hand towards her house.

"Yeah, it's definitely getting colder," I said with a shiver, putting my free hand in my pocket. She laughed.

"Oh Lucas, if you think this is cold, you're in for a rude awakening. Poor little Florida boy." She squeezed my hand.

"Don't remind me. Ugh, I'm not ready to start thinking of winter yet." The thought of the snow and ice sent a shiver through me, which reminded me of what we needed to talk about.

"You asked me earlier what I saw when I looked at Devin."

"Yes." Her smile faded. "You see something don't you? Something bad?"

We were walking by an old park with a few benches and a handful of swings. I stopped under a big tree that shaded the streetlight that was glaring down on top of us.

"Devin Donahue and his sister, are as dark as it gets, Mare." I looked at her, hoping that she would believe me.

"Dark like evil?"

"Yes," I said, hating to blanket the term, but not knowing another way to get the seriousness of this information through to her.

I could tell she was throwing the idea around in her head, but something wasn't clicking, and I can't blame her.

"But they're so nice. Mindy seems so nice. Maybe it's just because they haven't been around other kids their own age for so long. Do you know they used to live in Cambodia?"

"No, I didn't know that," I responded patiently.

"Okay, look. I know that there is something between you and Devin, and I know that you can *see things*. So maybe you do see darkness around him, but that can't just be it. There's something more isn't there? There's something more that you're not telling me."

"Mare," I said, cupping the side of her face. "You are probably one of the most observant people I have ever met. Nothing gets by you, does it?" I said, smiling into her eyes.

"I've spent a lot of time sitting back observing in the past few years, in hospitals, doctor's offices, at home. I'm right though, aren't I? There's something more."

"There is always something more, Mare. But now is not the time to get into that."

"Well, when?"

"I'm not sure," I said, shaking my head in frustration. "This isn't a game that we're playing here."

"Are you talking about us or about you and Devin?" she asked, getting frustrated.

"If I can see the essence of people, perhaps, I'm not the only one who has such abilities."

"You mean Devin can see it too?"

"I'm not one hundred percent sure, but I would guess yes."

"Okay. So then what? What exactly are you telling me?" she said, looking more confused. I was searching for the right words to say just as a large black dog came running across the park towards us. It was barking wildly and baring its teeth. Mare gasped, and I pushed her behind me.

"Friend of yours?" I asked.

"That looks like Mr. Diorgio's dog, he lives down the street from us. But I've never seen him like this."

The dog stopped in front of us. It was foaming at the mouth and hunched down ready to attack.

"Lucas," Mare nervously cried behind me. She pushed her face into my jacket blocking the dog from her view.

I closed my eyes and brought forth the light within me. My birthmark glowed as I held my hand towards the dog, and like a wave over a sandy beach I covered him with light. In an instant he sat down with a whelp and began wagging his tail. Mare peeled her face from my back and peered around me. The dog approached and began licking my hand.

"What just happened? How did you do that?" Mare asked.

"Shh, just a minute." I bent down grabbing the dogs face with my hands. I knew that Millie wasn't exactly your run of the mill dog, but she did say that it was possible to communicate. So I tried. The energy was very different than Millie, kind of like a Kindergartener versus a PhD student. Unlike Millie, I didn't hear words, but felt emotions. He was very confused and didn't know why he wasn't in his yard. He liked us and wanted to go home. And he was hungry, *very hungry*. I tried to ask him how he got here, but all I got was blackness. He didn't know. I stood up.

"I think he's ready to go home. You know where his house is?" I asked Mare, who was blankly staring at me.

"Yeah, that way. Lucas." She grabbed my arm. "That dog was about to attack us. What happened?"

"We got lucky. Come on." I whistled, and the dog walked alongside us until we reached his yard. The gate was wide open. He trotted in and went directly to his food bowl. I closed the gate, and we continued walking towards her house.

"This has been a most unusual night," Mare stated. "You know, life was pretty predictable until you showed up." She smiled a slanted smile towards me.

"Predictable? Where's the fun in that?"

"Well, it beats getting eaten by a fifty-pound dog."

"He wasn't going to eat you, he was just lost and scared. Although you do smell like a walking pizza," I said, smelling her hair.

"Look, I don't know what's really going on here, and I know that you're not ready to tell me, and that's okay. I'll be careful of Devin."

"And Mindy?" I asked.

"I promised her that I would take her to Guilford tomorrow after school, show her around town. Nothing bad will happen, Lucas. It's just two girls, shopping. And I really could use a day like that."

She was looking at her house that we were now standing in front of, and I sensed the turmoil that had set in.

"I know. Just be careful, okay?"

"Oh Lucas, it's not like she's going to turn into a werewolf. I'll be fine, I promise."

"I know you will." I kissed her on the forehead just as her mother opened the front door.

"Marianne? Oh, hi Lucas! Do you want to come in? I just pulled some biscotti from the oven," she asked.

ROBIN DONARUMA

"No thank you, Mrs. Rossi. I had better get home. But next time I'll take you up on it. I promise." She waved her goodbye and left the doorway, leaving the door open.

"That's my cue," Mare said. "See you tomorrow."

"Absolutely," I said, watching her walk up the path to her door.

"Lucas? Thanks for trusting me," she said, just before walking through the door. I put one hand over my heart and watched her close the door.

"With my life," I whispered.

: **THE UNDECIDED**

CHAPTER THIRTY-TWO

I sat up and looked around my room. Everything was as it should be; yet, something wasn't right. I could feel it. I opened my door and looked down the hallway. My parent's door was ajar, and I could faintly hear my dad's heavy breathing. I walked down the hall and peered over the railing into the den below. The soft glow of the kitchen light bounced over and around the furniture and wall hangings. Nothing unusual.

I started back down the hall, stopping to peek inside my parents' room. They were both sound asleep. I relaxed and went back to my room. The dread returned. I closed my door and locked it. I approached the window, and my pulse accelerated. It was out there. Pain shot through my head, and my hand hesitated on the curtain. I brought forth my light, willing my pain away, and in one quick motion I ripped the curtain away from the window.

Blackness.

I reached to unlock the latch and open the window.

"No Lucas."

"Millie." I wouldn't take my eyes away from the darkness outside my window.

"It is what it wants. To infect your house."

"It can't touch me." Out of the corner of my eye, I could see Millie standing beside me.

"Perhaps not tonight, but your parents are more vulnerable."

"Why can't I see him?" I asked her, my frustration mounting.

"I will show you." She bit my hand, and we were transported to the street in front of my house. A huge mass of blackness covered the entire side of our house where my bedroom was. It pulsated and moved trying to find a way in. I started to walk towards it but ended up back in my bedroom staring at the evil from the inside.

ROBIN DONARUMA

"It has begun its push. It wants to harm you, Lucas, for it knows that it cannot succeed with you alive."

"Well, then he's in for quite a disappointment, cause I'm not going anywhere." I grabbed my necklace from underneath my tee shirt and held onto it tightly. I created my own wall of white light, and I surrounded my entire house and everything inside.

"Yes, Lucas. This is very good," Millie said with an excited whimper.

I felt the power within the light, and I readied for battle. The black wall disappeared.

"Where did it go?" I asked, slightly disappointed.

"Away. Darkness cannot exist where there is light. The Council is quite pleased, Lucas. It is time for me to go."

I finally looked away from the window and into Millie's familiar face.

"Don't go. Can't you stay? Just for a while?"

"I miss you too, friend Lucas, but it is time for me to return."

I looked back to the window wondering what I could say to make her stay. When I turned around, she was gone. I put my hand on the window and leaned my head against it.

Devin's house was dark, but not dark enough. In a window on the second level he stood staring at me. Mindy walked up behind him putting her arms around his waist. She kissed his cheek, looked at me, smiled, and closed the curtain.

I woke up thinking about the dream. It seemed strange calling them dreams when in fact they were much more than that. But until someone comes up with some clever word for this in-between world battle of wills, I'll still call them dreams.

There was a freaky vibe going on with Devin and his sister. Not really wanting to think about that too much, I thought about the black wall that was outside my house. Millie called it the push, and that wasn't the first time I had heard that phrase. It was, however, the first time I actually saw what it meant. And realized that I too could create my own *push*.

THE UNDECIDED

When I walked into school, I made sure that I fortified myself with light. When other white energies walked near me, our lights melded together just like liquid mercury. It was spectacular.

I sat down in Mr. Holland's class having arrived just before Devin. I was stronger today and unaffected by his darkness as he entered the classroom. I could tell that he sensed as much, because his smile wavered ever so slightly. I tapped my pencil to my forehead in acknowledgment, and he widened his grin in response. Game on.

By lunch I was ready for a break. I felt as if I were on the defense all day, and it was starting to wear me down.

"Hey, you seem tired today," Mare said, passing me chocolate milk.

"Yeah, didn't sleep so great last night. Crazy dreams."

"Really? About what?" she asked, handing Muriel her money.

"I don't know, you know how dreams are. It makes sense while you're having it, but when you try to explain it to someone you sound like a lunatic. Hi Muriel." I handed her my money, and she gave me my change and a wink.

"Yeah, I know. Dreams are so whacked sometimes."

We sat down at our usual table, and after a healthy dose of tater tots, I began to feel back up to speed. Devin and Mindy walked into the cafeteria just as we were walking to the garbage bins.

"Hi Mare! I can't wait until after school. Should I meet you at your house?" Mindy said, looping her arm through Mares.

"See you later guys, I've got to run," Becca said as she threw away her tray and quickly left.

"Sounds great. Do you know where I live?"

"Oh, I can find it, don't worry." Mindy looked at me. "Hi Lucas."

"Hi, Mindy." Devin came out of the lunch line carrying an apple. "Devin."

"Lucas, my man." He crunched into the crisp apple. "So I heard you signed up for the *Battle*. Excellent."

"Yeah, it should be quite *enlightening*."

ROBIN DONARUMA

"I don't know about enlightening, but it will certainly not be a show you'd want to miss."

"So, I hear you're into heavy metal, the really heavy screamo stuff," Mare asked. He turned to her and gave her his undivided attention.

"Absolutely, the louder the better. Unfortunately, Mr. Kenzie has banned certain songs and bands from the playlist, so I'll have to dig further into my repertoire," he said playfully. Mare laughed, staring into his eyes. Between Mindy and Devin, their darkness was almost completely surrounding her. I grabbed her hand, which seemed to break the spell. Mindy immediately let go, and Devin backed up.

"We've gotta get to class, Mare."

"Right, I can't be late again to Mrs. Ruma's class. See you after school," she said to Mindy.

"Absolutely, can't wait," she sweetly responded. Devin took another bite of his apple and turned away. Mindy followed him, as did other dark entities, whether they realized it or not.

By the time I got home from school, I was exhausted. Apparently, projecting a force field all day will wear a guy out. I fell asleep for two wonderfully dreamless hours and only woke up because Mare called. She recounted her perfectly harmless trip to Guilford minute by minute and was positively convinced that Mindy wasn't as bad as I thought. I knew that this would happen, and wasn't quite sure how to handle it, so I let it go. Ultimately, I can't control what she feels, and in the end, it's all up to her anyway. Even if she hangs out with Mindy sporadically, I should be able to offset any negative effect that might bleed over.

The week ended just as it began. Teachers were assigning more homework and papers, and as a result, I saw less of Mare than I wanted. Her mother took the bull by the horns for me, though, and invited me to dinner on Friday night. Not just for Mare's sake but also for Grace's, who had been asking about me and badgering her mother to call.

CHAPTER THIRTY-THREE

The front door whipped open before I had a chance to knock.
"Lucas! There you are. Come in." Mrs. Rossi stepped aside, holding the door open. "Ooh, it's really starting to feel like fall out there."
Something wasn't right.
"It is definitely getting colder, I can attest to that."
"Mare! Lucas is here," she yelled into the living room. "A new friend of hers, Mindy, stopped by. You met her, I assume?"
"Yes ma'am. We've met. She and her family moved in right next door." I attempted to smile, but my stomach was roiling.
"You don't say," she replied. "Mare! Oh there you are. I wasn't sure you heard me."
"People three towns over heard you, Ma." She walked up to me, and kissed me on the cheek. "Hi."
"Hi." I looked at Mindy who was walking just behind her, staying as far from me as she could. "Hi Mindy."
"Hi Lucas." She smiled a near perfect smile just as Hairy the cat came strolling up beside her. The cat startled her, and her smile turned into a sneer of disgust. "Ugh, what a vile looking creature."
Hairy, much to his credit stopped and hissed at her.
"Hairy, be nice. He's harmless, I swear," Mare said as she attempted to pick him up. Hairy hissed again and emitted a low growl. Mindy was becoming quite agitated.
"I hate cats," she said with utter disgust before remembering that she wasn't alone. Her eyes shifted to Mrs. Rossi, and she immediately put her happy personae back on. "More of a dog person."
Mindy carefully walked around the perimeter of the room to avoid Harry who was staring back at her with his own discrimination.

"Well, I had better go," she said.
"Okay. Thanks again for bringing my sweater back. I didn't realize I left it in your car."
"No problem." She walked to the door and Hairy was two steps behind her. "Thanks for having me, Mrs. Rossi. Tell Grace it was really great to meet her too." In one quick movement, Mindy opened the door and stepped back towards Hairy landing on his paw. He squealed in pain and shot out the door. "Oops. Can he go outside?"
"No! He's never been outside, Lucas help me get him."
"I'm so sorry. It's my fault. I'll get him," Mindy said, appearing the innocent.
"No, really, it's fine Mindy. Lucas will help me. I'm sure he's just skulking around the bushes. Besides, I don't know how much help you would really be. He didn't seem to be too fond of you either," Mare said laughing. Mindy cocked her head to the side and bit the inside of her cheek making her dimple pop out.
"Really? You're so great Mare. And I really am sorry."
"Don't you worry about it, you get home to your parents, Mindy," Mrs. Rossi intervened. "Mare and Lucas here will get Mr. Hairy back right as rain." With a flash of her smile, Mindy was out on the porch and half way to her car.
"Okay. Bye Mare, maybe I'll see you around this weekend? Lucas, I know I'll be seeing you around," she said with a knowing look. I gave her a quick glance to acknowledge her statement then followed the sounds of growling.
"Mare? Where's Hairy?" A frail Grace was standing at the door's threshold. Mrs. Rossi threw a blanket around her shoulders.
"Gracie, come back to bed, there's nothing to worry about, Mare and Lucas will have him in before you know it." Mrs. Rossi attempted to pull her back in the house.
Mare walked towards Grace.
"He's fine, Grace, he just ran into the bushes, you can go back inside, we'll have him back..."
Like a shot of lightening, Hairy ran from beneath the bushes and darted into the street just as a car came barreling down the street.

THE UNDECIDED

"Hairy!" Grace called out.

"Oh no," Mare whispered.

I ran to the car that had stopped in the middle of the road. An older woman got out.

"I think I hit a squirrel, did you see that?" She bent down to look under her car.

"It was a cat, not a squirrel." I found Hairy lying very still on the other side of her rear tire.

"Oh, dear," the woman stated as she took in her surroundings. The severity of her actions slowly sank in. "I'm so sorry. I didn't see him, I swear. I've never even been down this road before, I just turned down here before I realized it and then…" She looked at the cat. "That's a cat?" she asked quietly.

"Yes," I said, gingerly picking him up. I could hear Grace's sobs in the background.

"Please go," Mare said from behind me.

"Let me take him to a vet. Please, I'm so sorry."

"I think you've done enough," Mare said in a cold, lifeless tone. I looked at her and saw black bits meshing with her gray. All white was gone. "Just go."

The woman looked at me, and I nodded that she should leave. Flustered, she got back in her car whispering her regrets once more.

"Tell your mother to take Grace inside. She doesn't need to see this," I said. Mare was staring at Hairy, unmoving. "Mare. Go, get Grace out of here." She snapped out of her reverie and walked back towards the house. I walked to the big tree separating the Rossi's house from their neighbors and sat down. I closed my eyes and listened to Hairy. He was very still and very hurt, but not quite gone.

I placed my hand over his body and infused my light with his fading one. I felt the cool, damp grass beneath me, and the prickly bark of the tree behind me. A cool breeze caressed me as I reached out to Hairy's life force. I began to feel warm and peaceful and knew that I was close. I no longer felt things around me, because it was all a part of me, no beginning and no end. Purring vibrated through the night air, and I knew I had connected.

"Hairy," I whispered aloud. Hairy, I thought to myself, come back to Grace, she needs you, friend. The purring got louder and beneath my hand I felt the subtle rise and fall of his hairless little body as life was pumped back into him.

"I would never leave my Gracie," a voice inside my head said. I laughed with joy.

"You can hear me?" I thought to myself.

"More importantly, I think, is that you can hear me. I don't like that girl," he said with a low growl replacing his purring.

"Me either. Do you feel okay?"

"I hurt, but I am happy to go back to my Gracie." He purred again. "I like you, Lucas."

"I like you too, Hairy." I slowly opened my eyes and watched Hairy slowly open his. With a slow, knowing blink I heard "Thank you" amid loud purring.

"My pleasure, friend. Let's keep to the house this time, shall we?" I said out loud as I stood up. Hairy rubbed his head against my jaw. "I think there's a little girl who would very much love to see you right now."

I turned around and found Mare staring at me with her mouth and eyes wide open.

"Lucas."

"Mare. I think he's going to be okay," I said, making my way to the front door. Not so lucky.

"Lucas. You. What did you do? He was dead." She watched Hairy who was happily purring in my arms. "I saw him get hit."

"He wasn't completely dead, Mare, just kind of stunned."

"No. I know what I saw. When I came out here, you were holding him and smiling and, I don't know." She looked around trying to find the right words then focused on my wrist. "Look! That! Your wrist, your whole body was doing that!"

I pushed my sleeve further down on my arm shifting Hairy to the other shoulder.

"I think what's important right now is that we let Gracie know that Hairy is okay. Right Mare?" I asked, looking deep into her eyes, willing her to not go any further with

THE UNDECIDED

this conversation right now. She let my words sink in and shook her head.

"Okay. But Lucas, I'm not letting this go."

"I didn't think for a second that you would," I said, walking into the house. Hairy leapt out of my arms and ran to the couch where Gracie was crying in her mother's arms.

"What's this?" Mrs. Rossi said, clearing her own tears from her face. "He's alive, he's all right, Gracie. Look!"

"Hairy!" Gracie said, laughing through her tears. He jumped onto the couch and started rubbing his head against Grace's.

"Lucas, you did it! I knew you could do it," Gracie said, hugging Hairy into her frail chest.

"I didn't do anything, Gracie. I think he was just a bit stunned from the hit. But one thing's for sure, I don't think you have to worry about him going outside anytime too soon."

"Lucas, what can I get you? A Coke? Sprite? I think I need a shot of whiskey," Mrs. Rossi said, walking into the kitchen.

"Lucas, will you help me back to my room please?"

"Here, I'll help you Gracie," Mare said, walking towards her.

"No. I want Lucas to help me," she said in a cutting tone.

"Fine. Lucas, do you mind?"

"Why, it would be my pleasure." I walked to the couch and bowed as deeply as any Knight Errant would. "Me lady." I offered her my arm.

Hairy jumped onto the bed first and waited for Grace to get settled before settling himself in.

"She did it, didn't she?"

"Who?" I asked, picking up a blanket from the floor that was previously wrapped around her shoulders.

"Mare's new friend, Mindy. I don't like her, Lucas. She's bad."

"Bad? Ah come on, she can't be too bad if Mare likes her," I answered cautiously.

"Hairy didn't like her."

"Well, if it's any consolation, I don't think she liked him either. Are you saying she's bad because she's not a cat person?"

"No. Well, yes." She laughed at herself. "It's more than that and I know that you know what I'm talking about."

I sat down on the bed beside her.

"Maybe."

"She looks so pretty on the outside, but she's really not, is she?"

"No, she's not Gracie."

"She scares me."

"She can't hurt you, you know," I said, growing concerned at her deep alarm.

"She hurt Hairy."

"A car hurt Hairy."

"She made him go outside. He has never tried to go outside before." Hairy licked her hand and looked back to me as if waiting for my reply. I took a deep breath thinking that I had better end this conversation soon.

"Maybe he got out because she held the door open, and yes he happened to have gotten hurt by a car driving down your street, but he's all better now, and she's gone, and nobody is ever going to hurt you. I promise."

"It's not me that I'm worried about."

"What do you mean?"

"I think she's trying to hurt Mare."

I didn't know what to say. What is it with these Rossi girls and their intense way of seeing to the heart of everything?

"Well, I guess it's up to us to not let that happen, then, isn't it?" I answered, trying to lighten things up.

"Yeah, it's up to us," she said, smiling through a yawn and offering her pinky finger. "Shake."

We shook pinkies.

"What's this?" Mrs. Rossi said, walking into the room with a Coke and a small glass of whiskey.

"It's a secret," Grace said coyly.

"A secret huh? Well, then you had best not tell me." She handed me a Coke and took a swig out of her glass. "Mare is setting the table. Daddy should be home any minute, do you feel up to coming to the table?"

THE UNDECIDED

"No, I'm kind of tired tonight," she said, petting Hairy.
"Of course, love." Mrs. Rossi kissed her forehead. "We'll be in when Daddy gets home, but you rest for now."
"Okay Momma."
I stood up to follow Mrs. Rossi.
"Remember Lucas." She held up her pinky finger and wiggled it. I wiggled mine back.
"Sleep well, Gracie."

Dinner was amazing. Though it appeared to be just a regular plate of spaghetti with meat sauce, it was none like I had ever tasted before. I inhaled two helpings, not allowing Mare's curious stares from across the table to interrupt my good food flow. Mr. Rossi brought home a bag of amaretti cookies that someone in his office baked. They certainly didn't look like much, kind of like a small off-white biscuit, but they tasted unlike anything I'd ever had. They were soft and crunchy, delicate and chewy and sweet and salty, all at the same time. Man, I loved coming over here.

"Lucas? You ready?" I snapped my head away from the plate of cookies to Mare who was putting on her jacket.
"For our walk?" she answered my confused expression.
"Yeah, sure." I grabbed one more cookie before meeting her at the door. Her parents were heading back to Grace's room where they would spend the rest of their evening reading and being with her. "Bye Mr. and Mrs. Rossi. Thanks for dinner."
"You come back soon Lucas. And tell your parents we said hello."
We walked outside and barely made it to the sidewalk before she started.
"Okay. I've been going over what I saw in my head for the past two hours, and you can't tell me that I didn't see what you know I saw." She stopped and looked at me with an awestricken expression. "Lucas, you brought Hairy back to life."
"Mare. Do you know how crazy that sounds?" I asked, squirming in my Nikes.
"Yes, as crazy as it looked. But you did." She was looking at me with complete adoration, and I gotta admit, I

was kind of digging it. I grabbed both of her hands. Maybe I could use this towards my advantage.

"Don't you think it a little odd that all of this happened because of Mindy?"

"Lucas. You can't blame a car hitting Hairy on Mindy."

"Maybe, maybe not. Funny how much Hairy didn't like Mindy. And how exactly did he happen to run outside for the first time in his life this one night that she happened to be over and in control of the door?"

Mare dropped my hands and began walking.

"Okay, fine. She's a dog person. That doesn't make her evil. And she left the door open, that doesn't either. That was just a mistake that you are twisting around to make her look guilty."

I saw the struggle mixing around in her gray essence. I didn't understand why she was already so attached to Mindy, but she definitely was.

"Okay, okay. But you have to admit, it was kind of eerie how that woman said that she turned down your street on a whim, for the first time ever."

"Eerie?" She let out an exasperated sigh. "I think you're really grasping at straws here, Lucas. It was an accident, all the way around." She sped up her pace leaving me behind her.

I grabbed her hand and pulled her back towards me.

"Okay. I'll stop. You really like her, don't you?" I asked, looking into her eyes that were swimming in confusion. The last thing I wanted to do was to make her feel like she had to take sides. Then I would lose her forever.

"I do. I don't expect you to understand. I don't know. I know that you think that she's evil or something, but when we hang out, we're just a couple of girls that like to shop and laugh and talk about boys." She smiled up at me coyly. "And, honestly, I really need that right now."

"Fair enough. As long as the only boy you're talking about is me." I pulled her into my arms and kissed her softly.

"As if there could be any other," she said before she kissed me back.

CHAPTER THIRTY-FOUR

"Lucas! You have a visitor!" my mother yelled from the kitchen. I ripped my ear buds out of my ears promising the Avett Brothers and my ipod that I would meet up with them later. I walked into the kitchen and found my mother and Mare sitting at the table chatting away as if long, lost friends.

"Mare," I said, totally surprised. She looked at me with stars in her eyes. White sparks floated around her light gray essence. Cool.

"Hi Lucas. I was in the neighborhood and thought I'd stop by."

"Awesome. We're still going to Lenny's tonight, right?"

"Definitely. Mr. Hotchkiss switched my shift at Stony Creek, so I actually have a whole day off," she said with a thrilled smile and an underlying meaning.

"Well, I've got to go finish my laundry. Help yourself to anything you want, Mare. It was wonderful to see you." My mother kissed my cheek and gave me a subtle wink. "You let me know before you leave the house, okay?"

"Yeah, Mom," I said, feeling redness creep under my skin.

"Nice to see you too, Mrs. Aarons." Mare stood up. "Ah, is Lucas blushing?"

"Alright, come on." I grabbed her hand and led her upstairs to my room.

"Wow. Very nice," she said turning around in circles studying all of my posters, concert stubs, and anything else that was tacked to the wall. I slyly shoved some dirty clothes under my bed when she wasn't looking and docked my ipod onto my stereo console.

"You ever heard of the Avett Brothers?"

"Avett Brothers? No. But you have, of course," she said, hopping onto my bed and sitting cross-legged.

ROBIN DONARUMA

"Of course." I started playing "Head Full of Doubt/Road Full of Promise." "They're two brothers out of North Carolina. They're really great, because they've kind of got a little bit of everything going on. A little punk, a little folk, a little rock and roll. They toured with Dave Mathews last year. If you haven't heard of them yet, you definitely will soon." I turned up the song that sang of darkness and light and let her get a taste. I picked up my guitar and began to play and sing along.

I lost track of what I was doing and didn't snap back until the song was over. I was slightly surprised to see Mare sitting on my bed, but in an instant it all came back to me.

"Pretty cool, huh?" I turned down my ipod and set my guitar against my bed. She was staring at me wide-eyed.

"Lucas. It's when you sing." She stood up and walked towards me.

"What is?" I tentatively asked. She grabbed my hand and held my wrist out in front of me. It was lit up like one of those glow stick bracelets. Oh boy. I shrugged my shoulders not really sure what to say.

"But it's not just that. Look at me, Lucas. You're so beautiful. When you sing, it's like you're putting your whole self out there. You sing from your heart." She touched my chest, and I looked down at her hand resting on my faded blue tee shirt. "And I can feel it here." She then placed her hand over her heart. I looked from her hand to her face and saw for the first time since I had met her that the gray was gone and white light was swirling around her. I let out a whoop of joyous laughter and hugged her tightly, spinning her around my room.

"Lucas! What are you doing?" She started laughing too. I put her down and held her face.

"Oh Mare. I can see..." My mother yelled both of our names from below. "Hold that thought." I dropped her face and grabbed her hand walking her down the hallway. "Yeah, Mom?"

"There's someone here to see you two. Can you come down here for a sec?" I started walking down the steps to the front door towing Mare behind me. The closer I got to the front door, the more my smile faded. Something wasn't

THE UNDECIDED

right. My mother looked back at me with a mixture of relief and remorse when I approached. Mindy.

"Thanks, Mom. We'll be outside," I said, ushering Mare outside and closing the door between my mother and Mindy.

"Mindy, hi!" Mare said, giving her a big hug. "What are you doing here?"

"Well, I saw your car in the driveway and was hoping that I would catch you. I stopped by Stony Creek, but they told me you weren't working, then I called your house and no one answered."

"My shift got switched. What's up?" Mare looked back to me. "Lucas, do you mind?"

"Oh, I'm sorry Lucas. I hope I wasn't interrupting anything," Mindy innocently offered.

"No, of course not." I stood back and watched Mindy grab Mare's arm causing the light to drain away from her being replaced with dark gray. "I'll wait right here." They just walked down a few steps, so I could still hear their conversation.

"I just wanted to make sure that you got your cat back. I felt so bad for letting him out. I should have stayed and helped find him."

"No, really, it's okay. Hairy is just fine, thanks to Lucas." She looked back at me with a smile, and her essence lightened immediately. Mindy grabbed her hand and it faded.

"Oh, I'm so glad. Thanks, Lucas," Mindy sweetly said to me with a cock of her head. "I was up all night worrying that it got lost or hit by a car or something."

Mare looked back at me and I raised my eyebrows as I walked towards them.

"Never fear, Hairy is back where he belongs, safe and sound."

"That's such a relief. Well, listen, the other reason I wanted to talk to you is to see if I could persuade you to come with me to Lenny's tonight. I know that it's the cool hang out, and I really want to go to check it out, but since I still don't have that many girlfriends...I would just be embarrassed to go by myself." She looked down coyly, and Mare looked back to me.

"Well, actually, I'm going with Lucas tonight."

Mindy feigned a pouty expression and looked at me then back to Mare.

"How 'bout this. You and I go together then when we get there, you two can hook up. That way I don't have to walk in like a total loser and you still get your date!" She smiled appearing quite pleased with herself. Mare looked back at me waffling with indecision.

"What do you think Lucas?"

"Please, Lucas. Just this one time, I promise."

I didn't like this plan one bit, but there really wasn't a whole lot that I could do about it. Evilness aside, two women against one guy, the guy is never going to win. Best cede now.

"Whatever you want, Mare. I can meet you there," I said.

"Yay!" Mindy clapped her hands and jumped up and down like a cheerleader witnessing her first touchdown.

"Okay, but I have to go home first and check in. Can you meet me at my house?"

"I suppose," she said, slightly deflated. "Are you sure you can't just come over to my house since you're right here? That way we can get ready together?"

The thought of Mare walking into their house terrified me. It would be the equivalent of walking into a crypt at the stroke of midnight. No telling what would be lurking in the corners.

"You promised Gracie that you'd see her later," I said to Mare. She looked at me and knew that I didn't want her going into Mindy's house.

"Yeah, I really do need to go spend a little time with Gracie. How about you pick me up around seven?"

"Seven it is," she said offering me a crooked smile. "See you at Lenny's. Thanks for sharing," she said jokingly then hopped down the steps and cut through the brush that separated our driveways.

She disappeared through her dark doorway. Mare grabbed my hand.

"Thanks Lucas. Thanks for understanding." She kissed my cheek. "Now what were you going to say when we were in your room? You said that you saw something?"

THE UNDECIDED

I looked down into her beautiful face and stroked her rosy cheek watching the gray overtake the white sparkling lights.

"I don't remember. You had better get home, I'll see you tonight." I kissed her forehead, and she grabbed my hand.

"Promise you'll sing for me tonight," she asked.

"Absolutely." I kissed her goodbye softly on the lips.

"Promise me one thing."

"Anything."

"Don't let Mindy come in your house. Please, promise me."

"Lucas, I already invited her."

"Meet her outside. Just don't let her in. Don't let Gracie see her."

"Okay, okay. I'll meet her outside, I promise."

"Good. And I will meet you at Lenny's, minus the fried food platter." She laughed as she walked towards her car.

"Uh, definitely no fried platter," she yelled through her passenger seat window as she backed out of the driveway.

At the Donahue's, a curtain fell back into place from an upstairs window.

***

I could tell from the parking lot that I was late to the scene. The music was already rocking out on the back deck and throngs of people were moving in and out of the restaurant.

I walked through the front doors, and my arm was taken hostage.

"You're late, Lucas." It was Barbara, the hostess I met last weekend.

"Late? It's only seven-thirty," I asked, totally confused.

"Well, they got here at seven. That's thirty minutes you'll never get back."

"Who got here?" And then I knew. "Mindy and Mare."

"And that's not all, Luke." She let go of my arm standing up as tall as her five foot two inch frame would allow her. "Devin came with."

"Somehow that doesn't surprise me."

"You need to get out there." She pushed me towards the restaurant. "Go protect that girl of yours. And keep them away from the rest of us." I glanced back at the very agitated host and grabbed her hand.

"I've got this." I infused my light with hers and watched her relax. With a slight squeezing of her fingers, I let go and headed towards the back.

Peter's parents were sitting at the same table as last week, but without Peter. As I passed their table his father held out his hand to me.

"Lucas Aarons, right? I'm Peter's dad."

"Yes, sir." I shook his hand.

"Well, we just wanted to thank you for taking Peter under your wing, so to speak." I looked at him with a slightly puzzled expression. "Peter doesn't have too many friends," his father explained. "At least, none that he ever talks about, so last week, when you asked him to come out there with you guys." He paused trying to overcome his emotion. "Well, we just wanted to thank you. It means a lot. To both of us."

"Peter's a great kid, it was a no brainer." I looked around the table for a sign of him. "Speaking of?"

"Oh! He's outside. He actually went outside," his father said beaming.

"Well then, I had best go and find him," I said more than anxious to get out there myself. "Enjoy your dinner."

I opened the door and felt like I ran into a wall of Jell-O. The air was thick. I saw Peter standing by himself looking as if he was about to make a run for it.

"Peter!" I walked over to him and extended my hand, which he awkwardly slapped. "Glad you could make it."

"Yeah, I was just about to go back inside. My parents are waiting for me." He started to leave, and I grabbed his shirt.

"Not so fast, man, I just got here. You can't leave me hanging. I talked with your parents, and they're not ready to go anywhere. I swear." Peter looked back to his two beaming parents who were staring at him through the window. His mother waved. I laughed and clapped him on the shoulder. "Come on. I see some friendly faces over here."

I took him over to John and his buddies, Paul and Kyle. I introduced them to Peter and John immediately began

THE UNDECIDED

interrogating him about his musical likes and dislikes. Mare was standing near the stage with Mindy appearing as if they had been best friends for years. Becca was there too, with Jeff and Scott, but didn't look very comfortable. Knowing that I was leaving Peter in good hands, I made my way across the deck.

Mindy saw me first and smiled a perfect smile, grabbed Mare's hand and turned her towards me.

"See? I got her here safe and sound, no harm done. She's all yours." She let go of her hand.

"Hi!" Mare grabbed my waist. "You're late," she teased.

"So you missed me?"

"Of course," she beamed. "Look, Jeff and Scott have been fighting over Mindy ever since we got here."

"Ah, that would explain why Becca doesn't seem as Becca-like." Mare looked at Becca.

"Oh, she's fine. Maybe a little jealous, but it's not like she thinks of them in *that* way."

Jeff and Scott stood on either side of Mindy looking like a couple of bookends. They were becoming riddled with black smoky flecks. Becca slowly edged away from them and moved towards other friends. I looked over at Peter who was talking animatedly with the drummer, Kyle. I smiled.

"What are you smiling about?" Mare asked me.

"Oh nothing."

"Hey! Mindy's on stage," Mare said.

"Hello! Test, test!" Mindy yelled into the mic. "My name's Mindy Donahue." All the guys began clapping and whistling, Jeff and Scott the loudest. "My brother and I just moved here from pretty far away. I've got to admit that we were pretty bummed at first, but then we heard that Branford was a pretty cool place." Everyone got louder. "But they were wrong." The crowd silenced. Branford isn't just a cool place. Branford's a *rocking* place!" The crowd went wild. "So put your hands together for my brother, Devin Donahue, who is about to *rock your world, Branford!*"

"Look! Jeff is going to play drums. I didn't even know he played!"

ROBIN DONARUMA

The crowd was cheering as Devin walked onto the stage wielding his *Dean* glossy black electric guitar, completely at ease with his surroundings. A lot of the girls in the crowd moved closer to the stage. Devin told Scott to come up on stage and put him behind the keyboard. He seemed thrilled, as did the crowd that was waiting anxiously for the music to begin.

"What's up Branford?" Devin said into the mic. The crowd screamed in response. "So. You ready to rock?" They screamed louder, including Mare. I looked around watching the shift. Dark entities moved closer to the stage as light energies fanned out to the sides.

"Let's move over here, out of the crowd," I suggested just as Devin hit his first lick. It was loud and insane and everyone loved it.

"Why did we move over here?" Mare complained.

"I was afraid we'd get trampled," I teased, never taking my eyes off of Devin who was playing the Black Sabbath song, "Paranoid," and playing it really well.

"He's really good," Mare said, waving to Mindy who was standing by the stage.

"Yeah, he is," I said truthfully. Devin looked at me as if he heard my comment and smiled, then his eyes shifted to Mare pinning her to her seat.

I headed over to where John, Peter, Becca, and some other guys were gathered, dragging Mare along behind me.

"He's pretty good, Bro," John said, seeming dismayed.

"You're better, man." I clapped him on his back and looked at Peter. "So what do you think? You like it out here?"

"It's awesome. But my parents are leaving, so I've got to go," he said dejectedly.

"I can take you home," I said.

"Really? Thanks, I'll be right back." He ran into the dining room to meet his parents who were ready to leave. And they weren't the only ones. Most of the white energies were standing up to leave. Looking around I realized that dark entities were bleeding outside while the white ones were being forced out.

Peter returned after walking the long way around the darkening crowd.

THE UNDECIDED

"Are we on?" I asked.
"Yeah, thanks Lucas."
"No problem, Pete."
"John, aren't you guys up next?" Becca asked.
"Oh yeah, baby. Get out your paper and pencil kids, you're about to get schooled." John, Kyle, and Paul all high-fived each other making their way to the stage. Devin finished, and the crowd went wild.
"Becca, I didn't know Jeff and Scott could play!" Mare exclaimed excitedly to Becca.
"Yeah, me either," she said, watching them get big hugs from Mindy.
"Don't worry about it. Hey besides, there's only one of her and two of them," Mare said, squeezing Becca's hand.
"Yeah, I know. It's not that. I don't know, I just feel like when they're with her they're different somehow."
"Different? Jeff and Scott?" Mare asked, and looked at me to see if I was following the conversation, which I was.
"Never mind. I don't want to talk about it. Johns up. Come on Peter, let's move over here." She grabbed Peter's hand and dragged him along with her to the stage.
　　John's band started playing "Break on Through" by the Doors. I was only half listening to the song, because I was too busy watching Devin and his new entourage.
"Don't you think, Lucas?" Mare asked me, shaking me out of my own little world.
"Hmm? Did you say something?"
"Never mind. Come on, let's go over by Becca and Peter." She pulled me towards them. People shifted as I walked into the crowd. "I think this Battle of the Bands is going to be absolutely amazing!"
"I couldn't agree more," said Devin as he approached us.
"Not bad, Devin," I said to his smirking face.
"I kept it light, you know, for the kids." He winked at Mare.
"Hey! There you are!" Mindy came up behind Devin and hugged him around his waist. "Isn't he awesome? He's so totally gonna win," she said, holding onto her brother tightly. "Oh! I'm sorry Lucas I forgot you signed up too. Well, I guess the battle's on!"

221

"I guess it is," I said directly to Devin, only momentarily shifting my eyes to Mindy. Jeff and Scott, who were now changed from light gray to a dark gray stepped up beside Devin.

"We're totally gonna rock it!" Jeff said as he slammed his fist into his chest.

"Rock and Roll all the way!" Scott added as he gave Jeff a slamming high five. Devin stood back and watched them rile up the audience for him. He lifted one eyebrow and looked at me.

"It should be fun," Devin said, looking at Mindy who was walking in between Jeff and Scott. She linked her petite arms around each of their beefy ones.

"Come on, boys, let's get out of here," Mindy said walking in front of Becca parading Jeff and Scott like arm candy. "Oh, hi Becca. I didn't notice you there."

Becca barely looked at Mindy instead keeping her eyes on the boys who were attached to her.

"Hi Jeff. Scott," Becca said weakly.

"Who's your new friend Becca?" Scott answered with a question. "Captain Dork of the Chess Club?"

The three of them fell into a fit of laughter as they walked towards the restaurant. Devin fell into step behind them and paused before Becca. He started to say something, looked around her and then back to Lucas.

"That's one for you." He laughed, then looked towards his sister. "Two for me," he said, walking away.

"Hey, look at me," I said to Becca, putting my hand on her shoulder. "It's okay. It will be okay, I promise."

"Will it? I thought they were my friends. I've known them since Kindergarten, how could they be so cruel to me?"

"Just ignore them. It's always worked for me," Peter offered. She looked at him with tears in her eyes and laughed.

"I'm sorry they said that about you Peter."

"Hey, that was nothing. It's all in how you look at it. To me, it was actually kind of like a twisted compliment. At least I wasn't some mignon dork chess member, I was the captain!"

THE UNDECIDED

"He's right, Becca. Don't let them bother you. It's totally hormonal," Mare interjected. "They'll grow bored once Mindy's newness has worn off, then they'll be back."

She glanced at them sitting along a bench adjacent to the restaurant door.

"I don't know if I want them back," she said sadly.

"Luke! You're up, man!" John said slapping me on the back.

"Cool. I'm on it." I kissed Mare on the cheek and headed to the stage.

"You need us man?" Kyle asked before leaving the drum set.

"No, I got this one, thanks Kyle." I picked up an acoustic guitar. The crowd began to move around and Devin stood up, observing the shift. I didn't say anything as I approached the mic, instead just began to play. Without any preparation, I played "Wild Horses" by the Stones. It was perfect, and I became lost in the lyrics and music. Everyone quieted from the concert like screaming to one of a serene calm. I closed my eyes and felt the audience responding. I could feel the shift happening faster, in darting movements.

When I opened my eyes Devin's table was empty. Mare, Becca, and Peter had their arms locked together and were swaying to the music. I finished, and the crowd roared with approval. In the parking lot Devin watched from a distance. Our eyes locked, and I took two steps towards the parking lot. He took two steps back. I put down the guitar and turned to walk towards him, but he was gone.

"Devin doesn't have a chance!" Mare said from behind me. "What are you looking at?"

"Nothing, nothing at all. You know, I'm suddenly a little hungry."

"Oh no, Lucas."

"Come on, we can split it," I said, kissing her on top of her head.

CHAPTER THIRTY-FIVE

The energy was building on both sides. Everywhere I went, in school, around town, in my neighborhood, people were vibrating at a much higher level. There were less gray energies now, and more gray with white or gray with black elements. The push was in full swing.

School had become divided. Not that anyone else would notice, but the two sides were most definitely separated. Where the dark walked the halls, the white were absent, and where there were white, the dark were nowhere to be seen.

The constant vigilance to protect myself and project out to others was exhausting. Nobody ever told me that being a leader would be so much work. And that's not to mention all of the homework and papers that I had to complete for actual school. I didn't see much of Mare during the school week thanks to a six-paged analysis of *The Giver* that I was way behind in, aside from our lunch dates in the school cafeteria. We were closer than ever, and as long as Mindy stuck to her side of the school, Mare was becoming more brilliant by the hour.

Thursday when I walked into the cafeteria, Becca and Peter were waiting for me at the door.

"Hey, what's up?" I asked their pained expressions. I looked around for Mare, but couldn't see a hair on her beautiful head.

"Lucas, Mare left just after second period today," Becca explained.

"Did she get sick?" I asked as an uneasy feeling began swirling in the pit of my stomach.

"No. It's Grace. They don't think..." Becca began to cry and looked away. Peter stepped up.

"Grace is real bad, Luke. We just thought you'd want to know."

THE UNDECIDED

It took a few seconds to digest what they were telling me.

"Thanks guys." I put my hand on Becca's shoulder and smiled. "It will be okay." I walked out the cafeteria door and out of school and headed straight to the Rossi's.

***

Cars that I didn't recognize lined their driveway. An older woman greeted me at the door.

"Are you a friend of the family, son?" she asked.

"Yes ma'am. May I come in?" I looked around for a familiar face.

"It's alright Betty, he can come in," said Mr. Rossi from behind her. She smiled and opened the door wider, allowing me to enter. Mr. Rossi looked like he had been beaten and left for dead.

"Mr. Rossi?" I asked with a lump in my throat. He grabbed me and held on as if his life depended on it. Unfortunately, it wasn't *his* life. His pain washed through me, and it was none like I had ever experienced.

"I'm sorry, come in Luke. Betty is from Hospice, they're here to, um, help us today." Tears unabashedly ran down his cheeks. "You see we don't think our Gracie is going to…" His voice cracked, and he walked away from me and into the kitchen. I looked at Betty who gave me a sympathetic nod.

"Can I go see her?" I asked hoarsely.

"Mrs. Rossi is with her now, if she feels she's up to it, dear, she'll let you know."

I headed back to the familiar hallway with much heavier steps. I turned the corner and saw Mare hunched in the corner of the hallway, her head between her legs.

"Mare," I whispered. Her head whipped up, and she lunged herself at me.

"Lucas! Lucas! Thank God you came. Thank God," she said, sobbing into my shirt. "It's Gracie. Gracie's not…" I held her head and tried to quiet her tears.

"I know. I know. Shhhh. It will be all right." I held her tightly again.

"Yes, yes!" She pulled away. "You can fix her, like Hairy. You can make her all better, Luke. I know it!"

225

ROBIN DONARUMA

"No sweetheart, it doesn't work that way." I wiped my thumb across her wet cheek.

"You're special, you can do things. I've seen it. You have to fix her, Lucas. Please," she whispered desperately. "Please Lucas, I can't lose her."

Grace's bedroom door opened and closed. Mrs. Rossi came out looking as if she had been through a war.

"Lucas. How nice of you to come. Would you like something to drink? Well, you know where the kitchen is, help yourself," she said as if on autopilot.

"I was wondering if I could see her?" I asked quietly.

"I think Gracie would like that very much." She brought a tissue up to her mouth to stop herself from an emotional outburst. "She's been a little tired today, but I know that she would love to see you."

Mrs. Rossi rushed from the hallway towards Betty who was standing in the dining room. Mare watched me expectantly as I approached Grace's door.

"I can't go in there," she said.

"Okay. You wait out here. I'll be right back." I opened the door a crack.

"Lucas?" Mare asked.

"Yes?" I asked without looking at her. I couldn't look away from Grace's room.

"Can you see her? Can you see her light?"

"Yes," I said smiling.

"Is it white?" she asked meekly.

"It's absolutely brilliant," I said, walking into Grace's room and closing the door behind me. The entire room was aglow as if the sun itself was nestled in the corner. Hairy got up from the bed to greet me. Grace stirred, and I realized that the light was coming from her.

"Lucas," she whispered with half opened eyes. "You came. I've been waiting for you."

"Hi Gracie." I approached the bed and took her frail, cool hand. "You've really got everyone worked into a tizzy out there, you know."

She smiled a shallow smile and closed her eyes.

"I want to show you something." Her eyes closed, and she stilled. The light in the room grew brighter.

"I'm here, Lucas." I heard her say, but her mouth didn't move.

I slowly turned around and found a glowing, vibrant vision of Grace standing in the middle of the room. A delicate silver chord connected her to her prone body on the bed.

"Gracie?" I stood up. "What is this?"

She giggled a youthful, girlish laugh and then leaped back into her sick body. Her eyelids fluttered and opened.

"Did you see? I thought you'd be proud of me."

"I don't understand," I said, desperate for some sort of explanation. Her eyes closed again, and in an instant, she jumped out of herself and was standing beside me.

"Of course you do, silly." She looked behind her towards the window and then back to me. "It's almost time for me to go home. My hair will be pretty again."

In the blink of an eye, she was back in her body. She opened her eyes.

"I think the next time I do that, I'm not going to come back," she said serenely.

"You can fight, Gracie. Fight to live, I can help you," I cried.

"Don't be sad, Lucas. I will be living. I just won't be living here anymore, and I won't be in pain. I don't want to hurt anymore, Lucas. I'm tired."

"I know," I whispered.

"Everyone keeps trying to fix me, but I'm not broken. Not in here." She tapped her heart. "And that is the part of me that will keep on living. Can you help them understand that?"

"I don't know," I answered honestly as tears ran down my cheeks.

"Don't cry, Lucas. For the first time in a long time I'm happy. I want to go home now."

"Gracie, you're so beautiful," I said as she became brighter and brighter.

"I love you too, Lucas. Promise me that you'll take care of her for me. Mare."

"I promise."

"I'm afraid for her, Lucas. She doesn't understand."

"I know. I'll take care of her, I promise."

ROBIN DONARUMA

She smiled, closed her eyes, and her hand fell out of mine.

"I know you will, Lucas." She stood beside me vibrant and full of life. The silver cord was gone. She glanced behind her and giggled. "I get to go now. Look Lucas, can you see it? It's so beautiful!" She began to fade. "I can run again!" She turned and ran until she disappeared. The room darkened, and I laughed and cried all at once.

Mare came in and screamed. Mr. and Mrs. Rossi were through the door seconds later followed by Betty and another woman. Mrs. Rossi fell onto Grace's body. Betty began writing things down on a clipboard attached to the foot of the bed. Mr. Rossi stared helplessly at his child's lifeless body, and Mare shrunk into the hallway staring at me with disgust and unabashed loathing.

"Mare." I started towards her. She jumped out of reach, and ran out of the house. I followed her.

"Hey." I touched her shoulder, and she shrugged off my hand.

"Don't! Don't you touch me!" She stared at me wildly. "Why didn't you save her? Why?"

"I can't." I held my hands out to my side. "It's not up to me to save lives. I'm not God."

"No, you certainly aren't." She took two steps towards me. "But you are something. What exactly are you Lucas Aarons?"

"Please, let's go inside. You should be with your parents. Your mother needs you." I tried to grab her elbow.

"What do you know about what anyone needs? Believe me, my parents haven't *needed* me for quite some time, they're not going to start now." She looked at me accusingly. "Why didn't you save her, was she not good enough for you?"

I stood there without any answers.

"You're a hypocrite and a liar. You'll save a cat, but not a sick little girl who never did anything to anyone. You know you keep telling me to stay away from Devin and Mindy because they're bad, but maybe you've been lying about that too. Maybe you're the one who's evil. You need to get out of here."

"Mare, please." She darkened. I was losing her.

THE UNDECIDED

"Get away from me. I wish I had never met you." She growled from between clenched teeth.

"Please." I held out my hand.

She lunged towards me and ripped the necklace from around my neck and threw it into the street.

"Get out of here!" she screamed before running into the house.

Slowly, I walked into the street and picked up my necklace. I clutched it tightly and held it up to my head wishing for some sort of divine direction for my next move. I stared at the house and felt the grief and despair pouring out of it. I walked to my car and drove home.

CHAPTER THIRTY-SIX

My mom was setting the table, and my dad was reading the newspaper when I got home.
"Lucas! Just in time. You didn't leave a note, so I wasn't sure where you were or when you'd be back. You know you really should..." My mother took one look at me and paused. My father's paper slowly lowered. "Lucas? What's happened? What's wrong?" My father stood, my mother approached me.
"She's gone. Gracie." My mother covered her mouth with her hands and suppressed a sob. My father rushed to me and held me.
"I'm so sorry, son. We didn't know," my dad said.
"Poor Rossi's, I can't imagine," my mother said, joining my dad. "And Mare. How's she holding up?" she asked me.
"Not very well," I stated flatly. "I think I'm gonna go upstairs, if you don't mind."
"Sure, son," my dad stated.
"Do you want any dinner?" my mother asked me as I walked up the stairs.
"Maybe later, thanks."
I shut my bedroom door and pulled my necklace out of my pocket re-fastening it around my neck. I immediately felt better. I turned on my ipod and fell back on my bed going over and over my last moments with Gracie. A smile spread across my face as I remembered her happiness just before she left her body. If only Mare could have seen that, or her parents. It was a gift to have witnessed it, but a curse to not be able to share it with those that, perhaps, needed to see it the most.
I wondered what Mare was doing. I had never seen a light extinguished so quickly as it did with her. But I wasn't giving up. She wasn't completely dark, which meant she could still come back to me.

THE UNDECIDED

I was clipping flowers for Ethan and putting them into a basket; however, the more flowers I put in, the larger the basket got. In frustration, I put the basket down and headed back to the house eager to tell Ethan what was happening. I walked into the kitchen and yelled for him. No answer. I opened the refrigerator to get something to drink and it was completely bare. I opened several cabinets and found them empty too. "Ethan!" No answer. I walked down the hall to my bedroom. Everything was just as I had left it, even Layla. I picked up my guitar, and it disintegrated in my hands. I backed out of the room and headed towards the back porch. I called for Ethan again. No answer. My pulse quickened. Something wasn't right. In a half run, half walk I headed towards our white Adirondack chairs overlooking the ocean. I called for Millie. She answered with a weak yelp. "Millie!" A tennis ball floated through the air and landed at my feet. It was covered in blood. "Millie!" I hollered at the top of my lungs. "Ethan!"

Laughter echoed behind me. Something wasn't right. I looked towards the flower garden. The flowers were all dead. The laughter returned and seemed to be coming from across the yard. A large crashing sound emanated from the house, and just as I turned, the right half of the house crashed into the ground. The back porch was next, and I watched with horror as the house continued to fold in on itself and disappear into the Earth. To steady myself, I put my hand out towards the Adirondack chairs but found two large rocks in their place. The surrounding ocean had become a marsh. My island was gone.

"This is going to be easier than I thought," a voice echoed from a dark corner of the marsh.

"Devin," I said with disgust.

"Especially if they keep extinguishing themselves." He smiled sinisterly.

"I wouldn't be so sure, if I were you."

"Really? And why is that?" He walked closer, always maintaining a safe distance from me.

"Because of something a friend showed me," I answered smugly.

"Really? And what could a friend of yours show you that could possibly threaten me?"

"Simple. We can never be extinguished. Unlike the darkness, the light can never be destroyed." With a wave of my arm an arc of light shot out in front of me illuminating the surrounding dark areas and forcing Devin to back far away. The truth brought fear into his blue eyes.

"We'll see about that. Survival can turn the gentlest lamb into the most ferocious beast. Should make for an interesting game."

I heard Millie approach before she put her head under my hand resting at my side. Devin shot a nervous glance towards her and continued to retreat.

"I'll be ready," I answered.

"That, I highly doubt," he laughingly answered then was gone.

"The battle nears, friend Lucas," Millie said with a whimper.

"I know."

"The lines have shifted. The grays are choosing their sides."

"Yes," I answered, staring out into the marsh.

"You are ready," she stated.

"Yes."

"You were lucky to have a friend Grace," Millie said, licking my hand. I shifted my eyes away from the marsh and looked at Millie who sat beside me looking as beautiful as ever.

"Yes, I was. She taught me a lot in very little time." I rubbed her head.

"She said to tell you that she is glad that you finally understood."

"You spoke with her?" I asked excitedly.

"Of course. She came to me with a message. She lives in the beyond with the others."

"With Ethan?"

"Yes, that is where he lives."

"Does she know about Mare? About her reaction?" I asked wearily.

"Yes. It was expected."

I sat down on the ground and put my hands on my knees.

"I think I lost her," I whispered.

THE UNDECIDED

"No one is ever lost, friend Lucas, this you already know."

"She thinks that I let Gracie die. She hates me," I said flatly.

"She hurts."

"She's gotten darker." I looked at Millie.

"And you've gotten lighter." She put her paw on my knee. "Don't give up, for if you do, then she will truly be gone."

"I'll never give up," I said into Millie's moist, brown eyes.

"Then wake up and lead." She licked my face.

I woke up ready for school. I got dressed, grabbed a donut, and was out the door before my mother even had the chance to interrogate me on my mental and emotional state, or make me eat an unwanted egg. I didn't have time for that. I needed to find Mare.

I got to Mr. Holland's class just before Devin. We both sat down at the same time and exchanged knowing glances. Mare's seat was empty. Becca looked at Mare's empty seat, then at me and gave me a doleful smile.

"I would like to take a moment, if you please." Mr. Holland addressed the class. "As some of you may know, your classmate, Marianne Rossi, lost her younger sister last night. If you would all take care to keep the Rossi family in your thoughts and perhaps set forth your own message of condolence that would, indeed, prove to be a lovely act. *Ah, this fell sergeant, death, is strict in his arrest.*" Mr. Holland was walking to the blackboard then paused in mid-stride. "Hamlet, Act Five, Scene Two."

There was an air of neutrality between Devin and me. Every move didn't feel as if it was a calculated step on his part to break me. It was kind of like we had called a sort of semi-truce. We were beyond the posturing stage. Well beyond that. The lines were shifting, and he now understood that I wasn't as weak as he first thought.

I walked the halls reaching out with my light to everyone that was near. Millie said that the lines between the light and dark armies were shifting, which meant that the end of this battle was near. And this was a battle we couldn't afford to lose.

ROBIN DONARUMA

Becca was standing outside the cafeteria waiting for me.

"Hi Becca," I said, giving her a big hug.

"Hi Lucas," she said, wiping tears from her eyes. "I just didn't want to go in there by myself."

"Come on," I said, putting my arm around her shoulder.

We went through the lunch line in silence. We sat at our usual table, minus Jeff and Scott who were sitting on the other side of the cafeteria with the other dark-lined kids.

"The funeral is today, you know," Becca said, stirring her ketchup with a soggy French fry.

"No. I didn't know."

"I was thinking of going, but didn't want to go by myself. Would you go with me?" she asked dejectedly.

"Sure. But Becca, Mare's your best friend, why are you nervous?" I asked.

"I went over to Mare's last night. It was late, but after I had heard what happened." She looked at me, and I nodded, understanding what she meant and encouraging her to continue. "Well, Mindy was there."

"Mindy?" I asked, alarm rushing through my veins.

"Yeah, before me. I mean, Mare and I have been best friends since Kindergarten, before that really, and here this Miss Perfect comes into town for two months, and now I'm totally invisible."

"I don't think that's the case. She loves you, Becca."

"Really? Well then why did she tell me to leave?"

"What?"

"I went over there to be with her, to help her, I don't know. I've known Gracie my whole life. I felt like I had lost my sister too." I handed her a paper napkin, and she blew her nose. "When I saw her, I ran to her and hugged her, and I might as well have been hugging a wall. She just stood there, like some sort of emotionless statue. Then Mindy walked over and said that maybe it would be better if I left, because Mare had had a pretty rough day. Me! She wanted me to leave!"

Becca sat back and pushed her tray away from her.

THE UNDECIDED

"All she did was stare at me. I put my hand on her shoulder and she shrugged it off and said that maybe Mindy was right and I should leave."

"So what did you do?"

"I left. What could I do?"

"I'm sorry, Becca. I know this is hard for you too." I grabbed one of her fidgeting hands. "Try not to take this too much to heart. Situations like this, emotional ones, are almost never as bad as they seem. Mare's been through a lot, for a long time. We should cut her a little slack."

Becca pulled her hand back and stood up forcing a smile onto her face.

"You're right. Here I am making this about me. I'm so stupid."

"No, you're just hurting."

We picked up our trays and walked to the trash compactor. Mindy chose that opportune moment to walk into the cafeteria. She walked directly to Becca.

"Hey Becca, sorry about last night. I was just worried for Mare, the last thing she needed was to get upset all over again."

"I didn't go there to upset her, Mindy. I went there because she's my best friend."

"Oh, I know!" She looked at me and at Becca with an innocent fluttering of her eyelashes. "Oh I've really messed this up, haven't I? I was just trying to do what's best for Mare, that's all. And I'm sure you understand that."

I stepped closer to Becca who was becoming more upset by the second and held onto her elbow. Mindy took a step back.

"Oh, I understand all sorts of things, Mindy," Becca said with an insincere smile and walked away. I followed directly behind her. Devin was watching from his lunch table, and I acknowledged him with a tilt of my head.

"Nice job, Becca," I said.

"Ugh, that girl gives me the creeps. I know she's beautiful, but I'm telling you there is something about her that isn't right."

"Tell me about it," I mumbled under my breath.

"So you'll pick me up about four-thirty? The service is at five."

ROBIN DONARUMA

"Absolutely."

THE UNDECIDED

CHAPTER THIRTY-SEVEN

I picked Becca up at four-thirty and we made our way to Branford Cemetery where Grace's ceremony and burial were taking place. The weather was cool and breezy with thin, grayish clouds blocking the sun. It added to the somber mood and made me wish that I had brought a heavier jacket.
There was a long row of cars already there, and I was amazed and pleased to see how many people had shown. I parked the car, and we walked up the gravel walkway winding our way through old, weathered tombstones. Leaves danced around our feet, and Becca's blonde hair flew wildly in the wind making a startling contrast with her black dress. My parents were talking with the Rossi's, my mother wiping away her own tears as she struggled to not glance at the small, white casket that sat directly beside her.
"There she is," Becca whispered. I wasn't sure if she referred to Gracie or Mare.
"There she is," I repeated as I spotted Mare standing beside her father looking very pale and withdrawn. Mindy walked up beside her in that moment and linked her arm with Mare's. Mare offered her a weak smile. Mindy whispered something in her ear, and Mare let out a small giggle and placed her hand over Mindy's.
"Let's just stay here. Becca pulled my arm and stopped me from walking towards Mare and instead directed us across from her where other kids from school were gathered.
It was strange seeing so many people dressed so drearily in one place. The leaves from the drying trees were falling as we stood there, not sure what sort of protocol to take. I thought the surroundings, including the people in it, a sad and drastic opposite to what Grace was, beauty and light.

ROBIN DONARUMA

    I felt Devin as he neared the site. He entered on the opposite side of where I stood moving closer to Mindy and Mare. I began to walk towards them, but Becca stilled me by grabbing my hand. It was in that same moment that Mare looked up and our eyes met. At first there was warmth, then she glanced beside me and saw that Becca and I were holding hands. Warmth in her eyes was replaced with loathing. Mindy took this opportunity to whisper something into her ear. Mare nodded and looked away from me.
    The minister took his place at the foot of the casket and began the ceremony. Mare stared at the casket as if nothing else existed. I glanced at Devin. His eyes were closed appearing as if he was praying. I knew better. In the distance a low rumble echoed through the air and a large raindrop fell onto the pristine casket. Low murmurs waved through the crowd as they scrambled to cover themselves from the moisture that was beginning to fall faster and heavier. Devin opened his eyes and smiled a slow, satisfied smile. In one swift movement, he pulled an umbrella from behind his back and walked over to Mare and Mindy offering shelter from the rain.
    The flower arrangement bled petals and the bright colors painted the browned ground surrounding the casket. Becca and several of the congregation moved underneath two large trees that lined the pathway directly behind us. I stood, oblivious to the wetness, watching as Devin put his arm around Mare and pulled her close. She turned her head into his chest. Devin looked at me as he lovingly cradled her head.
    Anger polluted my body. I shifted my eyes to Gracie's casket and remembered my promise to protect her sister. I closed my eyes and asked for help. I felt the breeze through the pelting cold raindrops, and I absorbed its energy. I heard the wind moving through the trees above, and I joined them. I let my anger fall away, and I tapped into the beauty of life that surrounded me. I felt the essence of those around me and felt their love for Gracie, and I blended it with my own. I asked the rain to stop. I asked for the breeze to remove the clouds from the sun so that we

THE UNDECIDED

could feel its warmth. I felt the birds hiding in their nests and willed them to sing.

The warmth of the sun hit my face, and I smiled in thanks. When I opened my eyes everyone was taking their previous positions through sighs of relief. Devin, with a jerk like motion, put away his umbrella. Mare stepped away from him and lifted her face to the sun laughing joyously. The minister continued with his sermon.

"Wow, can you believe this?" Becca whispered into my ear. "I never thought it would stop raining."

I smiled and attempted to listen to the reading, but something bright just beyond the trees caught my eye. I moved slightly to my right and caught the flash of a fluffy white tail.

"Millie?" I whispered to myself.

Millie walked from behind the tree walking alongside a little girl with long, shiny blonde hair. She was smiling at me as she whispered into Millie's ear. Then it hit me. Gracie. Gracie was here, and she was with Millie. I looked at Becca who was intently listening to the minister. Mare was staring at the casket. I wanted desperately to scream at the top of my lungs that she was okay, she was here, but I knew that no one else would be able to see her.

Gracie blew me a kiss, waved goodbye, and in a blink, they were gone.

***

Mare didn't go to school or work for the next two days. And my attempts at texting and calling her were done in vain. It was as if she fell off the face of Branford.

The air around school was thickening similar to that feeling right before a huge lightning storm. And a storm was definitely brewing. The entire city of Branford, not just the student body, seemed to be preparing for the Battle of the Bands, which was only four days away. Local businesses were closing their doors so that they could attend the competition. Even Lenny's was closing for the evening and directing everyone to attend the big Branford High battle taking place in the football arena.

Students had plastered the hallways with reminders and some bands even promoted themselves with full sized posters, like John and his band Ledz Rock. The community was definitely turning this competition into a big deal. For me, it wasn't the competing, it was the knowing that this would be the beginning of the end, at least for one of us.

Lines were being drawn on a daily basis. Classrooms, hallways, and lunchrooms were divided in half by the dark and the light. The gray were still scattered throughout, but each day there were less of them. They were gravitating towards their sides.

I met Peter and Becca at lunch and was glad to find them laughing about something when I walked up.

"What's happening guys?" I asked, placing my back against the window so I could observe the lunchroom.

"Hi Lucas. We were just talking about the Battle of the Bands."

"Of course you were." It seemed like that was all anyone was talking about these days.

"Yeah, we were just saying that it would be awesome if Principal Thomas played her accordion as an opening act," Peter chimed in, still laughing. "She has one in her office and can actually play it."

"That would be something to see, that's for sure," I answered just as Jeff and Scott walked by and purposely knocked Peter's lunch tray off of the table.

"Oops," Jeff said sarcastically as he kept walking.

"Hey!" Becca shouted as she pushed away from the table.

"Becca, don't worry about it, really, it's fine," Peter said quietly.

"No Peter, it's not fine. Jeff!" she yelled again. Jeff stopped and slowly turned around a sly smile wavering on his lips.

"Yes, your highness?" He bowed, and Scott laughed and clapped him on the back.

"Apologize."

"What?"

"You heard me. I said apologize. You owe Peter an apology." She walked around the table to stand face to face with Jeff.

"I don't owe Dweeber anything. Back off," he said and turned around. Becca grabbed his arm and pulled him

THE UNDECIDED

back towards her. Peter stood up nervously and begged her to stop, but she wasn't listening. No one was, everyone was watching Becca and Jeff.

"What has happened to you?" she asked, tears welling in her eyes. Jeff, in a quick jerk, pulled his arm free.

"Me? What has happened to you? You're the one hanging with losers." He motioned to Peter. "Or maybe it's more than that?" He walked closer to Becca. "Maybe you two are, you know, more than friends?" He ran his finger down one of Becca's arms, and she slapped it away. He stroked a lock of her blonde hair. "Does he give you what you need?" I stood up and grabbed his arm.

"Enough," I said. Jeff whipped his head around ready to attack but took one look at me and faltered. He looked at my hand grasping his arm and I knew, without looking, my birthmark was glowing. "I think you had better go Jeff. I'd hate for you to be late to class."

"What's this?" said a cold, calculated voice from behind me. Jeff looked over my shoulder and his resolve hardened. Devin put his hand on his shoulder. I let go. "He's right, Jeff, we don't want to be late to class." Jeff glanced at Becca and me with a slight tremor of confusion written across his face. Devin must have read that too because he grabbed his arm this time, forcing him to look at him. "Let's go, Jeff." Jeff hardened instantly and looked at Scott.

"Come on man, let's roll before anyone thinks we're actually friends with these losers." They boisterously left the lunchroom with about as much grace as a tidal wave. Devin started to follow them, then turned around to Peter.

"Looks like you had a little accident. Better clean it up before somebody gets hurt." Devin looked at me emphasizing the last two words before walking away.

Becca helped Peter pick up his lunch. I watched the energies dance around the lunchroom like a well-orchestrated waltz.

"Lucas. I don't know exactly what's going on between you and Devin," Becca said harshly. "But promise me one thing."

"What's that?"

"Promise me you'll kick Devin's ass this weekend."

ROBIN DONARUMA

My eyebrows shot up in surprise, and I looked at Peter who was also staring at Becca. She didn't wait for an answer as she grabbed her backpack and lunch tray and looked at Peter.

"Come on," she said to him. He followed, obediently giving me a slight wave goodbye.

"I'll see what I can do, Becca," I answered quietly.

THE UNDECIDED

CHAPTER THIRTY-EIGHT

I was already sitting in British Lit. when Mare walked into the classroom. She wasn't alone. Devin was beside her, his arm draped around her shoulders. She briefly glanced at me before looking away. He escorted her to an empty desk beside his. When the student that was supposed to sit there arrived, one look at Devin had him moving to a seat in the back of the room. Becca, who was watching the scene unfold, offered me a weak smile.

Mr. Holland closed the door and the next fifty-five minutes passed about as fast as a turtle scaling Mount Everest. I jumped out of my seat at the bell trying to make it to the door at the same time as Mare, but Mr. Holland stopped me.

"Mr. Aarons, if you please?" He motioned for me to join him at his desk. "Ah yes, I see that you have signed up for the prestigious Battle of the Bands contest."

"Yeah," I answered questioningly.

"Very good. We'll all be in attendance to cheer you on. And all of the other contestants, of course." He added the last comment as an afterthought.

"Thanks," I said, studying him a little bit closer. "I could use all the fans that I can get." I watched his light flare, and I knew then that he was one of my watchers. "Anything else?" I looked behind me and found the room now empty and the next class filing in.

"No, no, that was it. Just a bit of a pep talk as it were." He walked with me towards the door. "Lucas, as Helena once spoke, *Love looks not with the eyes, but with the mind.*"

"Helena?" I asked.

"From *Midsummer Night's Dream*, of course."

"Of course. I'll keep that in mind. Thank you Mr. Holland." I knew that he saw what was going on even though I really didn't get what he was trying to tell me, it felt good knowing I was being looked after. I just wish he would speak in English, not Shakespeare.

"Lucas." He grabbed my arm before I reached the door and spoke in a hushed tone. "Some Cupid kills with arrows, some with traps. You would do well to remember as much."

"Helena?" I asked a little breathlessly.

"Oh, don't be silly. That's Hero, *Much Ado About Nothing*. You really need to brush up on your Shakespeare, young man," he said letting go of my arm. "Heed my words, Lucas. There is a tide in the affairs of men."

I walked to my next class unable to shake the unease that was beginning to creep its way into my essence. Mr. Holland quite properly freaked me out. I knew that something big was building and apparently, I wasn't the only one.

The halls boasted more posters of the contest that was now only three days away. John and his band's posters looked just like the Beatles' *Abbey Road* album where they are all crossing the street, except that John, Kyle, and Paul were all wearing tee shirts and flip-flops. John added his own mark by looking at the camera and holding up his fingers in the classic devil-horned rock and roll signal. At the end of the hall, a group of girls gathered whispering excitedly. Normally, I wouldn't think twice about it, but since it was a group of dark energies, I thought I should check it out. I walked towards them and one left immediately. Two others watched as I approached looking as if they weren't sure what to do. The bell rang and that helped them with their decision. They all left. I was late for Mr. Kenzie's class, but looking at what they were so enrapt over, I didn't care. It was a poster of Devin wielding a shiny black Ibanez guitar. He was dressed in all black, which made his blue eyes seem even bluer, if that was possible. The picture was taken from a low angle, giving him the appearance of being much taller and larger than he really was. Jeff and Scott were blurrily positioned in the background standing on either side of him like his own personal bodyguards. With arms folded, he lazily smiled into the camera appearing self-assured and capable of

THE UNDECIDED

anything. There wasn't any writing on the poster except his name written in all capital letters at the bottom.

"Lucas!" Mr. Kenzie yelled down the hall. "Would you mind gracing us with your presence so we can get started?"

"Sorry, Mr. Kenzie." I walked to the door.

"You're not leaving me alone with him." He mumbled as I walked into the class. I sat down.

"Cool poster, John," I said.

"I thank you very much, and Ledz Rock thanks you. So what do you think about the name, pretty awesome, right?"

"Definitely. So you finally all agreed?"

"Well, not really, Kyle's mom had the final say and since she lets us use her garage to practice in, we kind of had to go with her decision. It's all good," he said with a wink.

"Absolutely," I said perusing the class. Devin was sitting on the opposite side of the class talking animatedly with a girl who used to be light gray but now was the color of charcoal. She laughed as she listened to him, a look of complete adoration lighting up her face.

"So quarter notes and syncopations aside, let's talk about this weekend," Mr. Kenzie said to the class. The class responded by whistling and clapping. "Okay good, for once we're all in agreement." He walked behind his desk and picked up a piece of chalk. "I know that many of you in this class have signed up for the Battle of the Bands this weekend, so I thought I would go over some of the rules." Everyone began talking excitedly. "But it won't do you any good if you can't hear me." The class quieted. "That's better. First of all, no death, thrash, black, or glam metal." He wrote that on the board then turned to look at Devin. "Sorry Mr. Donahue, there are just too many grandmothers who come to watch their precious kith and kin, and honestly, we don't have enough ambulances in Branford to handle them dropping. Second, no Miley Cyrus." A girl in the front row raised her hand.

"What's wrong with Miley Cyrus?" she asked desperately.

"There's a loaded question," he answered out loud, but more to himself. "To put it simply. I don't like her, I don't want to listen to her much less an imitation of her, and it's my contest, and I make the rules, so no Miley Cyrus." He wrote that on the board in all capital letters. "It's not a rule, but as a personal favor to me, who happens to be one of the judges, can we keep the country to a minimum? Thanks." He turned back to the board and began writing other, more specific rules like when to show up and where to go.

It was going to be held outside in the football stadium. The stage was being delivered today, thus cancelling any football programs. No one seemed to mind.

"What are you guys playing?" I asked John.

"I don't want to spoil the surprise, man, but between you and me we're playing "Ballroom Blitz" by Sweet because it will definitely be sweet, if you know what I mean. What about you?"

"You know, I'm not really sure," I answered honestly.

"Dude, it's like less than three days away."

"Yeah, I know," I said, frighteningly not worried at all that I wasn't prepared for the show in the slightest.

Class zoomed by, and before I knew it, I was out of there and on to my next one. Hopefully the next two would go by just as fast. I was determined to talk with Mare, alone, and lunch seemed the perfect place to do it.

She was at the head of the line, looking as if she was waiting for me and nothing had changed between us. I approached her, and her darkness faded.

"Hey," I said. "Do you think we could talk?"

"What is there to talk about?" she said cautiously.

"Everything," I answered honestly. I held my hand out to her. "Please." She started to take my hand, but Mindy got to her first.

"Hey, you ready?" she asked Mare, holding a tray filled with food. "I'm super hungry today, I have no idea why."

"Yeah, sure," Mare answered then looked at me, her darkness returning. "I don't have anything to say to you Lucas, at least nothing that I haven't already said."

"Bye, Lucas," Mindy pertly said as she escorted Mare to their table where Devin sat with Jeff and Scott.

My appetite was gone. At my lunch table Becca and Peter were watching me with sympathetic looks. Great. I was heading back out of the cafeteria when John approached me from behind slapping me on the back.

"Dude! That poster is rockin!" he said, smiling into my face.

"What poster?" I asked smiling back, infected by his happiness.

"Oh, that's so awesome! You don't even know do you? The poster of *you* my brotha!" John pointed over to Becca and Peter. "And I'm thinking those two are the geniuses behind it." John walked over to talk with Becca and Peter, and I slowly followed.

"Well?" Becca asked me.

"Did you see it?" Peter asked as his face flushed with pleasure.

"No, I haven't."

"It was totally Peter's idea," Becca announced proudly.

"I like to goof around with Photoshop," he answered coyly.

"Look." Becca pulled a rolled up poster out of her book bag. "We haven't finished putting them all up yet," she explained to Peter who was beaming.

She unrolled the poster, and there I was holding an acoustic guitar and leaning up against the side of a wall.

"Where did you get this picture?" I asked amazed.

"It's from that party we had at the puppet house during the Branford Festival, remember?" she asked proudly.

"I don't remember having my picture taken."

"Oh, I took lots of pictures, I was just lucky that I had this one of you, isn't it great?"

Wearing only jeans and a tee shirt, it was definitely nothing fancy, but then that's probably why I liked it. Then I noticed my wrist.

"Wait a minute," I whispered walking closer to the poster.

"Isn't it awesome?" John piped in.

"That's the photo shop part," Peter said.

Around my wrist my birthmark was glowing like some sort of white bracelet.

"And that's not all," Becca said, reaching back into her bag. She pulled out several white braided cloth bracelets. "Look." She pulled back her shirtsleeve, and I noticed that she was wearing one, so was Peter and John. "And we're not the only ones," she sang, motioning me to look around the cafeteria.

Everyone within throwing distance to our table was wearing a white bracelet. I was stunned. My wrist began to feel warm, and I tried not to look down, knowing that it was beginning to glow.

"I don't know what to say. This is amazing," I whispered, totally in awe.

"Thank Peter, it was his idea," Becca stated proudly.

"Thanks Peter. Really, thank you," I said, walking around the table and giving him a hug. Becca stood up.

"Come on, Peter, let's go hang the rest of these up."

"I don't think the school is that big, Becca," I said, looking at them.

"Oh, these aren't for school, these are for downtown," she said, smiling like I hadn't seen her do in a while. "Come on, Pete."

I grabbed some fries off of Becca's tray before she walked it to the trash compactor.

"Dude, this is going to be awesome!" John sang, walking away. I stood there, still slightly stunned by everything. I heard my name called from two tables over and Ruth, the girl from British Lit., held up her wrist showing me her bracelet. The other girls sitting around her did the same. I smiled and headed for the door. After being stopped three other times by people showing me their bracelets, I finally made it. I glanced at Mare across the lunchroom. She was staring at me. I took one step towards her, but Devin must have sensed it, because he swung his arm over her shoulder and whispered something into her ear. Her eyes dropped. I was off her radar.

CHAPTER THIRTY-NINE

Mare may not be talking to me, but luckily Mrs. Rossi still was. It didn't take much convincing for her to offer me Mare's work schedule. The Battle of the Bands was tomorrow, and this was probably going to be my only chance to try and get her back. I got to Stony Creek a few minutes before the end of her shift. I took a deep breath before reaching for the door.

"You sure that's a good idea, Luke?" muttered a raspy voice.

"Captain Bob," I said smiling. "Haven't given up that pipe, yet, huh?"

"Bah! Everyone needs to stop worrying so much about me and my pipe and worry more about their own dumb blame affairs." He stepped into the light of the streetlamp.

"Is that why you're here? To talk to me about my dumb blame affairs?" I teased.

"Don't be fresh." He limped closer and looked through the window at Mare. "She hasn't decided yet, has she?" he asked.

"No," I stated.

"You thinking of doing something about that, I take?"

"Well, I'm certainly going to try."

"I hear she's been keeping with some pretty heavy company lately. Don't you think that maybe you should worry more about tomorrow night and less about right now?"

"What, are you telling me to give up on her? Just walk away?"

"Well, not in so many words, but there are others who are still deciding too, son."

"You don't think I know that? You don't think that fact doesn't haunt me every second of every minute of every day?"

"We just want to make sure that you're keeping focus, is all Luke."

"We? You mean Ethan and the Council, right?" He nodded. "Well, if they care so much about me keeping focused, why have they blown me off? Why can't they come here instead of you? Where are they when I need them?"

"You know they can't come here," Captain Bob said soberly.

"Yeah, believe me, I know. And I think that really sucks."

"They haven't left you, Luke. They're always with you, you just can't see it."

"Well, then they should know that I'm not going to give up on her." I looked through the window. She was taking off her apron. It must be eight o'clock. "I made a promise."

"Very good. I was young once too, a very long time ago, but once never the less. There are some things that a man never forgets." He motioned towards the door. "See you tomorrow night." He put his pipe in his mouth and disappeared into the night.

"Good night," I said into the cool night air, just as Mare walked out of the door.

"Lucas," she said clutching her chest. "You scared me. What are you doing out here? Were you watching me?" she said cynically.

"More like waiting for you. You make it sound like I was stalking you or something." I attempted to explain. "Which I'm not. I just wanted to talk with you."

"I think I already told you, I don't have anything to say to you." She slung her purse over her shoulder and headed down the steps towards the back of the market.

"Well, I have something to say to you." I pulled her arm making her stop. She turned and faced me, tears glistening in her eyes. "I miss you," I whispered. A tear rolled down her cheek.

"Please let me go," she whispered. I dropped my hand. She stepped back two steps but didn't take off, for which I was eternally grateful.

"Please talk to me, Mare. Tell me you don't miss me a little too?"

She smiled, laughed, and sniffled all at the same time.

"I miss a lot of things, Lucas." She looked at me pointedly. I felt her pain and anger that dripped from her like hot molasses.

"I know," I whispered.

"Do you?" she said bitingly. "Do you really? Do you know what it's like to walk into a house and be totally invisible because your mom is so strung out on anti-depressants and your dad has become best friends with Jack Daniels? And I thought it was bad when she was sick." She angrily wiped the freely flowing tears off of her cheeks. "But I can handle that, it's really not too big of a change from what I was used to. What I *can't* deal with is walking by her bedroom every day knowing that I will never hear her laugh again, or call my name, or yell at me for changing the channel. I can't stand seeing people walk into our house and pick through her things like vultures, throwing her clothes and stuffed animals into big black bags and tossing it into the backs of their trucks like garbage."

I put my hand on her shoulder and poured light into her. She shrugged it off and stepped back.

"But what I can't stand the most is seeing that stupid cat. Because every time I see it, I remember what you did. And then I remember what you didn't do." She looked at me accusingly.

"Please don't do this," I whispered.

"You let her die," she cried. "Why didn't you light up your arm and save her, huh? Was she not good enough for you?"

"Stop!" I yelled. Mare jumped. "Your sister was sick, she was sick for a long time, everyone knows that." I took a deep breath. "If you want to blame me for her death, go ahead, I can't stop you, but what about Becca? What about your other friends? What have they done to you?"

"Nothing, I just..."

"Excuses are just that, Mare, excuses."

"You're just jealous I'm spending time with Devin, aren't you?" she said snidely.

"Yes," I answered honestly, and her resolve waivered.

"Do you remember that time I told you that when I'm with you I feel different, inside?" she asked softly. I nodded.

ROBIN DONARUMA

"Well, when I'm with Devin, I don't feel anything. It's like I become numb inside. The pain, the anger, everything, it all just sort of goes away, and I forget."

"Is that a good thing?"

"Maybe not. But it's what I need." She turned around and started walking to a parked car. "Go find someone else to save."

I didn't need any light to know who was behind the wheel.

CHAPTER FORTY

"Lucas! Don't you have to be there by now?" my mother frantically yelled through my bedroom door.

"Relax, Mom. I don't have to be there for at least a half hour." I opened my door.

"Lucas, you look wonderful," my mother said cupping my cheek.

"Thanks, Mom," I said, blushing appropriately. I hadn't veered too much from my normal look, just stepped it up a notch with a button down, white (of course) linen shirt over my faithfully worn jeans. I grabbed Layla and headed downstairs, my mother directly behind me. Dad was waiting at the foot of the stairs.

"Ready?" he asked.

"Absolutely."

"How are you feeling about all of this?" my dad asked, putting one hand on my shoulder and looking into my eyes, his head slightly cocked to one side. "About tonight. Something is happening tonight isn't it?"

"Yes."

"How?" my mother asked. "Do you know?"

"Not exactly, but I can feel it. It ends tonight."

"I thought as much," my mother responded. I looked at her questioningly, she continued. "I had a dream last night. I saw them, all of them."

"Do we have a chance?" I asked meekly.

"Yes. And so do they."

"I understand," I said, looking at them both. "Well, I've gotta go, if we're late for registration we can't perform." I grabbed my keys and made my way to the door. "And the show must go on!"

"Luke, what are you going to play tonight?" my mom asked expectantly.

ROBIN DONARUMA

"I haven't decided yet," I said, smiling at their blank expressions. "I'm sure it will come to me, don't worry. See you there."

"See you there," my dad said holding on to my mom. My mother attempted a half-hearted wave, but her mouth got in the way since it was hanging wide open.

***

It seemed as if the entire town, and maybe a couple of the adjacent ones were at Branford High tonight. Cars were still arriving when I got there and the line to get in wound around the front half of the stadium. As I walked through the parking lot, groups of kids that I didn't recognize shouted my name and held up their fisted left arms revealing their white armbands. Cool. I headed to the cafeteria to sign up. The air was humming with guitar chords, clicking drum sticks as well as violins, trumpets, and tambourines. Groups of twos and threes stood in corners of the room practicing their harmonies and choreographed dance steps. The energy was definitely at an all-time high. I approached the table and handed in my entry form.

"You left this one blank, sweetie," the woman said, looking over my application.

"Yeah, I know," I said.

"But how can you not know what you're going to perform?"

"Trust me," I said with a wink. She blushed in response and put my entry on the pile.

"To each his own, I suppose," she responded smiling. "You're number nine," she said, handing me a card with number nine on it.

"How many are performing tonight?" I asked her.

"Only ten sweetie." She winked, then looked behind me. "And here comes our number ten!"

"Devin," I whispered, feeling him approach.

"Lucas. I hope you're ready. It's going to be quite a show." He handed his form to the woman who then handed him his number ten card.

"I've been ready for a long time," I said, feeling confidence and strength that I'd never felt before. I really

THE UNDECIDED

believed what I had just told him. His smile slightly waivered, and he moved his application to look at mine beneath his.

"Funny, doesn't look like it to me."

"But Devin, you of all people should realize that looks can be quite deceiving." I took one step towards him and then sharply turned towards the door.

He was rattled. I could feel it. It was like a high-pitched buzzing alarm sounding off in his dark mind.

Mare was standing outside the cafeteria waiting for Devin, I supposed, since I knew I was out of the question. For a second I thought she was going to say something to me, but then opted out. I offered her a half smile then walked in the opposite direction.

Music was being channeled through the stadium. Performers in the Battle of the Bands were behind a stage constructed in the middle of the football field. Multi-colored lights from the stage filled the darkening sky making it look as respectable as any rock concert I'd ever been to.

"Dude! I was afraid you weren't going to make it!" John said, practically jumping me. "Man, I am so pumped! Woooot!" he yelled into the air. Kyle and Paul gave a call of the wild shout out right behind him in response.

"Never fear, I am here." I held up my card. "Number nine."

"Three," John said.

"You guys look good," I said, genuinely impressed with their whole look, which was a combination of Kiss and Twisted Sister, minus the makeup.

"We wanted to go for this whole kind of Rocky Horror thing, but my mom wouldn't let us use her make up," Kyle said.

"I told you not to ask," John said to Kyle.

"Well duh, I think she would kind of notice when we went out on stage. Then I'd be in real trouble."

"Yeah, but how would she know it was hers?" John asked, leaving a very confused expression on Kyle's face.

"Oh," Kyle responded.

John shook his head at Kyle as a parent would to their toddler then shifted his attention on me.

ROBIN DONARUMA

"So, what are you gonna shred up, my brotha?"
"I'm not sure yet," I answered serenely. It seemed the closer to show time, the calmer I got.
"What? You're kidding right?" John asked.
"Dude, you're totally whacked," Kyle added.
"I'm sure it will come to me." I spotted Mr. Kenzie and Mr. Holland standing behind John. "Hey, I'll catch up with you guys later." I walked away as John and Kyle went back to the discussion of their lack of make-up.

Mr. Kenzie and Mr. Holland were talking animatedly when I approached them.

"Trust me Jophiel, for once in your life, stop talking and just listen. Music is the answer, I know it," Mr. Kenzie said.

"But O, how bitter a thing it is to look into happiness through another man's eyes." Mr. Holland responded, closing his eyes and speaking up to the sky as if invoking the bard himself. "It's not that I don't listen to you Israfel, quite honestly, it's hard not to, but to risk everything for this one thing?"

"Sometimes, ole boy, all it takes is one thing." Mr. Kenzie responded before turning to me seeming as if he knew I was there the whole time. "Lucas, there you are."

"Mr. Kenzie, Mr. Holland." Mr. Holland was watching me, a soft smile pasted on his lips. "I didn't take you for a big music fan."

"See? He's hitting home runs already," Mr. Kenzie said to Mr. Holland.

"Are you referring to that baseball team again? Honestly Jophiel, you'd think you were still in high school, not teaching at one."

"*That* baseball team you are referring to is the Boston Red Sox, thank you very much."

"And to address your statement, Lucas." He rolled his eyes at Mr. Kenzie directing his attention back to me. "The man that hath no music in himself, nor is not moved by the concord of sweet sounds, is fit for treasons, stratagems and spoils."

I looked to Mr. Kenzie to translate for me.

"You keep saying that you're speaking English, but I don't understand a word you're saying," Mr. Kenzie said.

THE UNDECIDED

"I was merely taking this opportunity to infuse some literature into his young mind, is that so hard to ingest?" He calmly responded then looked at me. "Yes, Lucas. I do indeed enjoy an evening of music, very much so in fact."

"Great. I'm glad you're both here," I said sincerely.

"And we're not the only ones, kid," Mr. Kenzie said as he scanned the crowd. The stadium was practically full and the first band was on stage warming up. I followed Mr. Kenzie's gaze and saw Muriel from the lunchroom, Captain Bob, the hostess from Lenny's, my parents, a janitor from school, and three other adults who seemed familiar, but I couldn't ever remember talking with them. They all stood either in front of an exit or beside the stage, two stood directly in front of the stage. They stood out easily to me because their light was brighter than anyone else's.

"You're my watchers?" I asked, already knowing the answer.

"With pleasure," Mr. Holland answered with a slight bow.

"But that's it. We're all here for the battle, but only you can win the war, son," Mr. Kenzie said.

"It ends tonight, doesn't it?"

"Yes, one way or another. Hell is empty and all the devils are here," Mr. Holland stated soberly.

"Now that one I get," Mr. Kenzie said then looked back at me. The first band had already started playing, so he had to speak up to be heard. "The watchers are here to make sure that Devin and his minions stay far away from you. All exits are monitored, as well as the stage's entrances and the stage itself."

"To make sure no tomfoolery takes place, of course."

"Of course," I echoed.

"But Lucas, we are merely extra sets of eyes for you, our powers here are only those of observation."

"I think I understand." The first band exited the stage. The audience was screaming, and I had to pause a second to be heard. "Thank you, both of you."

"It is not you, but we that should be thankful, thankful for you, dear Lucas. You will succeed, I feel it in my bones." Mr. Holland placed one hand on my shoulder.

"Wisely and slow. They stumble that run fast." Mr. Kenzie placed his hand on my other shoulder. Mr. Holland looked at him sharply.

"Ah ha! I knew there was a bit of the bard inside that insanely white mop atop your head," he said, smiling widely.

"Yeah, well, let's get back to the topic, shall we?" Mr. Kenzie and Mr. Holland closed their eyes. Like bolts of lightning their energy merged with mine. I felt buoyant and free. My eyes closed of their own free will and everything around me disappeared. I heard music and laughter and waves of sparkling white lights repeatedly washed over me. I could hear Millie barking, and I knew that she was there with me too.

They both dropped their hands, and I was plunged back into reality.

"Whoa," I said, slightly dazed.

"Pretty cool, huh?"

"I always find that so refreshing!" Mr. Holland happily stated.

"What was that?" I whispered, looking down at my wrist, which was now aglow.

"Think of it as having just drank a six pack of Monster."

"Or a shot of B-12. Just a little inspiration to get your creative juices flowing, as it were."

"Now go on and get out of here, your buddy John is about to go on, and you're not too far behind," Mr. Kenzie said, dismissing me with a wave of his hand.

"Sure. Thanks. For everything." I walked away smiling to myself as I listened to Mr. Holland excitedly ask Mr. Kenzie what other works of literature he was familiar with, to which Mr. Kenzie responded *Hedwig and the Angry Inch*. Somehow, I don't think Mr. Holland would be familiar with that one.

I got to the side stage as John and his band took their places. Not only were the bleachers filled with people, but the front of the stage, which was the football field, was packed. I saw Becca and Peter standing in the third row, and upon locking eyes, they both raised up their left fists showing me their white bracelets.

THE UNDECIDED

John hit the first chord and the crowd went wild. He followed through with his promise and rocked the house to "Ballroom Blitz." Two beach balls bounced around from one side of the field to the other, and in one corner some students had even formed their own version of a mosh pit. It was definitely a rocking scene. They finished after an extended solo from each of them and ran off the stage looking as if they ruled the world.

"Did you see that? Man, that was so awesome!" John yelled as he ran into me for a hug.

"Dude, we totally rocked it out there!" Kyle chimed in with wide, wonder filled eyes.

"Amazing, man," I said, hugging him back. "Look." I pointed to the crowd that was still going wild and yelling "Ledz Rock!"

"Man, what a rush!" Paul chimed in.

"When are you up man? Nine?"

"Yup," I stated confidently.

"Excellent. Hey, anybody thirsty?" he asked in a raspy voice.

"On it," Kyle responded as they all made their way to a table in the back stacked with water bottles.

"Later Luke!" John said as he walked through the crowd backstage receiving multiple high fives and congratulations.

I stood back taking it all in, the screaming crowd, the stage, the friends. I looked at the watchers, including my parents that were standing in strategic places to make sure I was protected. The infusion from Mr. Kenzie and Holland still thrummed through my veins.

A cold nagging pain began to prick its way into my head. I scanned the stage and found Devin, his eyes boring into me. Hatred poured out of him like lava from a volcano, thick, scorching and deadly. I could feel his frustration. He wanted to come to me, but my watchers wouldn't let him. I smiled at him and his darkness pulsed larger and loomed over and around him. Mindy walked up to him and whispered in his ear. A smile curled around his mouth as he affectionately looked at her stroking her cheek with his finger. Mare wasn't near him, or anywhere around the stage.

ROBIN DONARUMA

Band five arrived on stage and started playing a Killers song pretty decently. I grabbed Layla to hopefully become inspired when I heard my name being harshly whispered behind me. Mare was standing near the bleachers a few feet from the stage. She was wearing a white scarf that was blowing in the wind along with her auburn hair. It felt as if time stood still.

"Lucas." She motioned for me to follow her. Still holding onto my guitar I left the backstage area following her to an exit. She walked out, and I was about to follow when Muriel stepped in front of me.

"Where are you off to Lucas? You don't want to be late and miss your performance," she said, smiling brightly.

"No, ma'am, of course not. I was just following a friend."

"I saw who you were following." She sobered immediately. "I've strict instructions that you aren't to leave our sight, Luke."

I ran my hand through my hair and began pacing back and forth.

"Please Muriel," I begged.

"I'm sorry, son. We just can't risk it."

"But it's Mare," I pleaded. She looked at me with partial sympathy, but I could tell it wasn't going to happen.

Then the sixth act came on stage. It was Mindy with three violinists. She approached the microphone, and the audience quieted in anticipation. She waited a few seconds longer than necessary to ensure that everyone had their eyes on her before she began to sing. "Nessun Dorma," an aria made famous by Pavarotti poured from her lips as naturally and exquisitely as any I had ever heard before. The audience held up lighters and swayed back and forth in cadence with the violinist's bows. Muriel, whose eyes were now closed had a serene smile pasted on her lips. Mr. Holland and Mr. Kenzie, as well as the rest of my watchers, were mesmerized as well. I took advantage of their distraction and headed out of the stadium.

She stood a few feet away near the practice field. Her scarf blew wildly about her emphasizing the pained expression written across her face. She held her hands out in front of her willing me to stop.

THE UNDECIDED

"Lucas, wait," she said, choking on a sob. "It's okay Mare. I'm here." I approached her carefully.

"Lucas!" she yelled as something was pulled over my head and everything went dark. I heard her scream as I was dragged across the field, my arms pinned behind my back. I hit a chain-linked fence and fell to my knees. I tried to stand but was kicked in the ribs. It not only kept me on the ground, but it also knocked the air out of my lungs. I attempted to get up again and was assisted by two hands.

"Stand up!" someone yelled.

I stood there shakily trying to catch my breath and ignore the sharp pain in my side. My back was pushed against the fence and each arm was stretched out to my sides. My wrists were tied to links of chain as the sack was ripped from my head. I willed my eyes to adjust to the bright field lights that were casting their light all around me. I tried to break free from my arm restraints, but they were too tight.

Jeff and Scott were on either side of me standing with their arms crossed. My heart sank.

"Jeff, what are you doing, man?" I asked. "Scott? What's going on?"

"Shut up," Scott said. Jeff averted his eyes and didn't respond.

"Mare," I whispered. A deep chilling laugh, one that I had heard many, many times before in my dreams echoed around me. I felt cold.

"It's over, Lucas. No one can help you now. No one is coming to save you." Devin stepped into the light along with Mare. Grabbing the back of her neck he kissed her harshly then cast her aside. He sauntered towards me as if he had all of the time in the world. "Some leader you turned out to be." He stopped leaving, barely an inch between us. "I'm going to love watching you suffer," he whispered in my ear.

I kicked him hard in the chest with my left knee throwing him off balance and leaving him gasping for air. After several seconds, he righted himself and attacked. His fist slammed repeatedly into my face. Something crunched after the third blow, and I calmly debated whether it was my nose or my cheek. He paused only to laugh maniacally.

ROBIN DONARUMA

"You don't actually think you have a chance here, do you?" He motioned to Jeff and Scott with a snap of his fingers. They turned to him like a dog to its master. He pointed to my legs and they quickly secured them to the fence.

"I think you're scared," I said through swelling lips.

"What? Scared? Of what? You? I don't think so." He punched me in the stomach then grabbed my hair pulling my head flush against the fence. "I'm thinking it's the other way around." He looked at my neck and with a curl of his upper lip he snarled. "Welcome to the beginning of the end." He ripped my necklace from my neck and threw it into the field behind him. I immediately weakened and pain began creeping in. He dropped my head and stood back, admiring his work. "Embrace the pain Lucas. Embrace the darkness."

I picked up my head as much as I was able and looked at him through the eye that wasn't swollen shut.

"If you weren't scared of me, then why am I tied up? Why not let me go and see what happens? If you're not scared."

Devin's smile wavered, and he began to shake with anger.

"What, so you can go running for your *watchers*? You see I know a lot more than you think. I know what you are, I know what you can do, and I know your weakness." He looked behind him where Mare had been standing, but she was gone. "And unfortunately for you, that is precisely what is going to kill you and as a bonus, for me, eliminate the White Army for good."

The crowd in the stadium began cheering as another act began performing. I looked towards the football field, hoping to see someone, anyone, but everyone who was there was inside the stadium. I glanced at Scott who watched me with a look of disgust. Jeff refused to look at me at all.

"I think that's band number eight," Devin said, following the direction of my gaze. "And you're number nine, right? Sorry buddy, it looks to me like you're going to be a no show. How sad for all of your little friends. But don't worry, I'll be there to take your place." He spotted my

THE UNDECIDED

guitar lying on the grass. Gingerly, he picked it up and inspected it from every angle. "So this is Layla? Kind of plain, don't you think? Then again, maybe that's how you like them. Figures." He spun my guitar around by its neck like a tennis racket and strummed a chord. His dark energy pulsated. He played another and another closing his eyes as his harsh rhythm increased. His darkness expanded around him and began to bleed out in search of victims.

He *was* like me.

"Ah! I see, pardon the pun, the *light* turning on. You understand now, don't you? What is that, a tear in your eye? I'm afraid defeat never tastes very good on the tongue, but you've got so much blood in there to mix with it, I'm sure you'll be right as rain in no time." He psychotically laughed and looked around him as if he had an audience, then sighed when he realized he didn't. "This has been so much fun, I can't even tell you. Man I wish I could spend more time with you out here, just the two of us and the two fools, but alas, the show must go on, and it seems that I'm performing a little earlier than expected!" He started towards the stadium then stopped. Slowly, he turned back to me. His eyes aglow with hatred and his lips curled into a malevolent grin. Darkness pulsated around him. He was the personification of evil, and I was chilled to the bone. Desolation crept through my veins.

"Oh, I suppose you want this, huh?" he asked, holding up my guitar. "Here you go."

On a wave of pure rage, Devin ran towards me smashing my guitar into the right side of my body. It shattered, and I cried out in pain as a large piece of wood lodged into my flesh. He laughed as he backed away his eyes shining with triumph.

"Come on boys, it's showtime!" He turned towards the stadium with Scott at his heels. Jeff hesitated.

"He's bleeding pretty bad, Dev. Shouldn't we tell someone?"

Devin's smile dropped as he looked at Jeff.

"Maybe you'd like to stay out here with him?" Jeff backed up, licking his lips nervously. He looked to Scott for help. "Forget him, buddy." Devin switched tactics. "Look, we just needed to get him out of the way so we can go on stage and put this competition to bed, right?"

"Yeah," he said meekly.

"And that's exactly what we did. Now come on, after our performance, I promise, you can tell anyone you want about his sorry state. By then, it won't matter anyway." He smiled and put his arm over Jeff's shoulder ushering him towards the stadium.

The warmth of my blood ran down my side, and I began to feel lightheaded. Darkness was creeping in around me and within seconds my world went black.

CHAPTER FORTY-ONE

I was numb. Something was wrong, but I couldn't remember what, and I didn't really care. Coldness deadened my senses as I floated along an endless sea of black. A pinprick of light penetrated the murkiness, and I was irritated by its intrusion and at the same time, drawn towards it.

I tried to float towards the light, and the closer I got, the bigger and brighter it became. The darkness tried to stop me. It muddied my movements making the strain of each stroke and stride excruciating. Sweat ran down my face mixing with tears of frustration. I screamed for help, but no sound came out. Desperately, I reached for the speck of white that was quickly diminishing and willed it to help me. *Help!* I yelled again, silently. I reached my other hand out to the light and the darkness took advantage by pulling me further back. *No!* I screamed. *No!* I stretched out my arms as far as they would reach and called to the light, begging for salvation. My wrist began to glow as light shot from my fingertips. It connected with the small white dot just before it disappeared. Warmth invaded my body and the darkness released my legs.

The light cocooned and carried me out of the abyss. Birds sang in the sky above and waves crashed off the shore. I was on the island. *Woof!* Millie was running towards me. I bent down and embraced her.

"Millie!"

"Yes, friend Lucas." She licked my face.

"Am I dead?" I asked, not caring what the answer was as long as I could stay here.

"No, but it is a possibility. One that makes me very sad," she whined. I pulled away, suddenly remembering everything.

"I failed," I whispered. "We lost." I looked at Mille, who was watching me with a tilted head. "I'm so sorry."

"Follow me." She led me to the flower garden and nudged me to enter. Inside, a man dressed all in white was clipping flowers.

"Ethan?" I whispered, afraid that my voice would scare him away. "Is it really you?"

He slowly turned and looked more radiant than I had ever seen him.

"Hello Lucas."

"But I thought. You said that you couldn't, that I wouldn't..." I was overwhelmed with emotion and ran to him, hugging him tightly. I was restored. "I'm sorry, I've failed you," I whispered into his shoulder. He pulled away and looked at me, the smile never wavering.

"No. You have not failed me or anyone else. The war is not yet won."

"What do you mean?" I sobered instantly.

"There are still moves in this game that have yet to be played," he said cryptically.

"But then why am I here, and why are you here? Here with me? I thought that I would never see you again," I finished quietly.

"I must admit, my being here is breaking a few rules, but then again so is beating a defenseless man." His smile dropped from his face, and he looked at me with grave sincerity. "You must go back, Lucas." I nodded. "I must warn you that your body is quite broken in many places, and you will experience great pain." I nodded and swallowed a lump in my throat. "But this pain will diminish as the light surrounds you."

"The light?"

"Of the others." He placed his hand on my shoulder. "You must perform, Lucas. It is imperative that you make it to the stage and play for the crowd."

"But Devin, he was going to take my spot..."

"Yes, and you shall take his." He dropped his hand and walked over to a rose bush inhaling the aroma from a dewy bud. "Do you remember your time on the island?"

"More than anything," I answered honestly.

"Then perhaps you'll recall your suggestion of gathering groups of people together in hopes to bring them light?"

I did remember.

"So it seems I owe you an apology."

"For what?" I asked, distracted from my thoughts.

"For not giving your idea more consideration. As it so happens, reaching to the masses through this Battle of the Bands may be the very act that saves our lives."

"I need to go back," I said with urgency.

"Good." He smiled and walked with me to the entrance of the garden. "This time, you will succeed Lucas." I turned towards him, knowing that this was goodbye.

"Can you come with me? Please?" As much as I needed to get back to the stadium, I didn't want to leave him.

"But Lucas, this is what you have failed to understand. I have never left you. I am always with you. Find strength in the truth, and you shall defeat the darkness."

Woof! Millie called from the entrance. I looked at her beautiful white bushy tail poking through the shrubs and laughed. I looked back to Ethan, but he was gone. Instead of despair, I felt a calm strength course through me. I could still feel him around me. I smiled and walked towards Millie who was patiently waiting for me.

"It is time, friend Lucas," she said.

"I know. I am ready." I looked at her. "Really ready," I said, patting her head.

"Don't forget what Ethan told you of your body's state," she warned.

"I know."

"Good. Then this shouldn't bother you very much," she said then sharply bit me on the right side of my body.

CHAPTER FORTY-TWO

Consciousness hit my body like a sledgehammer and a million knives, all at once. I tried my restraints, but they were too tight and I was too weak. It was a struggle just to keep from falling back into the darkness.

"Lucas!" someone yelled. "Lucas! I found him, Peter! He's over there. Oh my God, Lucas, what have they done to you?"

I opened my good eye to find Becca standing in front of me gingerly touching my hair.

"Becca," I uttered, attempting to smile. She sucked in a sob and turned away.

"Peter! Go get help! Find Mr. Holland! Hurry!" She turned back to me. "Oh Lucas, who did this to you? Never mind." She bent down to untie my feet. "I know who did this."

My head snapped back and hit the fence as the pain of blood rushing back into my feet hit me.

"Does that hurt? I'm sorry Lucas. I'm so sorry." Becca kept pausing to wipe tears from her eyes. "I'll untie your arms now, but I think it might hurt worse than your legs."

"Ah, I'm tough. Do your worst," I said in an attempt at levity just as we heard a giant roar from the stadium. Becca paused and looked at me. "Devin," I whispered. "Hurry Becca, undo my arms. Hurry, please."

She nodded and went back to work as the first lick of Devin's guitar echoed through the night air. She released my right arm, and it fell onto the wooden shard sticking out of my side. I inhaled sharply.

"Oh Lucas!" Becca cried. She touched the piece of wood. "I should pull this out. Should I pull this out?" she asked me. I lifted my head and saw three figures approaching, two of which seemed to be flying towards me.

THE UNDECIDED

"God's wounds!" Mr. Holland said as he worked on releasing my other hand. Becca backed up to let Mr. Kenzie look at Lucas.

"Lucas, this is going to hurt. A lot." Mr. Kenzie pulled the wooden slice out of my side and held both of his hands over my wound. My blood poured through his fingers. "Stay with me Lucas," he said, adding pressure to my side. Warmth began to replace the stabbing, cold pain making it much easier to breath. He dropped his hands and stood back satisfied. "That should stop the bleeding for now."

I screamed as my other arm was untied and blood fought its way back into my veins. I doubled over, sure that I was going to pass out, but Mr. Kenzie and Mr. Holland each grabbed me under an arm helping me stay afloat.

"Israfel, he needs rest and perhaps the attention of a physician," Mr. Holland said in hushed tones.

"We don't have time to rest Jophiel, listen."

We could all hear Devin playing and by the sound of the crowd, they were eating him up, or he was eating them up. A dark haze loomed over the stage and crept out over the football field like a snake getting ready to strike.

"I'm fine," I attempted. "And he's right. We don't have any time to lose." Mr. Holland stared at me sympathetically but knew I spoke the truth.

"Very well. The private wound is deepest. O time most accurst, 'Mongst all foes that a friend should be the worst."

"No time for that now. If you keep standing here talking, the show will be over and as a result, we will too. Come on."

Becca and Peter were walking beside us, holding hands trying to stifle their tears.

"Wait," I said, stopping. "Peter?" He ran over to me.

"I'm here, Lucas."

"Cool. Could you do me a solid?"

"What?" He looked around puzzled. "Of course, anything."

"Could you grab my necklace for me? It's over there, in the grass." Peter looked around helplessly at the huge field.

"Sure," he said quietly. "Becca help me," he pleaded.

I closed my eyes and whispered. "Millie, help please." In a matter of seconds Peter yelled out.

"I found it! Here it is! It's glowing!" Peter ran to me holding out the necklace. Mr. Kenzie took it from his hands before I could even acknowledge the retrieval. He brushed off the grass and tied it around my neck.

Waves of light washed over me. I looked at Peter.

"Thanks, buddy." I held out my hand to him. He took it and his love poured into me.

The music had stopped. Over the football field the darkness no longer loomed overhead; it had begun to descend down into the audience, looking for victims. The crowd was screaming louder than ever sounding almost frenzied.

"Let's go," I said, willing my legs to carry me. The pain in my side slowed my stride, but hearing the roaring crowd made me push ahead.

"Ah crap," Mr. Kenzie said, stopping.

"What is it Mr. Kenzie?" Becca said, looking all around in fear.

"Listen. They're going to call the competition."

"Then let's stop standing around talking like a couple of school girls and get in there," I said, dropping Mr. Kenzie's shoulder. "Go in there and tell them I'm coming."

"But Lucas, how are you going to..."

"Don't worry about that. Go," I said strongly. "Tell them I'm coming. But Israfel, don't let Devin hear you."

Mr. Kenzie nodded and ran towards the stage, appearing as if he was gliding. We approached the gate where Muriel was waiting for us.

"Lucas, thank goodness. I never should have taken my eyes off of you, it was all my fault."

"Shhh," I said, putting my hand on her cheek. "Everything happened exactly as it was meant to happen. There is no one to fault here but myself."

"Oh Lucas." She grabbed my hand, and I absorbed the love that she so willingly directed towards me. I smiled into her eyes as a flash of white caught my eye. Just behind Muriel, Mare stared at me with red rimmed eyes, tears coursing down her alabaster cheeks.

"Muriel, I need you to go inside now and make sure that Mr. Kenzie told them we're here. She obediently obeyed and shuffled off towards the stage.

THE UNDECIDED

"Mr. Holland?" I asked never taking my eyes off of Mare.

"Lucas, I can't possibly."

"Jophiel," I said, looking directly into his eyes. "I wasn't asking," I said with determination and strength. Mr. Holland shook his head, knowing that I couldn't be swayed.

"Very well, I shall be right over here should you need me." He pointed to the entrance gate. "The course of true love never did run smooth," he said as he let go of my arm and walked away.

Becca and Peter were standing behind me, and I looked back at them.

"I'm not leaving you with her," Becca spat.

"Me either," Peter said, moving in closer to me as Mare slowly walked towards me.

"I understand," I replied. "And I thank you, but, please, I need to do this. Alone."

Becca looked up at me and then looked at Mare who was now standing in front of me.

"We'll be right over there if you need us," Becca said as she and Peter walked towards Mr. Holland.

I looked at Mare who looked worse than I had ever seen her. My heart melted, and I knew that she would always be beautiful to me.

She slid her white scarf from her neck and stepped closer to me. Ever so gently, she wiped blood from my face. She looked into my eyes and sucked in an emotional breath.

"Oh Lucas, I'm so sorry. I didn't know..."

"Shhh," I said, stopping her. "None of that matters anymore. What's done is done."

"You're so hurt," she cried.

"Yes. But not where you can see it," I answered.

"I'll never forgive myself," she whispered, dropping her hands and looking down at the bloodied white scarf. "Never."

"Because there is nothing to forgive." I held out my hand to her, and she put her shaking, cold palm into mine.

"Listen, do you hear that?" she said, looking around wildly. "It's your name. They're calling your name!" she said smiling through her tears. "You should go. You must go." She said looking behind her and dropping her hand from mine.

"Come with me?" I asked softly. She shook her head. I smiled and loved her more than my heart could bear.

"Oh Mare, my sweet, silly Mare," I said, cupping her cheek. I awkwardly stepped toward her and kissed her forehead then bent towards her ear. "I can see you now. You have chosen." I pulled away, my smile still on my lips and gave her hair one more caress.

"Lucas, we must be off," Mr. Holland said, offering me his shoulder once more.

"Do you hear them Lucas?" Becca asked excitedly.

I smiled as I heard my name being chanted. I turned back to Mare, but she was gone, as I knew she would be. "Let's rock and roll," I said. As we entered the stadium a spot light hit us.

A hush descended over the crowd as they took in my abused state. The audience shifted, dark entities moved away from me while white moved towards me.

"The dark ones are moving, that is a good sign indeed," Mr. Holland said as he helped me walk to the stage. "We're not too late."

"You can see them too?" I asked him.

"Yes. Much more so now, I'm afraid, now that the end is so near."

"Good."

I stopped walking. Turning off the pain, the screaming of the crowd and the concerned questions being thrown at me, I stopped and listened. I listened with my mind and my heart reaching out to the light surrounding me. I was connected. Smiling, I slowly dropped my arm from Mr. Holland's shoulder. The light filled me with strength and my pain subsided.

"You've connected haven't you?" Mr. Holland asked me, a look of astonishment on his face. "Amazing."

I looked at him as Mr. Kenzie rushed to my side. I felt as I did when I was on the island when I was with Ethan. I was connected deeper than I had ever been before. Ethan was here. I could feel him. I laughed with joy and called to them in my mind. A rush of love hit me like a lightning bolt in return.

THE UNDECIDED

"Good God, he's connected hasn't he?" Mr. Kenzie said to Mr. Holland.

"Bloody right he's connected. He's magnificent," he whispered. "Bloody magnificent."

I continued to the stage, walking unassisted, my limp much less pronounced. With each step closer I became stronger.

"Wait, Lucas, let us help you," Becca said to my back.

I turned towards her, now able to see out of both eyes.

"Thanks Becca, I'm feeling much better now." I made my way towards the stage ignoring her wide-eyed look of astonishment.

The shock of my appearance faded, and the audience came back to life. The group in front of me parted creating a path to the stage. The dark entities bled out of the masses surfacing around the perimeter. Hands jutted out of the crowd bearing white bracelets. They grabbed my hands and gently clapped my back in support. Every touch strengthened me, and I became stronger with every step. They chanted my name as I neared the stage where Devin still stood with Jeff and Scott staring at me as if I were a ghost. Devin's eyes watched my approach with such loathing that I could actually see it oozing out of him, black, sticky and utterly vile. I started up the steps leading to the stage but was stopped by Jeff who stepped in front of me.

A hush fell over the audience once more. Jeff stood with his arms crossed, and looked back to Devin who nodded his head approvingly. Jeff took two steps towards me. I didn't move. In a jerk like motion, he offered his open hand to me. I grabbed it and was overcome with his remorse.

"I'm so sorry man. I didn't know," he stuttered, wetness now covering his face.

"I know." I squeezed his hand and watched with joy as his energy turned from a murky gray to a beautiful glowing white. "How 'bout a hand?"

He helped me onto the stage and the audience went wild. I looked past him to Scott, who still stood beside Devin. Standing at the edge of the stage, Devin was spitting darkness out like a sputtering engine about to overheat.

Jeff grabbed the mic and tapped it twice to get the crowd's attention just as the principal came onto the stage holding a large trophy in the shape of a guitar.

"It seems we have another contestant." He looked at Devin and held up the trophy. "I'm afraid Mr. Donahue, this isn't yours quite yet."

Devin pretended to laugh and bowed to the principal appearing calm and nonchalant.

"Mr. Aarons, are you prepared to go on?" he asked, looking at my disheveled appearance.

"Absolutely," I responded.

He looked at me questioningly, but then shrugged his shoulders and handed me the microphone.

The principal walked off stage with Devin and Scott. Jeff followed them but stopped at the edge of the stage. Apparently, I now had my own bodyguard.

I put the mic on the stand and stood in front of it, taking in the huge crowd and the even bigger moment that this was. My eyes were drawn to Mare who stood on the bleachers, away from everyone. She let go of her white scarf and I watched as it took flight into the black night. When I looked back to her, she was no longer there. Several people called out my name from the crowd, and my focus shifted.

"Hi. Sorry I'm late." The audience cheered. "I got tied up." Mr. Kenzie who was standing towards the front end of the stage gave me a thumbs-up sign. "But everything worked out, and here I am." Devin was beginning to appear less confident with each second that ticked by.

"A friend once told me that there are two elements needed to create a really spectacular event. Two elements that when they come together, they create an amazing, awe-inspiring event, one not to be missed." The audience was baited, listening to my every word, and I fed off of their love and energy.

Jeff sat down behind the drum set and began creating a rhythmic cadence. The audience began to clap in sync.

"I'm thinking that tonight is one of those nights." The crowd roared. I held my hands up to quiet them as Scott walked back onto the stage. I could see from the corner of my eye Captain Bob and Mr. Holland strategically

THE UNDECIDED

positioning themselves near me. Scott's light mutated, and I knew that he wasn't there to hurt me. I smiled and turned back to the audience. Scott picked up a guitar and began playing alongside Jeff. The audience livened up again.

"But what are these two elements I asked my friend? And then he told me, quite simply, what they were *not*. They're not things that you can buy or easily make. These elements are moments. Moments in time, moments of energy, moments of love." The audience's excitement was building along with Jeff and Scott's playing. John, Paul, and Kyle jumped up on stage with their instruments.

"It's a moment when the supernatural," I held up my left arm, my wrist glowing. The audience went wild and held up their wrists bearing white bracelets. I had to scream into the mic to be heard over their cheers. "It's a moment when the supernatural meets the natural. When those two moments collide, miracles happen. Lives are saved, and wars are won. And I'm thinking that tonight, right now, is one of those nights." Clapping and cheering overtook the stadium. The darkness began its retreat. "My name is Lucas Aarons." John handed me his guitar and got down on one knee mimicking lord and serf. I took it and helped him up, laughing. "Let's rock."

The words fell into my mouth and drifted out as sweet as any song ever sung. I sang about the push. I sang of lightness overtaking the dark, and I watched as the dark entities scrambled to escape from the stadium. The grays had changed, most of them for the good, and the darkness knew it. Devin knew it. He no longer had power here. With Mindy by his side, they left the stadium.

The battle was won.

My watchers stood together brighter than I had ever seen them. A flash of white tail caught my eye. Millie was here, standing with my watchers. "I knew you would do it, friend Lucas," she said to me. "I will miss you."

"Where are you going?" I asked her telepathically remembering that I wasn't alone on stage.

"Home."

"I'll miss you too," I said, watching her walk towards a figure all in white. "Ethan," I whispered aloud.

"You have done well, my son, as I always knew you would," he said. "Come on, girl, let's go home." Millie obediently followed him.

"Sleep well, Lucas," Ethan said. And then they were gone.

THE UNDECIDED

CHAPTER FORTY-THREE

The days following the Battle of the Bands seemed to go by so fast it's hard to say in what order events transpired.

The Donahues moved out of their house and out of Branford, as did a record number of people, according to a report on the news. Interestingly enough, a notable amount of people also found themselves moving to Branford.

School became that comfortable mix of calmness and angst. There were no more lines being drawn, no more threats of rejection or being ostracized. It wasn't perfect, after all it was still high school, but it was totally bearable.

Mare left Branford to go live with her grandparents in upstate New York for a while. I got her phone number from her mom, but hadn't called her yet. Sometimes I would walk by Stony Creek Market and pretend that she was inside working and that everything was like it was in the beginning, nothing had changed. But it had changed. We both had changed.

Graduation was a few days away, and I had yet to pick which college I was going to, but I had narrowed it down to four schools, two in the south, one on the east coast and one in the Midwest.

***

It was a wonderfully normal day, like the handful that preceded them, and I left school feeling grounded for the first time in a long time. My life was finally predictable and, dare I say it, typical, and I loved it. Graduation was within my grasp, and I felt as if I was finally in control of my life. I pulled my Saab into the driveway and was surprised to see both of my parents home already. I walked into the kitchen and stopped dead in my tracks. There were moving boxes everywhere.

"No," I whispered.

ROBIN DONARUMA

My mom turned the corner and jumped when she saw me.
"Lucas! You're home. Joey!" my mother yelled for my father who came running in from the living room holding a roll of tape.
"Luke, you're home," my dad echoed my mother.
"Am I?" I asked, referring to the moving materials scattered all over the kitchen.
"Well, think of it this way, this narrows down your college choices!" my mother offered.
"Did you have a dream?" I asked her. She nodded. "But I haven't," I answered.
"That's good, Lucas, that means we have more time. But you will."
I felt my necklace glowing and heard a distant woof. A familiar warm rush ran through me, and I smiled.
"Okay, so where are we headed?"
"South Bend, Indiana," my dad answered.
"Notre Dame, Lucas! You're going to Notre Dame!" my mother excitedly announced, giving me a big hug.
I hugged them both, took the roll of tape out of my dad's hands and headed back to my bedroom to start packing.
"Go Irish," I mumbled through my crooked smile.

ABOUT THE AUTHOR

Robin Donaruma was born in Virginia and raised in Texas where she lived life in the 70's to her fullest. At the ripe age of nine she relocated to Florida, where she remained for many hot, hair curling years. She obtained a degree from Florida State University and the University of Central Florida after which she secured a position with the Backlot Production Unit at Universal Studios Florida where she remained until opting out for motherhood.

Robin has written several award winning short films including a musical short, *Gotta Get Out* recently showcased at the Cannes Short Film Corner and has authored an historical romance novel, *Sweetest Confection*. Robin currently resides in South Bend, Indiana with her adoring husband, four children, two cats, and a turtle named George.